AF482794

Lester del Rey

A Trip to the Red Plane

e-artnow 2020

Lester del Rey

A Trip to the Red Plane

Two Mars Sci-Fi Novels: Police Your Planet & Badge of Infamy

e-artnow, 2020
Contact: info@e-artnow.org

ISBN 978-80-273-0904-7

Contents

Badge of Infamy

The computer seemed to work as it should. The speed was within acceptable limits. He gave up trying to see the ground and was forced to trust the machinery designed for amateur pilots. The flare bloomed, and he yanked down on the little lever.

It could have been worse. They hit the ground, bounced twice, and turned over. The ship was a mess when Feldman freed himself from the elastic straps of the seat. Chris had shrieked as they hit, but she was unbuckling herself now.

He threw her her spacesuit and one of the emergency bottles of oxygen from the rack. "Hurry up with that. We've sprung a leak and the pressure's dropping."

I

Pariah

The air of the city's cheapest flophouse was thick with the smells of harsh antiseptic and unwashed bodies. The early Christmas snowstorm had driven in every bum who could steal or beg the price of admission, and the long rows of cots were filled with fully clothed figures. Those who could afford the extra dime were huddled under thin, grimy blankets.

The pariah who had been Dr. Daniel Feldman enjoyed no such luxury. He tossed fitfully on a bare cot, bringing his face into the dim light. It had been a handsome face, but now the black stubble of beard lay over gaunt features and sunken cheeks. He looked ten years older than his scant thirty-two, and there were the beginnings of a snarl at the corners of his mouth. Clothes that had once been expensive were wrinkled and covered with grime that no amount of cleaning could remove. His tall, thin body was awkwardly curled up in a vain effort to conserve heat and one of his hands instinctively clutched at his tiny bag of possessions.

He stirred again, and suddenly jerked upright with a protest already forming on his lips. The ugly surroundings registered on his eyes, and he stared suspiciously at the other cots. But there was no sign that anyone had been trying to rob him of his bindle or the precious bag of cheap tobacco.

He started to relax back onto the couch when a sound caught his attention, even over the snoring of the others. It was a low wail, the sound of a man who can no longer control himself.

Feldman swung to the cot on his left as the moan hacked off. The man there was well fed and clean-shaven, but his face was gray with sickness. He was writhing and clutching his stomach, arching his back against the misery inside him.

"Space-stomach?" Feldman diagnosed.

He had no need of the weak answering nod. He'd treated such cases several times in the past. The disease was usually caused by the absence of gravity out in space, but it could be brought on later from abuse of the weakened internal organs, such as the intake of too much bad liquor. The man must have been frequenting the wrong space-front bars.

Now he was obviously dying. Violent peristaltic contractions seemed to be tearing the intestines out of him, and the paroxysms were coming faster. His eyes darted to Feldman's tobacco sack and there was animal appeal in them.

Feldman hesitated, then reluctantly rolled a smoke. He held the cigarette while the spaceman took a long, gasping drag on it. He smoked the remainder himself, letting the harsh tobacco burn against his lungs and sicken his empty stomach. Then he shrugged and threaded his way through the narrow aisles toward the attendant.

"Better get a doctor," he said bitterly, when the young punk looked up at him. "You've got a man dying of space-stomach on 214."

The sneer on the kid's face deepened. "Yeah? We don't pay for doctors every time some wino wants to throw up. Forget it and get back where you belong, bo."

"You'll have a corpse on your hands in an hour," Feldman insisted. "I know space-stomach, damn it."

The kid turned back to his lottery sheet. "Go treat yourself if you wanta play doctor. Go on, scram-before I toss you out in the snow!"

One of Feldman's white-knuckled hands reached for the attendant. Then he caught himself. He started to turn back, hesitated, and finally faced the kid again. "I'm not fooling. And I *was* a doctor," he stated. "My name is Daniel Feldman."

The attendant nodded absently, until the words finally penetrated. He looked up, studied Feldman with surprised curiosity and growing contempt, and reached for the phone. "Gimme Medical Directory," he muttered.

Feldman felt the kid's eyes on his back as he stumbled through the aisles to his cot again. He slumped down, rolling another cigarette in hands that shook. The sick man was approaching delirium now, and the moans were mixed with weak whining sounds of fear. Other men had wakened and were watching, but nobody made a move to help.

The retching and writhing of the sick man had begun to weaken, but it was still not too late to save him. Hot water and skillful massage could interrupt the paroxysms. In fifteen minutes, Feldman could have stopped the attack completely.

He found his feet on the floor and his hands already reaching out. Savagely he pulled himself back. Sure, he could save the man-and wind up in the gas chamber! There'd be no mercy for his second offense against Lobby laws. If the spaceman lived, Feldman might get off with a flogging-that was standard punishment for a pariah who stepped out of line. But with his luck, there would be a heart arrest and another juicy story for the papers.

Idealism! The Medical Lobby made a lot out of the word. But it wasn't for him. A pariah had no business thinking of others.

As Feldman sat there staring, the spaceman grew quieter. Sometimes, even at this stage, massage could help. It was harder without liberal supplies of hot water, but the massage was the really important treatment. It was the trembling of Feldman's hands that stopped him. He no longer had the strength or the certainty to make the massage effective.

He was glaring at his hands in self-disgust when the legal doctor arrived. The man was old and tired. Probably he had been another idealist who had wound up defeated, content to leave things up to the established procedures of the Medical Lobby. He looked it as he bent over the dying man.

The doctor turned back at last to the attendant. "Too late. The best I can do is ease his pain. The call should have been made half an hour earlier."

He had obviously never handled space-stomach before. He administered a hypo that probably held narconal. Feldman watched, his guts tightening sympathetically for the shock that would be to the sick man. But at least it would shorten his sufferings. The final seizure lasted only a minute or so.

"Hopeless," the doctor said. His eyes were clouded for a moment, and then he shrugged. "Well, I'll make out a death certificate. Anyone here know his name?"

His eyes swung about the cots until they came to rest on Feldman. He frowned, and a twisted smile curved his lips.

"Feldman, isn't it? You still look something like your pictures. Do you know the deceased?"

Feldman shook his head bitterly. "No. I don't know his name. I don't even know why he wasn't cyanotic at the end, *if* it was space-stomach. Do you, doctor?"

The old man threw a startled glance at the corpse. Then he shrugged and nodded to the attendant. "Well, go through his things. If he still has a space ticket, I can get his name from that."

The kid began pawing through the bag that had fallen from the cot. He dragged out a pair of shoes, half a bottle of cheap rum, a wallet and a bronze space ticket. He wasn't quick enough with the wallet, and the doctor took it from him.

"Medical Lobby authorization. If he has any money, it covers my fee and the rest goes to his own Lobby." There were several bills, all of large denominations. He turned the ticket over and began filling in the death certificate. "Arthur Billings. Space Lobby. Crewman. Cause of death, idiopathic gastroenteritis *and* delirium tremens."

There had been no evidence of delirium tremens, but apparently the doctor felt he had scored a point. He tossed the space ticket toward the shoes, closed his bag, and prepared to leave.

"Hey, doc!" The attendant's voice was indignant. "Hey, what about my reporting fee?"

The doctor stopped. He glanced at the kid, then toward Feldman, his face a mixture of speculation and dislike. He took a dollar bill from the wallet. "That's right," he admitted. "The fee for reporting a solvent case. Medical Lobby rules apply-even to a man who breaks them."

The kid's hand was out, but the doctor dropped the dollar onto Feldman's cot. "There's your fee, pariah." He left, forcing the protesting attendant to precede him.

Feldman reached for the bill. It was blood money for letting a man die-but it meant cigarettes and food-or shelter for another night, if he could get a mission meal. He no longer could afford pride. Grimly, he pocketed the bill, staring at the face of the dead man. It looked back sightlessly, now showing a faint speckling of tiny dots. They caught Feldman's eyes, and he bent closer. There should be no black dots on the skin of a man who died of space-stomach. And there should have been cyanosis....

He swore and bent down to find the wrecks of his shoes. He couldn't worry about anything now but getting away from here before the attendant made trouble. His eyes rested on the shoes of the dead man-sturdy boots that would last for another year. They could do the corpse no good; someone else would steal them if he didn't. But he hesitated, cursing himself.

The right boot fitted better than he could have expected, but something got in the way as he tried to put the left one on. His fingers found the bronze ticket. He turned it over, considering it. He wasn't ready to fraud his identity for what he'd heard of life on the spaceships, yet. But he shoved it into his pocket and finished lacing the boots.

Outside, the snow was still falling, but it had turned to slush, and the sidewalk was soggy underfoot. There was going to be no work shoveling snow, he realized. This would melt before the day was over. Feldman hunched the suitcoat up, shivering as the cold bit into him. The boots felt good, though; if he'd had socks, they would have been completely comfortable.

He passed a cheap restaurant, and the smell of the synthetics set his stomach churning. It had been two days since his last real meal, and the dollar burned in his pocket. But he had to wait. There was a fair chance this early that he could scavenge something edible.

He shuffled on. After a while, the cold bothered him less, and he passed through the hunger spell. He rolled another smoke and sucked at it, hardly thinking. It was better that way.

It was much later when the big caduceus set into the sidewalk snapped him back to awareness of where he'd traveled. His undirected feet had led him much too far uptown, following old habits. This was the Medical Lobby building, where he'd spent more than enough time, including three weeks in custody before they stripped him of all rank and status.

His eyes wandered to the ornate entrance where he'd first emerged as a pariah. He'd meant to walk down those steps as if he were still a man. But each step had drained his resolution, until he'd finally covered his face and slunk off, knowing himself for what the world had branded him.

He stood there now, staring at the smug young medical politicians and the tired old general practitioners filing in and out. One of the latter halted, fumbled in his pocket and drew out a quarter.

"Merry Christmas!" he said dully.

Feldman fingered the coin. Then he saw a gray Medical policeman watching him, and he knew it was time to move on. Sooner or later, someone would recognize him here.

He clutched the quarter and turned to look for a coffee shop that sold the synthetics to which his metabolism had been switched. No shop would serve him here, but he could buy coffee and a piece of cake to take out.

A flurry of motion registered from the corner of his eye, and he glanced back.

"Taxi! Taxi!"

The girl rushing down the steps had a clear soprano voice, cultured and commanding. The gray Medical uniform seemed molded to her shapely figure and her red hair glistened in the lights of the street. Her snub nose and determined mouth weren't the current fashion, but nobody stopped to think of fashions when they saw her. She didn't have to be the daughter of the president of Medical Lobby to rule.

It was Chris-Chris Feldman once, and now Chris Ryan again.

Feldman swung toward a cab. For a moment, his attitude was automatic and assured, and the cab stopped before the driver noticed his clothes. He picked up the bag Chris dropped and swung it onto the front seat. She was fumbling in her change purse as he turned back to shut the door.

"Thank you, my good man," she said. She could be gracious, even to a pariah, when his homage suited her. She dropped two quarters into his hand, raising her eyes.

Recognition flowed into them, followed by icy shock. She yanked the cab door shut and shouted something to the driver. The cab took off with a rush that left Feldman in a backwash of slush and mud.

He glanced down at the coins in his hand. It was his lucky day, he thought bitterly.

He moved across the street and away, not bothering about the squeal of brakes and the honking horns. He looked back only once, toward the glowing sign that topped the building. *Your health is our business!* Then the great symbol of the health business faded behind him, and he stumbled on, sucking incessantly at the cigarettes he rolled. One hand clutched the bronze badge belonging to the dead man and his stolen boots drove onward through the melting snow.

It was Christmas in the year 2100 on the protectorate of Earth.

Lobby

Feldman had set his legs the problem of heading for the great spaceport and escape from Earth, and he let them take him without further guidance. His mind was wrapped up in a whirl of the past-his past and that of the whole planet. Both pasts had in common the growth and sudden ruin of idealism.

Idealism! Throughout history, some men had sought the ideal, and most had called it freedom. Only fools expected absolute freedom, but wise men dreamed up many systems of relative freedom, including democracy. They had tried that in America, as the last fling of the dream. It had been a good attempt, too.

The men who drew the Constitution had been pretty practical dreamers. They came to their task after a bitter war and a worse period of wild chaos, and they had learned where idealism stopped and idiocy began. They set up a republic with all the elements of democracy that they considered safe. It had worked well enough to make America the number one power of the world. But the men who followed the framers of the new plan were a different sort, without the knowledge of practical limits.

The privileges their ancestors had earned in blood and care became automatic rights. Practical men tried to explain that there were no such rights-that each generation had to pay for its rights with responsibility. That kind of talk didn't get far. People wanted to hear about rights, not about duties.

They took the phrase that all men were created equal and left out the implied kicker that equality was in the sight of God and before the law. They wanted an equality with the greatest men without giving up their drive toward mediocrity, and they meant to have it. In a way, they got it.

They got the vote extended to everyone. The man on subsidy or public dole could vote to demand more. The man who read of nothing beyond sex crimes could vote on the great political issues of the world. No ability was needed for his vote. In fact, he was assured that voting alone was enough to make him a fine and noble citizen. He loved that, if he bothered to vote at all that year. He became a great man by listing his unthought, hungry desire for someone to take care of him without responsibility. So he went out and voted for the man who promised him most, or who looked most like what his limited dreams felt to be a father image or son image or hero image. He never bothered later to see how the men he'd elected had handled the jobs he had given them.

Someone had to look, of course, and someone did. Organized special interests stepped in where the mob had failed. Lobbies grew up. There had always been pressure groups, but now they developed into a third arm of the government.

The old Farm Lobby was unbeatable. The big farmers shaped the laws they wanted. They convinced the little farmers it was for the good of all, and they made the story stick well enough to swing the farm vote. They made the laws when it came to food and crops.

The last of the great lobbies was Space, probably. It was an accident that grew up so fast it never even knew it wasn't a real part of the government. It developed during a period of chaos when another country called Russia got the first hunk of metal above the atmosphere and when the representatives who had been picked for everything but their grasp of science and government went into panic over a myth of national prestige.

The space effort was turned over to the aircraft industry, which had never been able to manage itself successfully except under the stimulus of war or a threat of war. The failing airplane industry became the space combine overnight, and nobody kept track of how big it was, except a few sharp operators.

They worked out a system of subcontracts that spread the profits so wide that hardly a company of any size in the country wasn't getting a share. Thus a lot of patriotic, noble voters got their pay from companies in the lobby block and could be panicked by the lobby at the first mention of recession.

So Space Lobby took over completely in its own field. It developed enough pressure to get whatever appropriations it wanted, even over Presidential veto. It created the only space experts, which meant that the men placed in government agencies to regulate it came from its own ranks.

The other lobbies learned a lot from Space.

There had been a medical lobby long before, but it had been a conservative group, mostly concerned with protecting medical autonomy and ethics. It also tried to prevent government control of treatment and payment, feeling that it couldn't trust the people to know where to stop. But its history was a long series of retreats.

It fought what it called socialized medicine. But the people wanted their troubles handled free-which meant by government spending, since that could be added to the national debt, and thus didn't seem to cost anything. It lost, and eventually the government paid most medical costs, with doctors working on a fixed fee. Then quantity of treatment paid, rather than quality. Competence no longer mattered so much. The Lobby lost, but didn't know it-because the lowered standards of competence in the profession lowered the caliber of men running the political aspects of that profession as exemplified by the Lobby.

It took a world-wide plague to turn the tide. The plague began in old China; anything could start there, with more than a billion people huddled in one area and a few madmen planning to conquer the world. It might have been a laboratory mutation, but nobody could ever prove it.

It wiped out two billion people, depopulated Africa and most of Asia, and wrecked Europe, leaving only America comparatively safe to take over. An obscure scientist in one of the laboratories run by the Medical Lobby found a cure before the first waves of the epidemic hit America. Rutherford Ryan, then head of the Lobby, made sure that Medical Lobby got all the credit.

By the time the world recovered, America ran it and the Medical Lobby was untouchable. Ryan made a deal with Space Lobby, and the two effectively ran the world. None of the smaller lobbies could buck them, and neither could the government.

There was still a president and a congress, as there had been a Senate under the Roman Caesars. But the two Lobbies ran themselves as they chose. The real government had become a kind of oligarchy, as it always did after too much false democracy ruined the ideals of real and practical self-rule. A man belonged to his Lobby, just as a serf had belonged to his feudal landlord.

It was a safe world now. Maybe progress had been halted at about the level of 1980, but so long as the citizens didn't break the rules of their lobbies, they had very little to worry about. For that, for security and the right not to think, most people were willing to leave well enough alone.

Some rules seemed harsh, of course, such as the law that all operations had to be performed in Lobby hospitals. But that could be justified; it was the only safe kind of surgery and the only way to make sure there was no unsupervised experimentation, such as that which supposedly caused the plague. The rule was now an absolute ethic of medicine. It also made for better fees.

Feldman's father had stuck by the rule but had questioned it. Feldman learned not to question in medical school. He scored second in Medical Ethics only to Christina Ryan.

He had never figured why she singled him out for her attentions, but he gloried in both those attentions and the results. He became automatically a rising young man, the favorite of the daughter of the Lobby president. He went through internship without a sign of trouble. Chris humored him in his desire to spend three years of practice in a poor section loaded with disease, and her father approved; such selfless dedication was the perfect image projection for a future son-in-law. In return, he agreed to follow that period by becoming an administrator. A doctor's doctor, as they put it.

They were married in April and his office was ready in May, complete with a staff of eighty. The publicity releases had gone out, and the Public Relations Lobby that handled news and education was paid to begin the greatest build-up any young genius ever had.

They celebrated that, with a little party of some four hundred people and reporters at Ryan's lodge in Canada. It was to be a gala weekend.

It was then that Baxter shot himself.

Baxter had been Feldman's closest friend in the Lobby. He'd come along to handle press relations and had gotten romantic about the countryside, never having been out of a city before. He hired a guide and went hunting, eighty miles beyond the last outpost of civilization. Somehow, he got his hand on a gun, though only guides were supposed to touch them, managed to overcome its safety devices, and then pulled the trigger with the gun pointed the wrong way.

Chris, Feldman and Harnett from Public Relations had accompanied him on the trip. They were sitting in a nearby car while Feldman enjoyed the scenery, Chris made further plans, and Harnett gathered material. There was also a photographer and writer, but they hadn't been introduced by name.

Feldman reached Baxter first. The man was moaning and scared, and he was bleeding profusely. Only a miracle had saved him from instant death. The bullet had struck a rib, been deflected and robbed of some of its energy, and had barely reached the heart. But it had pierced the pericardium, as best Feldman could guess, and it could be fatal at any moment.

He'd reached for a probe without thinking. Chris knocked his hand aside.

She was right, of course. He couldn't operate outside a hospital. But they had no phone in the lodge where the guide lived and no way to summon an ambulance. They'd have to drive Baxter back in the car, which would almost certainly result in his death.

When Feldman seemed uncertain, Harnett had given his warning in a low but vehement voice. "You touch him, Dan, and I'll spread it in every one of our media. I'll have to. It's the only way to retain public confidence. There'd be a leak, with all the guides and others here, and we can't afford that. I like you-you have color. But touch that wound and I'll crucify you."

Chris added her own threats. She'd spent years making him the outlet for all her ambitions, denied because women were still only second-rate members of Medical Lobby. She couldn't let it go now. And she was probably genuinely shocked.

Baxter groaned again and started to bleed more profusely.

There wasn't much equipment. Feldman operated with a pocketknife sterilized in a bottle of expensive Scotch and only anodyne tablets in place of anesthesia. He got the bullet out and sewed up the wound with a bit of surgical thread he'd been using to tie up a torn good-luck emblem. The photographer and writer recorded the whole thing. Chris swore harshly and beat her fists against the bole of a tree. But Baxter lived. He recovered completely, and was shocked at the heinous thing that had been done to him.

They crucified Feldman.

Spaceman

Most crewmen lived rough, ugly lives-and usually, short ones. Passengers and officers on the big tubs were given the equivalent of gravity in spinning compartments, but the crews rode "free". The lucky crewmen lived through their accidents, got space-stomach now and then, and recovered. Nobody cared about the others.

Feldman's ticket was work-stamped for the *Navaho*, and nobody questioned his identity. He suffered through the agony of acceleration on the shuttle up to the orbital station, then was sick as acceleration stopped. But he was able to control himself enough to follow other crewmen down a hall of the station toward the *Navaho*. The big ships never touched a planet, always docking at the stations.

A checker met the crew and reached for their badges. He barely glanced at them, punched a mark for each on his checkoff sheet, and handed them back. "Deckmen forward, tubemen to the rear," he ordered. "*Navaho* blasts in fifteen minutes. Hey, you! You're tubes."

Feldman grunted. He should have expected it. Tubemen had the lowest lot of all the crew. Between the killing work, the heat of the tubes, and occasional doses of radiation, their lives weren't worth the metal value of their tickets.

He began pulling himself clumsily along a shaft, dodging freight the loaders were tossing from hand to hand. A bag hit his head, drawing blood, and another caught him in the groin.

"Watch it, bo," a loader yelled at him. "You dent that bag and they'll brig you. Cantcha see it's got a special courtesy stripe?"

It had a brilliant green stripe, he saw. It also had a name, printed in block letters that shouted their identity before he could read the words. *Dr. Christina Ryan, Southport, Mars.*

And he'd had to choose this time to leave Earth!

Suddenly he was glad he was assigned to the tubes. It was the one place on the ship where he'd be least likely to run into her. As a doctor and a courtesy passenger, she'd have complete run of the ship, but she'd hardly bother with the dangerous and unpleasant tube section.

He dragged his way back, beginning to sweat with the effort. The *Navaho* was an old ship. A lot of the handholds were missing, and he had to throw himself along by erratic leaps. He was gaining proficiency, but not enough to handle himself if the ship blasted off. Time was growing short when he reached the aft bunkroom where the other tubemen were waiting.

"Ben," one husky introduced himself. "Tube chief. Know how to work this?"

Feldman could see that they were assembling a small still. He'd heard of the phenomenal quantities of beer spacemen drank, and now he realized what really happened to it. Hard liquor was supposed to be forbidden, but they made their own. "I can work it," he decided. "I'm — uh-Dan."

"Okay, Dan." Ben glanced at the clock. "Hit the sacks, boys."

By the time Feldman could settle into the sacklike hammock, the *Navaho* began to shake faintly, and weight piled up. It was mild compared to that on the shuttle, since the big ships couldn't take high acceleration. Space had been conquered for more than a century, but the ships were still flimsy tubs that took months to reach Mars, using immense amounts of fuel. Only the valuable plant hormones from Mars made commerce possible at the ridiculously high freight rate.

Three hours later he began to find out why spacemen didn't seem to fear dying or turning pariah. The tube quarters had grown insufferably hot during the long blast, but the main tube-room was blistering as Ben led the men into it. The chief handed out spacesuits and motioned for Dan.

"Greenhorn, aincha? Okay, I'll take you with me. We go out in the tubes and pull the lining. I pry up the stuff, you carry it back here and stack it."

They sealed off the tube-room, pumped out the air, and went into the steaming, mildly radioactive tubes, just big enough for a man on hands and knees. Beyond the tube mouth was empty space, waiting for the man who slipped. Ben began ripping out the eroded blocks with a special tool. Feldman carried them back and stacked them along with others. A plasma furnace melted them down into new blocks. The work grew progressively worse as the distance to the tube-room increased. The tube mouth yawned closer and closer. There were no handholds there-only the friction of a man's body in the tube.

Life settled into a dull routine of labor, sleep, and the brief relief of the crude white mule from the still.

They were six weeks out and almost finished with the tube cleaning when Number Two tube blew. Bits of the remaining radioactive fuel must have collected slowly until they reached blow-point. Feldman in Number One would have gone sailing out into space, but Ben reacted at once. As the ship leaped slightly, Feldman brought up sharply against the chief's braced body. For a second their fate hung in the balance. Then it was over, and Ben shoved him back, grinning faintly.

He jerked his thumb and touched helmets briefly. "There they go, Dan."

The two men who had been working in Number Two were charred lumps, drifting out into space.

No further comment was made on it, except that they'd have to work harder from now on, since they were shorthanded.

That rest period Feldman came down with a mild attack of space-stomach —which meant no more drinking for him-and was off work for a day. Then the pace picked up. The tubes were cleared and they began laying the new lining for the landing blasts. There was no time for thought after that. Mars' orbital station lay close when the work was finished.

Ben slapped Feldman on the back. "Ya ain't bad for a greenie, Dan. We all get six-day passes on Mars. Hit the sack now so you won't waste time sleeping then. We'll hear it when the ship berths."

Feldman didn't hear it, but the others did. He felt Ben shaking his shoulder, trying to drag him out of the sack. "Grab your junk, Dan."

Ben picked up Feldman's nearly empty bag and tossed it toward him, before his eyes were fully open. He grabbed for it and missed. He grabbed again, with Ben's laughter in his ears. The bag hit the wall and fell open, spilling its contents.

Feldman began gathering it up, but the chief was no longer laughing. A big hand grabbed up the space ticket suddenly, and there was no friendliness now on Ben's face.

"Art Billing's card!" Ben told the other tubemen. "Five trips I made with Art. He was saving his money, going to buy a farm on Mars. Five trips and one more to go before he had enough. Now you show up with his ticket!"

The tubemen moved forward toward Feldman. There was no indecision. To them, apparently, trial had been held and sentence passed.

"Wait a minute," Feldman began. "Billings died of —"

A fist snaked past his raised hand and connected with his jaw. He bounced off a wall. A wrench sailed toward him, glanced off his arm, and ripped at his muscles. Another heavy fist struck.

Abruptly, Ben's voice cut through their yells. "Hold it!" He shoved through the group, tossing men backwards. "Stow it! We can take care of him later. Right now, this is captain's business. You fools want to lose your leave?" He indicated two of the others. "You two bring him along-and keep him quiet!"

The two grabbed Feldman's arms and dragged him along as the chief began pulling his way forward through the tubes up towards the control section of the ship. Feldman took a quick glance at their faces and made no effort to resist; they obviously would have enjoyed any chance to subdue him.

They were stopped twice by minor officers, then sent on. They finally found the captain near the exit lock, apparently assisting the passengers to leave. Most of them went on into the shuttle, but Chris Ryan remained behind as the captain listened to Ben's report and inspected the false ticket.

Finally the captain turned to Feldman. "You. What's your name?"

Chris' eyes were squarely on Feldman, cold and furious. "He *was* Doctor Daniel Feldman, Captain Marker," she stated.

Feldman stood paralyzed. He'd been unwilling to face Chris. He wanted to avoid all the past. But the idea that she would denounce him had never entered his head. There was no Medical rule involved. She knew that as a pariah he was forbidden to board a passenger ship, of course. But she'd been his wife once!

Marker bowed slightly to her. "Thank you, Dr. Ryan. I should take this criminal back to Earth in chains, I suppose. But he's hardly worth the freightage. You men. Want to take him down to Mars and ground him there?"

Ben grinned and touched his forelock. "Thank you, sir. We'd enjoy that."

"Good. His pay reverts to the ship's fund. That's all, men."

Feldman started to protest, but a fist lashed savagely against his mouth.

He made no other protests as they dragged him into the crew shuttle that took off for Southport. He avoided their eyes and sat hunched over. It was Ben who finally broke the silence.

"What happened to Art's money? He had a pile on him."

"Go to hell!"

"Give, I said!" Ben twisted his arm back toward his shoulder, applying increasing pressure.

"A doctor took it for his fee when Billings died of space-stomach. Damn you, I couldn't help him!"

Ben looked at the others. "Med Lobby fee, eh? All the market will take. Umm. It could be, maybe." He shrugged. "Okay, reasonable doubt. We won't kill you, bo. Not quite, we won't."

The shuttle landed and Ben handed out the little helmets and aspirators that made life possible in Mars' thin air. Outside, the tubemen took turns holding Feldman and beating him while the passengers disembarked from their shuttle. As he slumped into unconsciousness, he had a picture of Chris Ryan's frozen face as she moved steadily toward the port station.

Martian

It was night when Feldman came to, and the temperature was dropping rapidly. He struggled to sit up through a fog of pain. Somewhere in his bag, he should have an anodyne tablet that would kill any ache. He finally found the pill and swallowed it, fumbling with the aspirator lip opening.

The aspirator meant life to him now, he suddenly realized. He twisted to stare at the tiny charge-indicator for the battery. It showed half-charge. Then he saw that someone had attached another battery beside it. He puzzled briefly over it, but his immediate concern was for shelter.

Apparently he was still where he had been knocked out. There was a light coming from the little station, and he headed toward that, fumbling for the few quarters that represented his entire fortune.

Maybe it would have been better if the tubemen had killed him. Batteries were an absolute necessity here, food and shelter would be expensive, and he had no skills to earn his way. At most, he had only a day or so left. But meantime, he had to find warmth before the cold killed him.

The tiny restaurant in the station was still open, and the air was warm inside. He pulled off the aspirator, shutting off the battery.

The counterman didn't even glance up as he entered. Feldman gazed at the printed menu and flinched.

"Soup," he ordered. It was the cheapest item he could find.

The counterman stared at him, obviously spotting his Earth origin. "You adjusted to synthetics?"

Feldman nodded. Earth operated on a mixed diet, with synthetics for all who couldn't afford the natural foods there. But Mars was all synthetic. Many of the chemicals in food could exist in either of two forms, or isomers; they were chemically alike, but differently crystallized. Sometimes either form was digestible, but frequently the body could use only the isomer to which it was adjusted.

Martian plants produced different isomers from those on Earth. Since the synthetic foods turned out to be Mars-normal, that was probably the more natural form. Research designed to let the early colonists live off native food here had turned up an enzyme that enabled the body to handle either isomer. In a few weeks of eating Martian or synthetic food, the body adapted; without more enzyme, it lost its power to handle Earth-normal food.

The cheapness of synthetics and the discovery that many diseases common to Earth would not attack Mars-normal bodies led to the wide use of synthetics on Earth. No pariah could have been expected to afford Earth-normal.

Feldman finished the soup, and found a cigarette that was smokable. "Any objections if I sit in the waiting room?"

He'd expected a rejection, but the counterman only shrugged. The waiting room was almost dark and the air was chilly, but there was normal pressure. He found a bench and slumped onto it, lighting his cigarette. He'd miss the smokes-but probably not for long. He finished the cigarette reluctantly and sat huddled on the bench, waiting for morning.

The airlock opened later, and feet sounded on the boards of the waiting-room floor, but he didn't look up until a thin beam of light hit him. Then he sighed and nodded. The shoes, made of some odd fiber, didn't look like those of a cop, but this was Mars. He could see only a hulking shadow behind the light.

"You the man who was a medical doctor?" The voice was dry and old.

"Yeah," Feldman answered. "Once."

"Good. Thought that space crewman was just lying drunk at first. Come along, Doc."

"Why?" It didn't matter, but if they wanted him to move on, they'd have to push a little harder.

The light swung up to show the other. He was the shade of old leather with a bleached patch of sandy hair and the deepest gray eyes Feldman had ever seen. It was a face that could have belonged to a country storekeeper in New England, with the same hint of dry humor. The man was dressed in padded levis and a leather jacket of unguessable age. His aspirator seemed worn and patched, and one big hand fumbled with it.

"Because we're friends, Doc," the voice drawled at him. "Because you might as well come with us as sit here. Maybe we have a job for you."

Feldman shrugged and stood up. If the man was a Lobby policeman, he was different from the usual kind. Nothing could be worse than the present prospects.

They went out through the doors of the waiting room toward a rattletrap vehicle. It looked something like a cross between a schoolboy's jalopy and a scaled-down army tank of former times. The treads were caterpillar style, and the stubby body was completely enclosed. A tiny airlock stuck out from the rear.

Two men were inside, both bearded. The old man grinned at them. "Mark, Lou, meet Doc Feldman. Sit, Doc. I'm Jake Mullens, and you might say we were farmers."

The motor started with a wheeze. The tractor swung about and began heading away from Southport toward the desert dunes. It shook and rattled, but it seemed to make good time.

"I don't know anything about farming," Feldman protested.

Jake shrugged. "No, of course not. Couple of our friends heard about you where a spaceman was getting drunk and tipped us off. We know who you are. Here, try a bracky?"

Feldman took what seemed to be a cigarette and studied it doubtfully. It was coarse and fibrous inside, with a thin, hard shell that seemed to be a natural growth, as if it had been chopped from some vine. He lighted it, not knowing what to expect. Then he coughed as the bitter, rancid smoke burned at his throat. He started to throw it down, and hesitated. Jake was smoking one, and it had killed the craving for tobacco almost instantly.

"Some like 'em, most don't," Jake said. "They won't hurt you. Look-see that? Old Martian ruins. Built by some race a million years ago. Only half a dozen on Mars."

It was only a clump of weathered stone buildings in the light from the tractor, and Feldman had seen better in the stereo shots. It was interesting only because it connected with the legendary Martian race, like the canals that showed from space but could not be seen on the surface of the planet.

Feldman waited for the other to go on, but Jake was silent. Finally, he ground out the butt of the weed. "Okay, Jake. What do you want with me?"

"Consultation, maybe. Ever hear of herb doctors? I'm one of them."

Feldman knew that the Lobby permitted some leniency here, due to the scarcity of real medical help. There was only one decent hospital at Northport, on the opposite side of the planet.

Jake sighed and reached for another bracky weed. "Yeah, I'm pretty good with herbs. But I got a sick village on my hands and I can't handle it. We can't all mortgage our work to pay for a trip to Northport. Southport's all messed up while the new she-doctor gets her metabolism changed. Maybe the old guy there would have helped, but he died a couple months ago. So it looks like you're our only hope."

"Then you have no hope," Feldman told him sickly. "I'm a pariah, Jake. I can't do a thing for you."

"We heard about your argument with the Lobby. News reaches Mars. But these are mighty sick people, Doc."

Feldman shook his head. "Better take me back. I'm not allowed to practice medicine. The charge would be first-degree murder if anything happened."

Lou leaned forward. "Shall I talk to him, Jake?"

The old man grimaced. "Time enough. Let him see what we got first."

Sand howled against the windshield and the tractor bumped and surged along. Feldman took another of the weeds and tried to estimate their course. But he had no idea where they were when the tractor finally stopped. There was a village of small huts that seemed to be merely entrances to living quarters dug under the surface. They led him into one and through a tunnel into a large room filled with simple cots and the unhappy sounds of sick people.

Two women were disconsolately trying to attend to the half-dozen sick-four children and two adults. Their faces brightened as they saw Jake, then fell. "Eb and Tilda died," they reported.

Feldman looked at the two figures under the sheets and whistled. The same black specks he had seen on the face of Billings covered the skins of the two old people who had died.

"Funny," Jake said slowly. "They didn't quite act like the others and they sure died mighty fast. Darn it, I had it figured for that stuff in the book. Infantile paralysis. How about it, Doc? Sort of like a cold, stiff sore neck."

It was clearly polio-one of the diseases that could attack Mars-normal flesh. Feldman nodded at the symptoms, staring at the sick kids. He shrugged, finally. "There's a cure for it, but I don't have the serum. Neither do you, or you wouldn't have brought me here. I couldn't help if I wanted to."

"That old book didn't list a cure," Jake told him. "But it said the kids didn't have to be crippled. There was something about a Kenny treatment. Doc, does the stuff really cripple for life?"

Feldman saw one of the boys flinch. He dropped his eyes, remembering the Lobby's efficient spy service on Earth and wondering what it was like here. But he knew the outcome.

"Damn you, Jake!"

Jake chuckled. "Thought you would. We sure appreciate it. Just tell us what to do, Doc."

Feldman began writing down his requirements, trying to remember the details of the treatment. Exercise, hot compresses, massage. It was coming back to him. He'd have to do it himself, of course, to get the feel of it. He couldn't explain it well enough. But he couldn't turn his back on the kids, either.

"Maybe I can help," he said doubtfully as he moved toward a cot.

"No, Doc." Jake's voice wasn't amused any longer, and he held the younger man back. "You're doing us a favor, and I'll be darned if I'll let you stick your neck out too far. You can't treat 'em yourself. Mars is tougher than Earth. You should live under Space Lobby *and* Medical Lobby here a while. Oh, maybe they don't mind a few fools like me being herb doctors, but they'd sure hate to have a man who can do real medicine outside their hands. You let me do it, or get in the tractor and I'll have Lou drive you back. Once you start in here, there'll be no stopping. Believe me."

Feldman looked at him, seeing the colonials around him for the first time as people. It had been a long time since he'd been treated as a fellow human by anyone.

Jake was right, he knew. Once he put his hand to the bandage, eventually there'd be no turning back from the scalpel. These people needed medical help too desperately. Eventually, the news would spread, and the Lobby police would come for him. Chris couldn't afford to shield him. In fact, he was sure now that she'd hunt him night and day.

"Don't be a fool, Jake," he ordered brusquely. He handed his list to one of the women. "You'll have to learn to do what I do," he told the people there. "You'll have to work like fools for weeks. But there won't be many crippled children. I can promise that much!"

He blinked sharply at the sudden hope in their eyes. But his mind went on wondering how long it would be before the inevitable would catch up with him. With luck, maybe a few months. But he hadn't been blessed with any superabundance of luck. It would probably be less time than he thought.

V
Surgery

Doc Feldman's luck was better than he had expected. For an Earth year, he was a doctor again, moving about from village to village as he was needed and doing what he could.

The village had been isolated during the early colonization when Mars made a feeble attempt to break free of Space Lobby. Their supplies had been cut off and they had been forced to do for themselves. Now they were largely self-sufficient. They grew native plants and extracted hormones in crude little chemical plants. The hormones were traded to the big chemical plants for a pittance to buy what had to come from Earth. Other jury-rigged affairs synthesized much of their food. But mostly they learned to get along on what Mars provided.

Doc Feldman learned from them. Money was no longer part of his life. He ate with whatever family needed him and slipped into the life around him.

He was learning Martian medicine and finding that his Earth courses were mostly useless. No wonder the villagers distrusted Lobby doctors. Doc had his own little laboratory where he had managed to start making Mars-normal penicillin —a primitive antibiotic, but better than nothing.

Jake had come to remind him that it was his first anniversary, and now they were smoking bracky together.

"Sheer luck, Jake," Doc repeated. "You Martians are tough. But some day someone is going to die under my care, with the little equipment I have. Then —"

Jake nodded slowly. "Maybe, Doc. And maybe some day Mars will break free of the Lobbies. You'd better pray for that."

"I've been —" Doc stopped, realizing what he'd started to say. The old man chuckled.

"You've been talking rebellion for months, Doc. I hear rumors. Whenever you get mad, you want us to secede. But you don't really mean it yet. You can't picture any government but the one you're used to."

Doc grinned. Jake had a point, but it was not as strong as it would have been a few months before. The towns under the Lobby were cheap imitations of Earth, but here, divorced to a large extent from the lobbies, the villages were making Mars their own. Their ways might be strange; but they worked.

Jake shifted his body in the weak sunlight. "Newton village forgot to report a death on time. I hear Ryan is sweating them out, trying to prove it was your fault."

There was no evidence against him yet, Doc was sure. But Chris was out to prove something, and to get a reputation as a top-flight administrator. It must have hurt when they shipped her here as head of the lesser hemisphere of Mars. She'd expected to use Feldman as a front while she became the actual ruler of the whole Lobby. Now she wanted to strike back.

"She's using blackmail," he said, and some of his old bitterness was in his voice. "Anyone taking treatment from an herb doctor in this section is cut off from Medical Lobby service. Damn it, Jake, that could mean letting people die!"

"Yeah." Jake sighed softly. "It could mean letting people begin to think about getting rid of the Lobby, too. Well, I gotta help harvest the bracky. Take it easy on operating for a while, will you, Doc?"

"All right, Jake. But stop keeping the serious cases a secret. Two men died last month because you wouldn't call me for surgery. I've broken all my oaths already. It doesn't matter anymore."

"It matters, boy. We've been lucky, but some day one case will go to the hospital and they'll find your former work. Then they'll really be after you. The less you do the better."

Doc watched Jake slump off, then turned down into the little root cellar and back toward the room concealed behind it, where his crude laboratory lay. For the moment, he was free to work on the mystery of the black spots.

He kept running into them-always on the body of someone who died of something that seemed like a normal disease. Without a microscope, he was almost helpless, but he had taken specimens and tried to culture them. Some of his cultures had grown, though they might be nothing but unknown Martian fungi or bacteria. Mars was dry and almost devoid of air, but plants and a few smaller insects had survived and adapted. It wasn't by any means lifeless.

Without a microscope, he could do little but depend on his files of cases. But today there was new evidence. A villager had filched an Earth *Medical Journal* from the tractor driven by Chris Ryan and forwarded it to him. He found the black specks mentioned in a single paragraph, under skin diseases. Investigation of the diet was being made, since all cases were among people eating synthetics.

There was another article on aberrant cases —a few strange little misbehaviors in classical syndromes. He studied that, wondering. It had to be the same thing. Diet didn't account for the fact that the specks appeared only when the patient was near death.

Nor did it account for the hard lump at the base of the neck which he found in every case he could check. That might be coincidence, but he doubted it.

Whatever it was, it aggravated any other disease the patient had and made seemingly simple diseases turn out to be completely and rapidly fatal. Once syphilis had been called "The Great Imitator". This gave promise of being worse.

He shook his head, cursing his lack of equipment. Each month more people were dying with these specks-and he was helpless.

The concealed door broke open suddenly and a boy thrust his head in. "Doc, there's a man here from Einstein. Says his wife's dying."

The man was already coming into the room.

"She's powerful sick, Doc. Had a bellyache, fever, began throwing up. Pains under her belly, like she's had before. But this time it's awful."

Doc shot a few questions at him, frowning at what he heard. Then he began packing the few things that might help. There should be no appendicitis on Mars. The bugs responsible for that shouldn't have adapted to Mars-normal. But more and more infections found ways to cross the border. Gangrene had been able to get by without change, it seemed. So far, none of the contagious infections except polio and the common cold had made the jump.

This sounded like an advanced case, perhaps already involving peritonitis.

So far, he'd been lucky with penicillin, but each time he used it with grave doubts of its action on the Mars-adapted patients. If the appendix had burst, however, it was the only possible treatment.

He riffled through his stores; There was ether enough, fortunately. The villagers had made that for him out of Martian plants, using their complicated fermentation processes. He yelled for Jake, and the boy brought the old man back a moment later.

"Jake, I'll need more of that narcotic stuff. I don't want the woman writhing and tearing her stitches after the ether wears off."

"Can't get it, Doc." Jake's eyes seemed to cloud as he said it. "Distilling plant broke down. Doc, I don't like this case. That woman's been to the hospital three times. I hear she just got out recently. This might be a plant, or they figure they can't help her."

"They're afraid to try anything on Mars-normal flesh. They can't be proved wrong if they do nothing." Doc finished packing his bag and got ready to go out. "Jake, either I'm a doctor or I'm not. I can't worry when a woman may be dying."

For a second, Jake's expression was stubborn. Then the little crow's feet around his eyes deepened and the dry chuckle was back in his voice. "Right, Dr. Feldman." He flipped up his thumb and went off at a shuffling run toward the tractor. Lou and the man from Einstein followed Doc into the machine.

It was a silent ride, except for Doc's questions about the sick woman. Her husband, George Lynn, was evasive and probably ignorant. He admitted that Harriet had been to the dispensary and small infirmary that Southport called a hospital.

It was the only place in the entire Southern hemisphere where an operation could be performed legally. Most cases had to go to Northport, but Chris had been trying to expand. Apparently, she was determined to make Southport into another major center before she was called back to Earth.

Doc wondered why the villagers went there. They had no medical insurance with the Lobby; they couldn't afford it. Most villagers didn't have the cash, either. They were forced to mortgage their future work and that of their families to the drug plants that were run by the Lobby.

"And they just turned your wife away?" Doc asked. He couldn't quite believe that of Chris.

"Well, I dunno. She wouldn't talk much. Twice she went and they gave her something. Cost every cent I could borrow. Then this last time, they kept her a couple days before they let me come and get her. But now she's a lot worse."

Jake spun about, suddenly tense. "How'd you pay them last time, George?"

"Why, they didn't ask. I told her she could put up six months from me and the kids, but nobody said nothing about it. Just gave her back to me." He frowned slowly, his dull voice uncertain. "They told me they'd done all they could, not to bring her back. That's why she was so strong on getting Doc."

"I don't like it," Jake said flatly. "It stinks. They always charge. George, did they suggest she get in touch with Doc here?"

"Maybe they did, maybe not. Harriet did all the talking with them. I just do what she tells me, and she said to get Doc."

Jake swore. "It smells like a trap. Are you sure she's sick, George?"

"I felt her head and she sure had a fever." George Lynn was torn between his loyalties. "You know me, Doc. You fixed me up that time I had the red pip. I wouldn't pull nothing on you."

Doc had a feeling that Jake was probably right, but he vetoed the suggestion that they stop to look for spies. He had no time for that. If the woman was really sick, he had to get to her at once, and even that might be too late.

He remembered the woman, sickly from other treatment. He'd been forced to remove her inflamed tonsils a few months before. She'd whined and complained because he couldn't spend all his time attending her. She was a nag, a shrew, and a totally selfish woman. But that was her husband's worry, not his.

He dashed into the little house when they reached Einstein, and his first glance confirmed what George Lynn had said. The woman was sick, all right. She was running a high fever. Much too high.

She began whining and protesting at his having taken so long, but the pain soon forced her to stop.

"There may still be a chance," Doc told her husband brusquely. He threw the cleanest sheet onto a table and shoved it under the single light. "Keep out of the way-in the other room, if you can all pile in there. This isn't exactly aseptic, anyhow. You can boil a lot of water, if you want to help."

It would give them something to do and he could use the water to clean up. There was no time to wait for it, however. He had to sterilize with alcohol and carbolic acid, and hope. He bent over the woman, ripping her thin gown across to make room for the operation.

Then he swore.

Across her abdomen was the unhealed wound of a previous operation. They'd worked on her at Southport. They must have removed the appendix and then been shocked by the signs of infection. They weren't supposed to release a sick patient, but there was an easy out for them; they could remove her from the danger of spreading an unknown infection. Some doctors must have doped her up on sedatives and painkillers and sent her home, knowing that she would call him. For that matter, they might have noticed her unrecorded tonsillectomy and considered her fair bait.

He grabbed the ether and slapped a cone over her nose. She tried to protest; she never cooperated in anything. But the fumes of the ether he dipped onto the packing of the cone soon overcame that.

It was peritonitis, of course. The only thing to do was to go in and scrape and clean as best he could. It was a rotten job to have to do, and he should have had help. But he gritted his teeth and began. He couldn't trust anyone else to hold the instruments, even.

He cleaned the infection as best he could, knowing there was almost no chance. He used all the penicillin he dared. Then he began sewing up the incision. It was all he could do, except for dressing the wound with a sterile bandage. He reached for one, and stopped.

While he'd been working, the woman had died, far more quietly than she had ever lived.

It was probably the only gracious act of her life. But it was damning to Doc. They couldn't hide her death, and any investigation would show that someone had worked on her. To the Lobby, he would be the one who had murdered her.

Jake was waiting in the tractor. He took one look at Doc's face and made no inquiries.

They were more than a mile away when Jake pointed back. Small in the distance, but distinct against the sands, a gray Medical Corps tractor was coming. Either they'd had a spy in the village or they'd guessed the rate of her infection very closely. They must have hoped to catch Doc in the act, and they'd barely missed.

It wouldn't matter. Their pictures and what testimony they could force from the village should be enough to hang Doc.

There had been a council the night following the death of Harriet Lynn. Somehow the word had spread through the villages and the chiefs had assembled in Jake's village. But they had brought no solution, and in the long run had been forced to accept Doc's decision.

"I'm not going to retire and hide," he'd told them, surprised at his own decision, but grimly determined. "You need me and I need you. I'll move every day in hopes the Lobby police won't find me, but I won't quit."

Now he was packing the things he most needed and getting ready to move. The small bottles in which he was trying to grow his cultures would need warmth. He shoved them into an inner pocket, and began surveying what must be left.

He was heading for his tractor when another battered machine drove up. It had a girl of about fourteen, with tears streaming down her face. She held out a pleading hand, and her voice was scared. "It's —it's mama!"

"Where?"

"Leibnitz."

Leibnitz was near enough. Doc started his tractor, motioning for the girl to lead the way. The little dwelling she led him to was at the edge of the village, looking more poverty-stricken than most.

Chris Ryan, and three of the Medical Lobby police were inside, waiting. The girl's mother was tied to the bed, with a collection of medical instruments laid out, but apparently the threat had been enough. No actual injury had been inflicted. Probably none had been intended seriously.

"I knew you'd answer that kind of call," Chris said coldly.

He grinned sickly. They'd wasted no time. "I hear it's more than you'll do, Chris. Congratulations! My patient died. You're lucky."

"She was certainly dead when my men took her picture. The print shows the death grimace clearly."

"Pretty. Frame it and keep it to comfort you when you feel lonely," he snapped.

She struck him across the mouth with the handle of her gun. Then she twisted out through the door quickly, heading for the tractor that had been camouflaged to look like those used by the villagers. The three police led him behind her.

A shout went up, and people began to rush onto the village street. But they were too late. By the time they reached Southport, Doc could see a trail of battered tractors behind, but there was nothing more the people could do. Chris had her evidence and her prisoner.

Judge Ben Wilson might have been Jake's brother. He was older and grayer, but the same expression lay on his face. He must have been the family black sheep, since his father had been president of Space Lobby. Instead of inheriting the position, Wilson had remained on Mars, safely out of the family's way.

He dropped the paper he was reading to frown at Chris. "This the fellow?"

She began formal charges, but he cut them off. "Your lawyer already had all that drawn up. I've been expecting you, Doctor. Doctor! Hnnf! You'd do a lot better home somewhere raising a flock of babies. Well, young fellow-so you're Feldman. Okay, your trial comes up day after tomorrow. Be a shame to lock you in Southport jail, a man of your importance. We'll just keep you here in the pending-trial room. It's a lot more comfortable."

Chris had been boiling slowly, and now she seemed to blow her safety valve. "Judge Wilson, your methods are your own business in local affairs. But this involves Earth Medical Lobby. I demand —"

"Tch, *tch!*" The judge stared at her reprovingly. "Young woman, you don't demand anything. This is Mars. If Space Lobby can stand me, I guess our friends over at Medical will have to. Or should I hold trial right now and find Feldman innocent for lack of evidence?"

"You wouldn't!" Chris cried. Then her face sobered suddenly. "I apologize. Medical is pleased to leave things in your hands, of course."

Wilson smiled. "Court's closed for today. Doc, I'll show you your cell. It's right next to my study, so I'm heading there anyhow."

He began shucking his robe while Chris went out with the police, her voice sharp and continual.

The cell was both reasonably escape-proof and comfortable, Doc saw, and he tried to thank the judge.

But the old man waved it aside. "Forget it. I just like to see that little termagant taken down. But don't count on my being soft. My methods may be a bit unusual—I always did like the courtroom scenes in the old books by that fellow Smith-but Space Lobby never had any reason to reverse my decisions. Anything you need?"

"Sure," Doc told him, grinning in spite of his bitterness. "A good biology lab and an electron microscope."

"Umm. How about a good optical mike and some stains? Just got them in on the last shipment. Figure they were meant for you anyhow, since Jake Mullens asked me to order them."

He went out and came back with the box almost at once. He snorted at Doc's incredulous thanks and moved off, his bedroom slippers slapping against the hard floor.

Doc stared after him. If he were a friend of Jake, willing to invent some excuse to get a microscope here ...but it didn't matter. Friend or foe, his death sentence would be equally fatal. And there were other things to be thought of now. The little microscope was an excellent one, though only a monocular.

Doc's hands trembled as he drew his cultures out and began making up a slide. The sun offered the best source of light near the window, and he adjusted the instrument. Something began to come into view, but too faintly to be really visible.

He remembered the stains, trying to recall his biology courses. More by luck than skill, his fourth try gave him results.

Under two thousand powers, he could just see details. There were dozens of cells in his impure culture, but only one seemed unfamiliar. It was a long, worm-like thing, sharpened at both ends, with the three separate nuclei that were typical of Martian life forms. Nearby were a host of little rodlike squiggles just too small to see clearly.

Martian life! No Martian bug had ever proved harmful to men. Yet this was no mutated cell or virus from Earth; it was a new disease, completely different from all others. It was one where all Earth's centuries of experience with bacteria would be valueless-the first Martian disease. Unless this was simply some accidental contamination of his culture, not common to the other samples. He worked on until the light was too faint before putting the microscope aside.

By the time the trial commenced, however, he was sure of the cause of the disease. It *was* Martian. Crude as his cultures were, they had proved that.

The little courtroom was filled, mostly from the villages. Lou was there, along with others he had come to know. Then the sight of Jake caught Doc's eyes. The darned fool had no business there; he could get too closely mixed into the whole mess.

"Court's in session," Wilson announced. "Doc, you represented by counsel?"

Jake's voice answered. "Your Honor, I represent the defendant. I think you'll find my credentials in order."

Chris started to protest, but Wilson grinned. "Never lost your standing in spite of that little fracas thirty years ago, so far as I know. But the police thought you were a witness when you came walking in. Figured you were giving up."

"I never said so," Jake answered.

Chris was squirming angrily, but the florid man acting as counsel for Medical Lobby shook his head, bending over to whisper in her ear. He straightened. "No objection to counsel for the defense. We recognize his credentials."

"You're a fool, Matthews," the judge told him. "Jake was smarter than half the rest of Legal Lobby before he went native. Still can tie your tail to a can. Okay, let's start things. I'm too old to dawdle."

Doc lost track of most of what happened. This was totally unlike anything on Earth, though it might have been in keeping with the general casualness of the villages. Maybe the ritualistic routine of the Lobbies was driving those who could resist to the opposite extreme.

Chris was the final witness. Matthews drew comment of Feldman's former crime from her, and Jake made no protest, though Wilson seemed to expect one. Then she began sewing his shroud. There wasn't a fact that managed to emerge without slanting, though technically correct. Jake sat quietly, smiling faintly, and making no protests.

He got up lazily to cross-examine Chris. "Dr. Ryan, when Daniel Feldman was examined by the Captain of the *Navaho* after arriving at Mars station, did you identify him then as having been Dr. Daniel Feldman?"

She glanced at Matthews, who seemed puzzled but unconcerned. "That's correct," she admitted. "But —"

"And you later saw him delivered to the surface of Mars. Is that also correct?" When she assented, Jake hesitated. Then he frowned. "What did you do then? Did you report him or send anyone to look after him or anything like that?"

"Certainly not," she answered. "He was no —"

"You did absolutely nothing about him after you identified him and saw him delivered here? You're quite sure of that?"

"I did nothing."

Jake stood quietly for a moment, then shrugged. "No more questions."

Matthews finished things in a plea for the salvation of all humanity from the danger of such men as Daniel Feldman. He was looking smug, as was Chris.

Wilson turned to Jake. "Has the defense anything to say?"

"A few things, Your Honor." Jake stood up, suddenly looking certain and pleased. "We are happy to admit everything factual the Lobby had testified. Daniel Feldman performed a surgical operation on Harriet Lynn in the village of Einstein. But when has it been illegal for a member of the Medical profession to perform an operation, even with small chance of success, within an accepted area for such operation? There has been no evidence adduced that any crime or act of even unethical conduct was committed."

That brought Chris and Matthews to their feet. Wilson was relaxed again, looking as if he'd swallowed a whole cage of canaries. He banged his gavel down.

Jake picked up two ragged and dog-eared volumes from his table. "Case of Harding vs. Southport, 2043, establishes that a Lobby is responsible for any member on Mars. It is also responsible for informing the authorities of any criminal conduct on the part of its members or any former member known to it. Failure to report shall be considered an admission that the Lobby recognizes the member as one in good standing and accepts responsibility for that member's conduct.

"At the time Daniel Feldman arrived, Dr. Christina Ryan was the highest appointed representative of Medical Lobby in Southport, with full authority. She identified Feldman as having been a doctor, without stipulating any change in status. She made no further report to any authority concerning Daniel Feldman's presence here. It seems obvious that Medical Lobby at Southport thereby accepted Daniel Feldman as a doctor in good standing for whose conduct the Lobby accepted full responsibility."

Wilson studied the book Jake held out, and nodded. "Seems pretty clear-cut to me," he agreed, passing the book on to Matthews. "There's still the charge that Dr. Feldman operated outside a hospital."

"No reason he shouldn't," Jake said. He handed over the other volume. "This is the charter for Medical Lobby on Mars. Medical Lobby agrees to perform all necessary surgical and medical services for the planet, though at the signing of this charter there was no hospital on Mars. Necessarily, Medical Lobby agreed to perform surgery outside of any hospital, then. But to make it plainer, there's a later paragraph-page 181 —that defines each hospital zone as extending not less than three nor more than one hundred miles. Einstein is about one hundred and ten miles from the nearest hospital at Southport, so Einstein comes under the original charter provisions. Dr. Feldman was forced by charter provisions to protect the good name of his Lobby by undertaking any necessary surgery in Einstein."

He waited until Matthews had scanned that book, then took it back and began packing a big bag. Doc saw that his possessions and the microscope were already in the bag. The old man paid no attention to the arguments of Matthews before the bench.

Abruptly Wilson pounded his gavel. "This court finds that Dr. Daniel Feldman is qualified to practice all the arts and skills of the medical profession on Mars and that he acted ethically in the performance of his duties in the case of the deceased Harriet Lynn," he ruled. "The costs of the case shall be billed to Medical Lobby of Southport."

He took off his robe and moved rapidly toward his private quarters. Court was closed.

Doc got up shakily, not daring to believe fully what he had heard. He started toward Jake, trying to avoid bumping into Chris. But she would not be avoided. She stood in front of him, screaming accusations and threats that reminded him of the only fight they'd ever had during their brief marriage.

When she ran down, he finally met her eyes. "You're a helluva doctor," he told her harshly. "You spend all your time fighting me when there's a plague out there that may be worse than any disease we've ever known. Take a look at what lies under the black specks on your corpses. You'll find the first Martian disease. And maybe if you begin working on that now, you can learn to be a real doctor in time to do something about it. But I doubt it."

She fell back from him then. "Research! You've been doing unauthorized research!"

"Prove it," he suggested. "But you'd be a lot smarter to try some yourself, and to hell with your precious rules."

He followed Jake out to the tractor.

Surprisingly, the old man was sweating now. He shook his head at Doc's look, and his grin was uncertain.

"Matthews is an incompetent," he said. "They could have had you, Doc. That charter is so sloppy a man can prove anything by it, and building a hospital here did bring in Earth rules. Wilson went out on a limb in letting you go. But I guess we got away with it. Let's get out of here."

Doc climbed into the tractor more soberly. They had escaped this time. But there would be another time, and he was pretty sure that would be Chris' round. He had no intention of giving up his research.

Plague

Dr. Feldman leaned back from his microscope and lighted another bracky weed. He glanced about the room and sighed wearily. Maybe he'd been better off when he had no friends and couldn't risk the safety of others in an effort to do research that was the highest crime on two worlds.

The evidence of his work was hidden thirty feet beyond his former laboratory in Jake's village, with a tunnel that led from another root-cellar. The theory was the old one that the best place to avoid discovery was where you had already been discovered. If their spies had identified his former hangout, they'd never expect to have him set up research nearby. It was a nice theory, but he wasn't sure of it.

Jake looked up from a cot where he'd been watching the improvised culture incubator. "Stop tearing yourself to bits, Doc. We know the danger and we're still darned glad to have you here working on this."

"I'm trying to put myself together into a whole man," Doc told him. "But I seem to come out wholly a fool."

"Yeah, sure. Sometimes it takes a fool to get things done; wise men wait too long for the right time. How's the bug hunt?"

Doc grunted in disgust and swung back to the microscope. Then he gave up as his tired eyes refused to focus. "Why don't you people revolt?"

"They tried it twice. But they were just a bunch of pariahs shipped here to live in peonage. They couldn't do much. The first time Earth cut off shipments and starved them. Next time the villages had the answer to that but the cities had to fight for Earth or starve, so they whipped us. And there's always the threat that Earth could send over unmanned war rockets loaded with fissionables."

"So it's hopeless?"

"So nothing! The Lobbies are poisoning themselves, like cutting off Medical service until they cut themselves out of a job. It's just a matter of time. Go back to the bugs, Doc."

Doc sighed and reached for his notes. "I wish I knew more Martian history. I've been wondering whether this bug may not have been what killed off the old Martians. Something had to do it, the way they disappeared. I wish I knew enough to make an investigation of those ruins out there."

"Durwood!" Jake had propped himself on an elbow, staring at Doc in surprise.

Doc scowled. "Clive Durwood, you mean? The archeologist who dug up what little we know about the ruins?"

"Yeah, before he went back to Earth and started living off his lectures. He came here again three years ago and dropped dead in Edison on the way to some other ruins. Heart failure, they called it, though it was more like the two old farmers who ran themselves to death last month. I saw him when they buried him. His face looked funny, and I think he had those little specks, though I may remember wrong." He grimaced. "Mars is tough, Doc; it has to be. Some of the plant seeds Durwood found in the ruins grew! Maybe your bugs waited a million years till we came along."

"What about the farmers? Did they meet Durwood?"

Jake nodded. "Must have. He lived in their village most of the time."

Doc went through his notes. He'd asked for reports on all deaths, and he finally found the account. The two old men had been nervous and fidgety for weeks. They were twins, living by themselves, and nobody paid much attention. Then one morning both were seen running wildly in circles. The village managed to tie them up, but they died of exhaustion shortly after.

It wasn't a pretty picture. The disease might have an incubation period of nearly fifteen years, judging by the length of time it had taken to hit Durwood. It must spread from person to person during an early contagious stage, leaving widening circles behind Durwood and those first infected. When matured, any other sickness would set it off, with few symptoms of its own. But without help, it still killed its victims, apparently driving them madly toward frenzied physical effort.

He studied the culture on a slide again. He'd tried Koch's method to get a pure strain, splattering the bugs onto a native starchy root and plucking off individual colonies. About twenty specimens had been treated with every chemical he could find. So far he'd found a few things that seemed to stop their growth, but nothing that killed them, except stuff far too harsh to use in living tissue.

He had nearly forty cases of deaths that showed symptoms now, and he went back over them, looking for anything in common that went back ten to twenty years before death. There were no rashes nor blisters. A few had had apparent colds, but such were too common to mean anything.

Only one thing appeared, about fourteen years before their deaths. The people interviewed about the victims might be vague about most things, but they remembered the time when "Jim had the jumping headache."

"Jake," Doc called, "what's jumping headache? Most people seem to have it some time or other, but I haven't run across a case of it."

"Sure you have, Doc. Mamie Brander's little girl a few weeks ago. Feels like your pulse is going to rip your skull off, right here. Can't eat because chewing drives you crazy. Back of your head, neck and shoulders swell up for about a week. Then it goes away."

Then it goes away-for fourteen years, until it comes back to kill!

Doc stared at his charts in sudden horror. It was a new disease-thought to be some virus, but not considered dangerous. Selznik's migraine, according to medical usage; you treated it with hot pads and anodyne, and it went away easily enough.

He'd seen hundreds of such cases on Earth. There must be millions who had been hit by it. The patent-medicine branch of the Lobby had even brought out something called Nograine to use for self-treatment.

"Something important?" Jake wanted to know.

Feldman nodded. "How much weight do you swing in other villages, Jake?"

"People sort of do me favors when I ask," Jake admitted. "Like swiping those medical journals from Northport for you, or like Molly Badger getting that job as maid to spy on Chris Ryan. Name it and I'll do my best."

Doc had a vague idea of village politics, but he had more important things to think of. Most of his foul mood had disappeared with the clue he'd stumbled on, and his chief worry now was to clinch the facts.

Feldman considered the problem. "I want a report on every case of jumping headache in every village-who had it, when, and how old they were. This place first, but every village you can reach. And I'll want someone to take a letter to Chris Ryan."

Jake frowned at that, but went out to issue instructions. Doc sat down at a battered old typewriter. Writing Chris might do no good, but some warning had to be gotten through to Earth, where the vast resources of Medical Lobby could be thrown into the task of finding the cause and cure of the disease. The connection with Selznik's migraine had to be reported. If something could blast the Lobby into action, it wouldn't matter quite so much what they did to him. He wasn't foolish enough to expect gratitude from them, but he was getting used to the idea that his days were numbered. The plague was more important than what happened to him.

The letter had been dispatched by the time Jake returned. "Here's the dope for this village. Everybody accounted for except you."

"Never had it, Jake." Feldman went down the list. "Most of it fourteen years ago. That fits. About the only exceptions are the kids who seem to get it between the ages of two and three. Eighty-seven out of ninety-one!"

He stared at the figures sickly. Most of the village not only had the plague but must be near the end of the incubation period. It looked as if most of the village would be dead before another year passed.

"Bad?" Jake asked.

"The first symptom of Martian fever."

The old man whistled, the lines around his eyes tightening. "Must be me," he decided. "I'm the guy who must have brought it here, then. I used to spend a lot of time with Durwood at his diggings!"

There was a constant commotion all that day and the next as runners went out to the villages and came back with reports. The variation from village to village was only slight. Most of Mars seemed to have advanced cases of Martian fever.

Without animals for investigation and study, real research was difficult. Doc also needed an electron microscope. He was reasonably sure that the disease must travel through the nerves, but he had found no proof beyond the hard lump at the base of the neck. There it was a fair-sized organism. Elsewhere he could find nothing, until the black specks developed.

His eyes ached from trying to see more than was visible in the microscope. The tantalizing suggestions of filaments around the nuclei might be the form of plague that was contagious. They might even be the true form of the bug, with the bigger cell only a transition stage. There were a number of diseases that involved complicated changes in the organisms that caused them. But he couldn't be sure.

He finally buried his head in his hands, trying to do by pure thought what he couldn't do in any other way. And even there, he lacked training. He was a doctor, not a xenobiologist. Research training had been taboo in school, except for a favored few.

The reports continued to come in, confirming the danger. They seemed to have the worst plague on their hands in all human history; and nobody who could do anything about it even knew of it.

"Molly reports that your letter got some results," Jake reported. "Chris Ryan brought home one of the electron microscopes and a bunch of equipment from the hospital pathology room. Think she'll get anywhere?"

Doc doubted it. Damn it, he hadn't meant for her to try it, though she might have authority for routine experiments. But it was like her to refuse to pass on the word without trying to prove her own suspicion of him first.

He tried to comfort himself with the fact that some men were immune, or seemed so; about three out of a hundred showed no signs. If that immunity was hereditary, it might save the race. If not....

Jake came in at twilight with a grim face. "More news from Molly. The Lobby is starting out to comb every village with a fault-finder, starting here. And this hole will show up like a sore thumb. Better start packing. We gotta be out of here in less than an hour!"

VIII
Fool

Three days later, Doc saw his first runner.

The tractor was churning through the sand just before sundown, heading toward another one-night stand at a new village. Lou was driving, while Doc and Jake brooded silently in the back, paying no attention to the colors that were blazoned over the dunes. The cat-and-mouse game was getting to Doc. There was no real assurance that the village they were approaching might not be the target the Lobby had chosen for the next investigation.

Lou braked the tractor to a sudden halt, and pointed.

A figure was running frantically over one of the low dunes with the little red sun behind him. He seemed headed toward them, but as he drew nearer they could see that he had no definite direction. He simply ran, pumping his legs frantically as if all the devils of hell were after him. His body swayed from side to side in exhaustion, but his arms and legs pumped on.

"Stop him!" Jake ordered, and Lou swung the tractor. It halted squarely in the runner's path, and the figure struck against it and toppled.

The legs went on pumping, digging into the dirt and gravel, but the man was too far gone to rise. Jake and Lou shoved him through the doors into the tractor and Doc yanked off his aspirator.

The man was giving vent to a kind of ululating cry, weakened now almost to a whine that rose and fell with the motion of his legs. Sweat had once streaked his haggard face, but it was dry and blanched to a pasty gray.

Doc injected enough narcotic to quiet a maddened bull. It had no effect, except to upset the rhythm of the arms and legs. It took five more minutes for the man to die.

The specks were larger this time-the size of periods in twelve-point type. The lump at the base of the skull was as big as a small hen's egg.

"From Edison, like the others so far. Jack Kooley," Jake answered Doc's question. "Durwood spent a lot of time here on his first expedition, so it's getting the worst of it."

Doc pulled the aspirator mask back over the man's face and they carried him out and laid him on a low dune. They couldn't risk returning the corpse to its people.

This was only the primary circle of infection, direct from Durwood. The second circle could be ten times as large, as the infection spread from one to a few to many. So far it was localized. But it wouldn't stay that way.

Doc climbed slowly out of the tractor, lugging his small supplies of equipment, while Jake made arrangements for them to spend the night in a deserted house. But the figure of the runner and his own failures to find more about the disease kept haunting Doc. He began setting up his equipment grimly.

"Better get some sleep," Jake suggested. "You're a mite more tired than you think. Anyhow, I thought you told me you couldn't do any more with what you've got."

Feldman looked at the supplies he had spread out, and shook his head wearily. He'd been over every chemical and combination a dozen times, without results that showed in the limited magnification of the optical mike.

He snapped the case shut and hit the rude table with the heel of his hand. "There are other supplies. Jake, do you have any signal to get in touch with Molly at the Ryan house?"

"Three raps on the rear left window. I'll get Lou."

"No!" Doc came to his feet, reaching for his jacket. "They're looking for three men now. It's safer if I go alone-and I'm the only one who knows what supplies are needed. With luck, I may even get the electron mike. Got a gun I can borrow?"

Jake found one somewhere, an old revolver with a few loads. He began protesting, but Doc overruled him sharply. Three men could no more fight off the police than one, if they were spotted. He swung toward the tractor.

"You'd better start spreading the word on everything we know. If people realize they're already safe or doomed it'll be better than having them going crazy to avoid contagion."

"Most of the villages know already," Jake told him. "And damn it, get back here, Doc. If you can't make it, turn tail quick, and we'll think of something else."

Southport seemed normal enough as Doc drove through its streets. The stereo house was open, and the little shops were brightly lighted. He stopped once to pull a copy of Southport's little newspaper from a dispenser. All was quiet on its front page, too.

As usual, though, the facts were buried inside. The editorial was pouring too much oil on the waters in its lauding of the role of Medical Lobby on Mars for no apparent reason. The death notices no longer listed the cause of death. Medical knew something was up, at least, and was worried.

He parked the tractor behind Chris' house and slipped to the proper window. Everything was seemingly quiet there. At his knock, the shade was drawn back, and he caught a brief glimpse of Molly looking out. A moment later she opened the rear lock to let him into the kitchen.

"Shh. She's still up, I think. What can I do, Doc?"

He tried to smile at her. "Hide me until it's safe to get into her laboratory. I've got to —"

The inner kitchen was kicked open and Chris stood beyond it, holding a cocked gun in her hand.

"It took longer than I expected, Dan," she said quietly. "But after your letter, I knew you'd swallow the bait. You bloody fool! Did you really believe I'd start doing research here just because of your imaginings?"

He slumped slowly back against the sink. "So this is a fool's errand, then? There never was any equipment here?"

"The equipment's here-in my office. I guessed your spies would report it, so it had to be here. But it won't help you now, pariah Feldman!"

He came from his braced position against the sink like a spring uncoiling. He expected her to shoot, but hoped the surprise would ruin her aim. Then it was too late, and his boot hit the gun savagely, knocking it from her hand. Life in the villages had hardened him surprisingly. She was comparatively helpless in his hands. A few minutes later, he had her bound securely with surgical tape Molly brought him. She raged furiously in the chair where he'd dumped her, then gave up.

"They'll get you, Daniel Feldman!" Surprisingly, there was no rage in her voice now. "You won't get away from us. The planet isn't big enough."

"I got away from your trial," he reminded her. "And I got away and lived when you left me without a chance on the ground of the spaceport."

She laughed harshly. "*You* got away then? You fool, who do you think gave you the extra battery so you could live long enough to be helped at the spaceport? Who hired a fool like Matthews so you wouldn't get the death sentence you deserved? Who let you get away as an herb doctor for months before you set yourself up as God and a traitor to mankind again?"

It shook him, as it was probably intended to do. How had she known about the extra battery? He'd always assumed that Ben had returned to give it to him. But in that case, Chris couldn't know of it. Then he hardened himself again. In the old days, she'd always had one trump card he couldn't beat and hadn't expected. But too much was involved for games now.

"Any police around, Molly?" he asked.

Molly came back a minute later to report that everything looked clear and to show him where the equipment had been set up in Chris' office. It was all there, including the electron mike —a beautiful little portable model. There was even a small incubator with its own heat source into which he immediately transferred the little bottles he'd been keeping warm against his skin. Most of the equipment had never been unpacked, which made loading it onto his tractor ridiculously easy.

"Better come with me now, Molly," he suggested at last. Then he turned to Chris, who was watching him with almost no expression. "You can wriggle your chair to the phone in half an hour, I guess. Knock the phone off and yell for help. It's better than you deserve, unless you really did leave me that battery."

"You won't get away with it," she told him again, calmly this time.

"No," he admitted. "Probably not. But maybe the human race will, if I have time to find an answer to the plague you won't see under your nose. But you won't get away with it, either. In the long run, your kind never do."

Molly was sniffling as they drove away. It had probably been the best life she'd known, Doc supposed. Chris could be kind to menials. But now Molly's work was done, and she'd have to disappear into the villages. He let her off at the first village and drove on alone. He was itching to get to the microscope now, hardly able to wait through the long journey back to Jake. His impatience grew with each mile.

Finally he gave up. He swung the tractor into a small gulley between sand dunes, left the motor idling and pulled down the shades the villagers used for blackout traveling. There was power enough for the mike here, and the cab was big enough for what he had to do.

He mounted the mike on the tractor seat and began laying out the collection of smears and cultures he had brought. It had been years since he'd made a film for the electron mike, but he found it all came back to him as he worked.

His hands were sweating with tension as he inserted the first film into the chamber. He had the magnetic "lenses" set for twenty thousand power, but a quick glance showed it was too weak. He raised the power to fifty thousand.

The filaments were there, clear and distinct.

He turned on the little tape recorder that had been part of Chris' equipment and set the microphone where he could dictate into it without stopping to make clumsy notes. He readjusted the focus carefully, carrying on a running commentary.

Then he gasped. Each of the little filaments carried three tiny darker sections; each was a cell, complete in itself, with the typical Martian triple nucleus.

He put a film with a tiny section of the nerve tissue from a corpse into the chamber next, and again a quick glance at the screen was enough. The filaments were there, thickly crowded among nerve cells. They *did* travel along the nerves to reach the base of the brain before the larger lump could form.

A specimen from one of the black specks was even more interesting. The filaments were there, but some were changed or changing into tiny, round cells, also with the triple dark spots of nuclei. Those must be the final form that was released to infect others. Probably at first these multiplied directly in epithelial tissue, so that there was a rapid contagion of infection. Eventually, they must form the filaments that invaded the nerves and caused the brief bodily reaction that was Selznik's migraine. Then the body adapted to them and they began to incubate slowly, developing into the large cells he had first seen. When "ripe", the big cells broke apart into millions of the tiny round ones that went back to the nerve endings, causing the black spots and killing the host.

He knew his enemy now, at least.

He reached for the controls, increasing the magnification. He would lose resolution, but he might find something more at the extreme limits of the mike.

Something wet and cold gushed into his face. He jerked back, trying to wipe it off, but it was already evaporating, and there was a thick, acrid odor in the cab. He grabbed for his aspirator, then tried to reach the airlock. But paralysis was already spreading through him, and he toppled to the floor before he could escape.

When he came to, it was morning outside, and Chris was waiting inside the cab with two big Lobby policemen. A hypo in her hand must have been what revived him.

She touched the electron microscope with something like affection. "The Lobby technicians did a good job on this, don't you think, Dan? I warned you, but you wouldn't listen. And now we've even got your own taped words to prove you were doing forbidden research. Fool!"

She shook her head pityingly as the tractor began moving with two others toward Southport.

"You and your phony diseases. A little skin disorder, Selznik's migraine, and a few cases of psychosis to make a new disease. Do you think Medical Lobby can't check on such simple things? Or didn't you expect us to hear of your open talk of revolt and realize you were planning to create some new germ to wipe out the Earth forces. Maybe those runners of yours were real, mass murderer!"

She drew out another hypo and shoved the needle into his arm. Necrosynth-enough to keep him unconscious for twenty-four hours. He started to curse her, but the drug acted before he could complete the thought.

Doc woke to see sunlight shining through a heavily barred window that must be in the official Southport jail. He waited a few minutes for his head to clear and then sat up; necrosynth left no hangover, at least.

The sound of steps outside was followed by the squeak of a key in the lock. "Fifteen minutes, Judge Wilson," a voice said.

"Thank you, officer." Wilson came into the cell, carrying a tray of breakfast and a copy of the Northport *Gazette*. He began unloading bracky weeds from his pocket while Doc attacked the breakfast.

"They tossed the book at you, Doc," he said. "You haven't got a chance, and there's nothing the villages can do. Trial's set for tomorrow at Northport, and it's in closed session. We can't get you off this time."

Doc nodded. "Thanks for coming, even if there's nothing you can do. I've been living on borrowed time for a year, anyhow, so I have no right to kick. But who's 'we'?"

"The villages. I've been part of their organization for years." The old man sighed heavily. "You might say a revolution has been going on since I can remember, though most villagers don't know it. We've just been waiting our time. Now we've stopped waiting and the rifles will be coming out-rifles made in village shops. The villages are going to rebel, even if we're all dead of plague in a month."

Doc Feldman nodded and reached for the bracky. He knew that this was their way of trying to make him feel his work hadn't been for nothing, and he was grateful for Wilson's visit. "It was a good year for me. Damned good. But time's running short. I'd better brief you on the latest on the plague."

Wilson began making notes until Doc was finished. Finally he got up as steps sounded from the hall. "Anything else?"

"Just a guess. A lot of Earth germs can't live in Mars-normal flesh; maybe this can't live in Earth-normal. Tell them so long for me."

"So long, Doc." He shook hands briefly and was waiting at the door when the guard opened it.

An hour later, the Lobby police took Feldman to the Northport shuttle rocket. They had some trouble on the way; a runner cut down the street, with the crowds frantically rushing out of his way. Terror was reaching the cities already.

Doc flashed a look at Chris. "Mob hysteria. Like flying saucers and wriggly tops, I suppose?" he asked, before the guard could stop him.

They locked his legs, but left his hands free in the rocket. He unfolded the paper Wilson had brought and buried his face in it. Then he swore. They *were* explaining the runners as a case of mob hysteria!

Northport was calmer. Apparently they had yet to have first-hand experience with the plague. But now nothing seemed quite real to Doc, even when they locked him into the big Northport jail. The whole ritual of the Lobbies seemed like a fantasy after the villages.

It snapped back into focus, however, when they led him into the trial room of the Medical Lobby building. It was a smaller version of his trial on Earth. Fear washed in by association. The complete lack of humanity in the procedure was something from a half-remembered and horrible past.

The presiding officer asked the routine question: "Is the prisoner represented by counsel?"

Blane, the dapper little prosecutor, arose quickly. "The prisoner is a pariah, Sir Magistrate."

"Very well. The court will accept the protective function for the prisoner. You may proceed."

I'll be judge, I'll be jury. And prosecution and defense. It made for a lot less trouble. Of course, if Space Lobby had asserted interest, it would have gone to a supposedly neutral court. But as usual, Space was happy to leave it in the hands of Medical.

The tape was played as evidence. Doc frowned. The words were his, but there had been a lot of editing that subtly changed the import of his notes.

"I protest," he challenged. "It's not an accurate version."

The Lobby magistrate turned a wooden face to him. "Does the prisoner have a different version to introduce?"

"No, but —"

"The evidence is accepted. One of the prisoner's six protests will be charged against him."

Blane smiled smoothly and held up a small package. "We wish to introduce this drug as evidence that the prisoner is a confirmed addict, morally irresponsible under addiction. This is a package of so-called bracky weed, a vile and noxious substance found in his possession."

"It has alkaloids no more harmful than nicotine," Feldman stated sharply.

"Do you contend that you find the taste pleasing?" Blane asked.

"It's bitter, but I've gotten used to it."

"I've tasted it," the magistrate said. "Evidence accepted. Two deductions, one for irregularity of presentation."

Doc shrugged and sat back. He'd tested his rights and found what he expected. It was hard to see now how he had ever accepted such procedure. Jake must be right; they'd been in power too long, and were making the mistake of taking the velvet glove off the iron fist and flailing about for the sheer pleasure of power.

It dragged on, while he became a greater and greater monster on the record. But finally it was over, and the magistrate turned to Feldman. "You may present your defense."

"I ask complete freedom of expression," Doc said formally.

The magistrate nodded. "This is a closed court. Permission granted. The recording will be scrambled."

The last bit ruined most of the purpose Doc had in mind. But it was too late to change. He could only hope that some one of the Medical men present would remember something of what he said.

"I have nothing to say for myself," he began. "It would be useless. But I had to do what I did. There's a plague outside. I've studied that plague, and I have knowledge which must be used against it...."

He sat down in three minutes. It had been useless.

Blane arose, with a smile still plastered on his face. "We, of course, recognize the existence of a new contagion, but I believe we have established that this is one disseminated by the prisoner himself, and probably not directly contagious. There have been many cases of fanatics ready to destroy humanity to eliminate those they hate. Now, surely, the prisoner has himself left no question of his attitude. He asserts he has knowledge and skill greater than the entire Medical Research staff. He has attempted to intimidate us by threats. He is clearly psychopathic, and dangerously so. The prosecution rests."

The guards took Doc into the anteroom, where he was supposed to hear nothing that went on. But their curiosity was stronger than their discretion, and the door remained a trifle ajar.

The magistrate began the discussion. "The case seems firm enough. It's fortunate Dr. Ryan acted so quickly, with some of the people getting nervous. Perhaps it might be wise to publicize our verdict."

"My thought exactly," Blane agreed. "If we show Feldman is responsible and that Medical is eliminating the source of the infection, it may have a stabilizing effect."

"Let's hope so. The sentence will have to be death, of course. We can't let such a rebellious psychopath live. But this needs something more, it seems. You've prepared a recommendation, I suppose."

"There was the case of Albrecht Delier," Blane suggested. "Something like that should have good publicity impact."

It struck Doc that they sounded as if they believed themselves-as the witch-burners had believed in witches. He was sweating when the guards led him before the bench.

The magistrate rolled a pen slowly across his fingers as his eyes raked Feldman. "Pariah Daniel Feldman, you have been found guilty on all counts. Furthermore, your guilt must be shared by that entire section of Mars known as the villages. Therefore the entire section shall be banned and forbidden any and all services of the Medical Lobby for a period of one year."

"Sir Magistrate!" One of the members of Southport Hospital staff was on his feet. "Sir Magistrate, we can't cut them off completely."

"We must, Dr. Harkness. I appreciate the fine humanitarian tradition of our Lobby which lies behind your protest, but at such a time as this the good of the body politic requires drastic measures. Why not see me after court, and we can discuss it then?"

He turned back to Feldman, and his face was severe.

"The same education which has produced such fine young men as Dr. Harkness was wasted on you and perverted to endanger the whole race. No punishment can equal your crimes, but there is one previously invoked for a particularly horrible case, and it seems fitting that you should be the fourth so sentenced.

"Daniel Feldman, you are sentenced to be taken in to space beyond planetary limits, together with all material used by you in the furtherance of your criminal acts. There you shall be placed into a spacesuit containing sufficient oxygen for one hour of life, and no more. You and your contaminated possessions shall then be released into space, to drift there through all eternity as a warning to other men.

"This sentence shall be executed at the earliest possible moment, and Dr. Christina Ryan is hereby commissioned to observe such execution. And may God have mercy on your soul!"

Execution

The hours of waiting were blurred for Doc. There were periods when fear clogged his throat and left him gasping with the need to scream and beat his cell walls. There were also times when it didn't seem to matter, and when his only thoughts were for the villages and the plague.

They brought him the papers, where he was painted as a monster beside whom Jack the Ripper and Albrecht Delier were gentle amateurs. They were trying to focus all fear and resentment on him. Maybe it was working. There were screaming crowds outside the jail, and the noise of their hatred was strong enough to carry through even the atmosphere of Mars. But there were also signs that the Lobby was worried, as if afraid that some attempt might still be made to rescue him.

He'd looked forward to the trip to the airport as a way of judging public reaction. But apparently the Lobby had no desire to test that. The guards led him up to the roof of the jail, where a rocket was waiting. The landing space was too small for one of the station shuttles, but a little Northport-Southport shuttle was parked there after what must have been a difficult set-down. The guards tested Doc's manacles and forced him into the shuttle.

Inside, Chris was waiting, carrying an official automatic. There was also a young pilot, looking nervous and unhappy. He was muttering under his breath as the guards locked Doc's legs to a seat and left.

"All right," Chris ordered. "Up ship!"

"I tell you we're overweight with you. I wasn't counting on three for the trip," the pilot protested. "The only thing that will get this into orbit with the station is faith. I'm loaded with every drop of fuel she'll hold and it still isn't enough."

"That's your problem," Chris told him firmly. "You've got your orders, and so have I. Up ship!"

If she had her own worries about the shuttle, she didn't show it. Chris had never been afraid to do what she felt she should. The pilot stared at her doubtfully and finally turned back to his controls, still muttering.

The shuttle lifted sluggishly, but there was no great difficulty. Doc could see that there was even some fuel remaining when they slipped into the tube at the orbital station. Chris went out, and other guards came in to free him.

"So long, Dr. Feldman," the pilot called softly as they led him out. Then the guards shoved him through the airlock into the station. Fifteen minutes later he was locked into one of the cabins of the *Iroquois*, with all his possessions stacked beside him.

He grinned wryly. As an honest worker on the *Navaho* he'd been treated like an animal. Now, as a human fiend, he was installed in a luxury cabin of the finest ship of the fleet, with constant spin to give a feeling of weight and more room than the entire tube crew had known.

He roamed the cabin until he found a little collapsible table. He set the electron microscope up on that and plugged it in. It seemed a shame that good equipment should be wasted along with his life. He wondered if they would really throw it out into space with him. Probably they would.

He pushed a button on the call board over the table and asked for the steward. There was a long wait, as if the procedure were being checked with some authority, but finally he received a surly acknowledgement. "Steward. Whatcha want?"

"How's the chance of getting some food?"

"You're on first-class."

They could afford it, Doc decided. He wouldn't cost them much, considering the distance he was going. "Bring me two complete dinners-one Earth-normal and one Mars-normal."

"Okay, Feldman. But if you think you can suicide that way, you're wrong. You may be sick, but you'll be alive when they dump you."

A sharp click interrupted him. "That's enough, Steward. Captain Everts speaking. Dr. Feldman, you have my apologies. Until you reach your destination, you are my passenger and entitled to every consideration of any other passenger except freedom of movement through the ship. I am always available for legitimate complaints."

Feldman shook his head. He'd heard of such men. But he'd thought the species extinct.

The steward brought his food in a thoroughly chastened manner. He managed to find space for it and came to attention. "Is that all—sir?"

For a moment, as the smell of real steak reached him, Doc regretted the fact that his metabolism had been switched. Then he shrugged. A little wouldn't hurt him, though there was no proper nourishment in it. He squeezed some of the gravy and bits of meat into one of his bottles, sticking to his purpose; then he fell to on the rest. But after a few bites, it was queerly unsatisfactory. The seemingly unappealing Mars-normal ragout suited his current tastes better, after all.

Once the steward had cleared away the dishes, Doc went to work. It was better than wasting his time in dread. He might even be able to leave some notes behind.

A gong sounded, and a red light warned him that acceleration was due. He finished with his bottles, put them into the incubator, and piled into his bunk, swallowing one of the tablets of morphetal the ship furnished.

Acceleration had ended, and a simple breakfast was waiting when he awoke. There was also a red flashing light over the call board. He flipped the switch while reaching for the coffee.

"Captain Everts," the speaker said. "May I join you in your cabin?"

"Come ahead," Feldman invited. He cut off the switch and glanced at the clock on the wall. There were less than eleven hours left to him.

Everts was a trim man of forty, erect but not rigid. There was neither friendliness nor hostility in his glance. His words were courteous as Doc motioned toward the tray of breakfast. "I've already eaten, thank you."

He accepted a chair. His voice was apologetic when he began. "This is a personal matter which I perhaps have no right to bring up. But my wife is greatly worried about this plague. I violate no confidence in telling you there is considerable unease, even on Earth, according to messages I have received. The ship physician believes Mrs. Everts may have the plague, but isn't sure of the symptoms. I understand you are quite expert."

Doc wondered about the physician. Apparently there was another man who placed his patients above anything else, though he was probably meticulous about obeying all actual rules. There was no law against listening to a pariah, at least.

"When did she have Selznik's migraine?" he asked.

"About thirteen years ago. We went through it together, shortly after having our metabolism switched during the food shortage of '88."

Doc felt carefully at the base of the Captain's skull; the swelling was there. He asked a few questions, but there could be no doubt.

"Both of you must have it, Captain, though it won't mature for another year. I'm sorry."

"There's no hope, then?"

Doc studied the man. But Everts wasn't the sort to dicker even for his life. "Nothing that I've found, Captain. I have a clue, but I'm still working on it. Perhaps if I could leave a few notes for your physician —"

It was Everts' turn to shake his head. "I'm sorry, Dr. Feldman. I have orders to burn out your cabin when you leave. But thank you." He got to his feet and left as quietly and erectly as he had entered.

Doc tore up his notes bitterly. He paced his cabin slowly, reading out the hours while his eyes lingered on the little bottle of cultures. At times the fear grew in him, but he mastered it. There was half an hour left when he began opening the little bottles and making his films.

He was still not finished when steps echoed down the hall, but he was reasonably sure of his results. The bug could not grow in Earth-normal tissue.

Three men entered the room. One of them, dressed in a spacesuit, held out another suit to him. The other two began gathering up everything in the cabin and stowing it neatly into a sack designed to protect freight for a limited time in a vacuum.

Doc forced his hands to steadiness with foolish pride and began climbing into the suit. He reached for the helmet, but the man shook his head, pointing to the oxygen gauge. There would be exactly one hour's supply of oxygen when he was thrown out and it still lacked five minutes of the deadline.

They marched him down the hallway, to meet Everts coming toward them. There were still three minutes left when they reached the airlock, with its inner door already open. The spacesuited man climbed into it and began strapping down so that the rush of air would not sweep him outward when the other seal was released.

Doc had saved one bracky weed. Now he raised it to his lips, fumbling for a light.

Everts stepped forward and flipped a lighter. Doc inhaled deeply. Fear was thick in every muscle, and he needed the smoke desperately. Then he caught himself.

"Better change your metabolism back to Earth-normal, Captain Everts," he said, and his voice was so normal that he hardly recognized it.

Everts' eyes widened briefly. The man bowed faintly. "Thank you, Dr. Feldman."

It was ridiculous, impossible, and yet there was a curious relief at the formality of it. It was like something from a play, too unreal to affect his life.

Everts nodded to the man holding the helmet. Doc dropped his bracky weed and felt the helmet snap down. A hiss of oxygen reached him and the suit ballooned out. There was no gravity; the two men handed him up easily to the one in the airlock while the inner seal began to close.

There was still ten seconds to go, according to the big chronometer that had been installed in the lock. The spaceman used it in tying the sack of possessions firmly to Doc's suit.

A red light went on. The man caught Doc and held him against the outer seal. The red light blinked. Four seconds ... three ... two....

There was a sudden heavy thudding sound, and the *Iroquois* seemed to jerk sideways slightly. The spaceman's face swung around in surprise.

The red light blinked and stayed on. Zero!

The outer seal snapped open and the spaceman heaved. Air exploded outwards, and Doc went with it. He was alone in space, gliding away from the ship, with oxygen hissing softly through the valve and ticking away his life.

Convert

Feldman fought for control of himself, forced himself to think, to hold onto his sanity. It was sheer stupidity, since nothing could have been more merciful than to lose this reality. But the will to be himself was stronger than logic. And bit by bit, he forced the fear and horror away from him until he could examine his situation.

He was spinning slowly, so that stars ahead of him seemed to crawl across his view. The ship was retreating from him already hundreds of yards away. Mars was a shrunken pill far away.

Then something blinked to one side. He turned his head to stare.

A little ship was less than three hundred yards away. He recognized it as a life raft. Now his spin brought him around to face it, and he saw it was parallelling his course. The ejection of the life raft must have caused the thump he'd heard before he was cast adrift.

It meant someone was trying to save him. It meant *life*!

He flailed his arms and beat his legs together, senselessly trying to force himself closer, while trying to guess who could have taken the chance. No one he could think of could have booked passage on the *Iroquois*. There wasn't that much free money in the villages.

Something flashed a hot blue, and the little ship leaped forward. Whoever was handling it knew nothing about piloting. It picked up too much speed at too great an angle.

Again blue spurts came, but this time matters were even worse. Then there was a long wait before a third try was made. He estimated the course. It would miss him by a good hundred feet, but it was probably the best the amateur pilot could do. The ship drifted closer, but to one side. It would soon pass him completely.

A spacesuited figure suddenly appeared in the tiny airlock, holding a coil of rope. The rope shot out, well thrown. But it was too short. It would pass within ten feet-and might as well have been ten miles for all the good it would do him.

Every film he had seen on space seemed to form a mad jumble in his mind, but he seized on the first idea he could remember. He inhaled deeply and yanked the oxygen tank free. An automatic seal on the suit cut off the connection. He aimed the hissing bottle, fumbling for the manual valve.

It almost worked. It kicked him toward the rope slightly, but most of the energy was wasted in setting him into a wilder spin. He blinked, trying to spot the rope. It was within five feet now.

Again he waited, until he seemed to be in position. This time he threw the bottle away from it. It added spin to his vertical axis, but the rope came into view within arm's reach.

He grasped it, just as his lungs seemed about to burst. He couldn't hold on long enough to tie the rope....

His lungs gave up suddenly, collapsing and then sucking in greedily. Clean air rushed in, letting his head clear. He'd forgotten that the inflated suit held enough oxygen for several minutes.

His body struck the edge of the airlock and a hand jerked him inside. The outer seal was slammed shut and locked, and there was a hiss of air entering.

He threw back his helmet just as Chris Ryan jerked hers off.

Her voice shook almost hysterically. "Thank God. Dan, I almost gave up!"

"I liked the air out there better," he told her bitterly. "If you'll open the lock again, I'll leave. Or am I supposed to believe this is rescue and that you came along just to save me?"

"I came along to see you killed, as you know very well. Saving you wasn't in my orders."

He grunted and reached for the handle that would release the outer lock. "Better get back inside if you don't want to blow out with me."

"It's up to you, Dan," she told him, and there was all the sincerity in the world in her blue eyes. "I'm on your side now."

He began counting on his fingers. "Let's see. The spare battery, the delay in arresting me, the choice of Matthews —"

"It was all true." Anger began to grow in her eyes. "Dan Feldman, you get inside this raft! If you don't care about me, you might consider the people dying of the plague who need you!"

She'd played her trump, and it took the round. He followed her.

"All right," he said grudgingly. "Spill your story."

She held out a copy of a space radiogram, addressed to Mrs. D. E. Everts, and signed by one of the best doctors on the Lobby Board of Directors.

> Regret confirm diagnosis. Topsecret. Repeat topsecret. Martian fever incubates fourteen years, believed highly fatal. No cure, research beginning immediately. Penalty violation topsecret, death all concerned.

"Mrs. Everts rates a topsecret break?" Doc commented dryly. "Come off it, Chris!"

"She's the daughter of Elmers of Space Lobby!" Chris answered. She pointed to the message, underlining words with her finger. "*Fourteen years.* You couldn't have caused it. *Highly fatal.* And people are being told it's only a skin disease. *Research beginning.* But you've already done most of the research. I can see that now. I can see a lot of things."

"You've got me beat then," he said. "I can't see how such a reformed young noblewoman calmly walked over and stole a life raft. I can't see how your brilliant mind concocted this whole scheme in almost no time. And to be honest, I can't even see why Medical Lobby decided to save me at the last minute and sent you to do the job. You didn't have to spy out knowledge from me. I've been trying all along to get it to your Research division."

She sighed and dropped onto a little seat.

"I can't prove my motives. You'll just have to believe me. But it wasn't hard to do what I've done. That shuttle pilot was found in a routine check, stowed away on the life raft. I was with Captain Everts when he was found, so I discovered how to get into the raft. And I heard his whole confession. He wasn't the real pilot. He'd come from the villages to save you. The whole scheme was his. I just used it, hoping I could reach you."

As always her story had a convincing element she shouldn't have known. The pilot's farewell, addressing him as Dr. Feldman, had been too low for her to hear, but it was something that fitted her story. It was probably a deliberate clue to give him hope, to assure him the villages were still trying. It shook his confidence.

"And your motive-your real motive?" he insisted.

She swore at him, then began ripping off the spacesuit. She turned her back, pulling a thin blouse down from her neck. He stared, then reached out to touch the lump there.

"So you've had Selznik's migraine and know you're carrying plague. And you've decided your precious Lobby won't save you?"

She dropped her eyes, then raised them to meet his defiantly. "I'm not just scared and selfish. Dad caught it, too, and it must be close to the time for him. He switched to Mars-normal when he was a liaison agent and never changed back. Dan, are we all going to have to die? Can't you save him?"

Feldman was out of his suit and at the control panel. There was a manual lever, which Chris must have used before. It might work out here where there was room to maneuver and nothing to hit. But trying to make a landing was going to be different.

"Dan?" she repeated.

He shrugged. "I don't know. They've started research too late and they'll be under so much pressure that the real brains won't have a chance. The topsecret stuff looks bad for research. Maybe there's a cure. It works in culture bottles, but it may fail in person. When I'm convinced I'm safe with you, I may tell you about it."

"Oh." Her voice was low. Then she sighed. "I suppose I can understand why you hate me, Dan."

"I don't hate you. I'm too mixed up. Tomorrow maybe, but not now. Shut up and let me see if I can figure out how to land this thing."

He found that the fuel tanks were nearly full, but that still didn't leave much margin. Mars must have been notified by Everts and be ready to pick the raft up. He had to reach the wastelands away from any of the shuttle ports. They had no aspirators, however, and they couldn't cover much territory in the spacesuits they would have to use. It meant he'd have to land close to a village where he was known.

He jockeyed the ship around by trial and error, studying the manual that was lying prominently on the control panel. According to the booklet, the ship was simple to operate. It was self-leveling in an atmosphere, and automatic flare computers were supposed to make it possible for an amateur to judge the rate of descent near the surface. It looked reassuring-and was probably written with that in mind.

Finally he reached for the control, hoping he'd figured his landing orbit reasonably well by simple logic. He smoothed it out in the following hours as he watched the markings on Mars. When they were near turnover point, he began cranking the little gyroscope to swing the ship. It saved fuel to turn without power, and he wasn't sure he could have turned accurately by blasting.

He was gaining some proficiency, however, he felt. But now he had to waste fuel and ruin his orbit again. There was no way to practice maneuvering without actually doing so.

In the end, he compromised, leaving a small margin for a bad landing that would require a second attempt, but with less practice than he wanted.

He had located Jake's village through the little telescope when he finally reached for the main blast control. The thin haze of Mars' atmosphere came rushing up, while the blast lashed out. Then they were in the outer fringes of the sky and the blast was beginning to show a corona that ruined visibility.

He turned to the flare computer and back to what he could see through the quartz viewport. He was going to land about half a mile from the village, as nearly as he could judge.

The computer seemed to work as it should. The speed was within acceptable limits. He gave up trying to see the ground and was forced to trust the machinery designed for amateur pilots. The flare bloomed, and he yanked down on the little lever.

It could have been worse. They hit the ground, bounced twice, and turned over. The ship was a mess when Feldman freed himself from the elastic straps of the seat. Chris had shrieked as they hit, but she was unbuckling herself now.

He threw her her spacesuit and one of the emergency bottles of oxygen from the rack. "Hurry up with that. We've sprung a leak and the pressure's dropping."

They were halfway to the village when a dozen tractors came racing up and Jake piled out of the lead one to drag the two in with him.

"Heard about it from the broadcasts and figured you might land around here. Good to see you, Doc." He started the tractor off at full speed, back to the wastelands, while Doc stared at the armed men who were riding the tractors.

Jake caught his look and nodded. "You're in enemy territory, Doc. There's a war going on!"

Sometimes it seemed to Doc that war was nothing but an endurance race to see how many times they could run before they were bombed. He was just beginning to drop off to sleep after a long trip for the sixth consecutive day when the little alarm shrilled. He sighed and shook Chris awake.

"Again?" she protested. But she got up and began helping him pack.

Jake came in, his eyes weary, pulling on the old jacket with the big star on its sleeve. Doc hadn't been too surprised to learn that Jake was the actual leader of the rebels. "Shuttles spotted taking off this way. And I still can't find where the leak is. They haven't missed our location once this week. Here, give me that."

He took the electron mike that had been among Doc's' possessions, but Chris recaptured it. "I can manage," she told him, and headed out for the tractor where Lou was waiting.

Doc scowled after her. He and Jake had been watching her. She was too useful to Doc's research to be turned away, but they didn't trust her yet. So far, however, they had found nothing wrong with her conduct. Still....

He swung suddenly into Jake's tractor. "Just remembered something. How'd they find me that time I stopped in the tractor to use the mike? I was pretty well hidden, and no tracks last in the sand long enough for them to have followed. But they were there when I came to. Somehow, they must have put a radio tracer on me."

Jake waited while they lighted up, his eyes suddenly bright. "You mean something you got from her house was bugged? It figures."

"And I've still got all the stuff. Now they find wherever we set up headquarters, though they've always managed to miss my laboratory, even when they've hit the troops around us. Jake, I think it's the microscope." Doc managed to push enough junk off one of the seats to make a cramped bed, and stretched out. "Sure, we figured they sent her because they want to keep tabs on what I discover. They've finally gotten scared of the plague, and she's the perfect Judas goat. But they have to have some way to get in touch with her. I'll bet there's a tracer in the mike and a switch so she can modulate it or key it to send out Morse."

"Yeah," Jake nodded. "Well, she does her own dirty work. I might get to like her if she was on our side. Okay, Doc. If they've put things into the mike, I've got a boy who'll find and fix it so she won't guess it's been touched."

Doc relaxed. For the moment, there would be no power in the instrument, nor any excuse for her to use it. But she must have handled some secret arrangement during the work periods. She used the mike more than he did. The switch could be camouflaged easily enough. If anyone detected the signal, they'd probably only think it was some leak in the electrical circuit.

Far away, the shuttle rockets had appeared as tiny dots in the sky. They were standing on their tails a second later, just off the ground, letting the full force of their blasts bake the area where headquarters had been.

Jake watched grimly, driving by something close to instinct. Then he looked back. "Know anything about a Dr. Harkness?"

"Not much, except that he protested sealing off the villages. Why?"

"He and five other doctors were picked up, trying to get through to us. Claimed they wanted to give us medical help. We can use them, God knows. I guess I'll have to chance it."

They stopped at a halfway village and hid the tractors before looking for a place to rest. Doc found Chris curled up asleep against the microscope. He had a hard time getting her to leave it in the tractor, but she was too genuinely tired to put up any real argument.

Jake reported in the morning before they set out again. "You were right, Doc. It was a nice job of work. Must have taken the best guys in Southport to hide the circuit so well. But it's safe now. It just makes a kind of meaningless static nobody can trace. Maybe we can get you a permanent lab now."

Doc debated again having Chris left behind and decided against it. The Lobby was determined to let him find a cure for them if he could. That meant Chris would work herself to exhaustion trying to help. Let her think she was doing it for the Lobby! It was time she was on the receiving end of a double cross.

"It's a stinking way to run a war," he decided.

Jake chuckled without much humor. "It's the war you wanted, remember? They forced our hand, but it had to come sometime. Right now the Lobby's fighting to get their hands on your work before we can use it; they're just using holding tactics, which helps our side. And we're hoping you get the cure so we can win. With that, maybe we'll whip them."

It was a crazy war, with each side killing more of its own men than of the enemy. The runners were increasing, and Jake's army was learning to shoot the poor devils mercifully and go on. They knew, at least, that there was no current danger of infection. In the Lobby towns, more were dying of panic in their efforts to escape the runners.

Desert towns had joined the villages, reluctantly but inevitably, to give the rebels nearly three-quarters of the total population. But the Lobby forces and the few cities held most of the real fighting equipment and they were ready to wait until Earth could send out unmanned rockets, loaded with atomics, which could cut through space at ten times normal speed.

There were vague lines of battle, but time was the vital factor. The Lobbies waited to steal a cure for the plague and the villages waited until they could announce it and demand surrender as its price.

It looked as if both sides were doomed to disappointment, however. He and Chris had put in every spare minute between moving and the minimum of sleep in searching for something that would check the disease. It couldn't grow in an Earth-normal body, but it didn't die, either. And there wasn't enough normal food available to permit the switch-over for more than a handful of people. Even Earth was out of luck, since eighty percent of her population ate synthetics. There were ways to synthesize Earth-normal food, but they were still hopelessly inefficient.

Jake had ordered one of the villages to rebuild their plant for such a purpose, while another was producing the enzyme that would permit switching. But it looked hopeless for more than a few of the most valuable men.

"No progress?" Jake asked for the hundredth time.

Doc grinned wryly. "A lot, but no help. We've found a fine accelerator for the bug. We can speed up its incubation or even make someone already infected catch it all over again. But we can't slow it down or stop it."

The new laboratory was still being fitted when they arrived. It had been dug into one of the few real cliffs in this section of Mars. The power plant had been installed, complete with a steam plant that would operate off sunlight in the daytime through a series of heat valves that took in a lot of warm air and produced smaller amounts hot enough to boil water.

"I'll see you whenever I can," Jake said. "But mostly, you're going to be somewhat isolated so they won't trace you. Let them think they goofed with the shuttles and hit you and Chris. Anything you need?"

"Guinea pigs," Doc told him sarcastically. It was meant as a joke, though a highly bitter one. Jake nodded and left them.

Doc opened the cots as Chris came in, not bothering to unpack the equipment. "Hit the sack, Chris," he told her.

She looked at him doubtfully. "You almost said that the way you'd address a human being, Dan. You're slipping. One of these days you'll like me again."

"Maybe." He was too tired to argue. "I doubt it, though. Forget it and get some sleep."

She watched him silently until he got up to turn out the light. Then she sighed heavily. "Dan?"

"Yeah?"

"I never got a divorce. The publicity would have been bad. But anyway, we're still married."

"That's nice." He swung to face her briefly. "And they found the radio in the microscope. Better get to sleep, Chris."

"Oh." It was a quiet exclamation, barely audible. There was a sound that might have been a sniffle if it had come from anyone else. Then she rolled over. "All right, Dan. I still want to help you."

He cursed himself for a stupid fool for telling her. Fatigue was ruining what judgment he had. From now on, he'd have to watch her every minute. Or had she really seen the value of the research by now? She wasn't a fool. It should have registered on even her stubborn mind. But he was too sleepy to think about it.

She had breakfast ready in the morning. She made no comment on what had been said during the night. Instead, she began discussing a way to keep one of the organic antibiotics from splitting into simpler compounds when they tried to switch it over to Mars-normal. They were both hopelessly bad chemists and biologists, but there was no one else to do the work.

Chris worked harder than ever during the day.

Just after sundown, Jake came in with a heavy box. He dropped it onto the floor. "Mice!"

Doc ripped off the cover, exposing fine screening. There were at least six dozen mice inside!

"Harkness found them," Jake explained. "A hormone extraction plant used them for testing some of the products. Had them sent by regular shipments from Earth. Getting them cost a couple of men, but Harkness claims it's worth it. He's a good man on a raid. Here!"

He'd gone to the doorway again and came back with another box, this one crammed with bottles and boxes. "They had quite a laboratory, and Harkness picked out whatever he thought you could use."

Chris and Doc were going through it. The labels were engineering ones, but the chemical formulae were identification enough. There were dozens of chemicals they hadn't hoped to get.

"Anything else?" Doc finally asked as they began arranging the supplies.

"More runners. A lot more. We're still holding things down, but it's reaching a limit. Panic will start in the camps if this keeps on. But that's my worry. You stick to yours."

Several of the new chemicals showed promise in the tubes. But two of them proved fatal to the mice and the others were completely innocuous in the little animal's bodies, both to mouse and to germ. The plague was much hardier in contact with living cells than in the artificial environment of the culture jars.

They lost seven mice in two days, but that seemed unimportant; the females were already living up to their reputations, nearly all pregnant. Doc didn't know the gestation period, but he remembered that it was short.

"Funny they all started at the same time," he commented. "Must have been shipped out separately or else been kept apart while they were switched over to Mars-normal. Something interrupted their habits, anyhow."

A few nights later they learned what it was. There was a horrible squealing that woke him out of the depths of his sleep. Chris was already at the light switch. As light came on, they turned to the mouse box.

All the animals were charging about in their limited space, their little legs driving madly and their mouths open. What they lacked in size they made up in numbers, and the din was terrific.

But it didn't last. One by one, the mice began dropping to the floor of the cage. In fifteen minutes, they were all dead!

It was obviously the plague, contracted after having their metabolism switched. Women were sterile for some time after Selznik's migraine struck, and the same must have been true of the mice. They must have contracted the plague at about the same time and reached fertility together. Somehow, the plague incubation period had been shortened to fit their life span; the disease was nothing if not adaptive.

Chris prepared a slide in dull silence. The familiar cell was there when Doc looked through the microscope. He picked up one of the little creatures and cut it open, removing one of the foetuses.

"Make a film of that," he suggested.

She worked rapidly, scraping out the almost microscopic brain, dissolving out the fatty substance, and transferring the result to a film. This time, even at full magnification, there was no sign of the filaments that were always present in diseased flesh. The results were the same for the other samples they made.

"Something about the very young animal or a secretion from the mother's organs keeps the bug from working." Doc reached for a bracky weed and accepted a light from Chris without thinking of it. "Every kid I've heard about contracted the plague between the second and third year. None are born with it, none get it earlier. I've suspected this, but now here's confirmation."

Chris began preparing specimens, while Doc got busy with tubes of the culture. They'd have to test various fluids from the tiny bodies, but there were enough cultures prepared. Then, if the substance only inhibited growth, there would be a long, slow test; if it killed the bugs, they might know more quickly.

Jake came in before the final tests, but waited on them. Doc was studying a film in the microscope. He suddenly motioned excitedly for Chris.

"See the filaments? They're completely disintegrated. And there's one of the big cells broken open. We've got it! It's in the blood of the foetus. And it must be in the blood of newborn children, too!"

Jake looked at the slide, but his face was doubtful.

"Maybe you've got something, Doc. I hope so. And I hope you can use it." He shook his head wearily. "We need good news right now. A couple of big rockets just reached the station and they've been sending shuttles back and forth a mile a minute. Nobody can figure how they got here so fast or what they're for. But it doesn't look good for us!"

Susceptibility

Doc could feel the tension in the village where GHQ was temporarily located long before they were close enough for details to register. The people were gathered in clusters, staring at the sky where the station must be. A few were pacing up and down, gesticulating with tight sweeps of their arms.

One woman suddenly went into even more violent action. She leaped into the air and then took off at a rapid trot, then a run. Her hands were tearing at her clothes and her mouth seemed to be working violently. She was halfway to the top of the nearest dune before a rifle cracked. She dropped, to twitch once and lie still.

Almost with her death, another figure leaped from one of the houses, his face bare of the necessary aspirator. He took off at a violent run, but he was falling from lack of air before the bullet ended his struggles.

The people suddenly began to move apart, as if trying to get away from each other. For weeks they had faced the horror with courage; now it was finally too much for them.

Tension mounted as no news came from the cities. Doc noticed that it seemed to aggravate or speed up the disease. He saw three men shot in the next half-hour.

He was trying to calm them with word of a possible cure for the plague, but their reactions were as curiously dull as those of Jake had been. As he spoke, they faced him with set expressions. At his mention of the need for the blood of young children, they turned from him, sullenly silent.

Jake came over, nodding unhappily. "It's what I was afraid might happen, Doc. George Lynn! Tell Doc what's wrong."

Lynn was reluctant, but he finally stumbled out his explanation. "It ain't like you, Doc. Comes from that Lobby woman you got. It's her dirty idea. We've seen the Lobby doctors cutting open our kids, poisoning their blood, and bleeding them dry. That ain't gonna happen again, Doc. You tell her it ain't!"

Doc swore as he realized their ignorance. An unexplained vaccination looked like poisoning of the blood. But he couldn't understand the bleeding part until Jake filled him in.

"Northport infant's wing. Each department has its own blood bank and donation is compulsory. Southport started it a couple months ago, too."

The long arm of the Lobby had reached out again. Now if he ever got them to try the treatment, it would be only after long sessions of preparing them with the facts, and there was hardly enough time for the crucial work!

By afternoon, Judge Ben Wilson reached them. His voice shook with fatigue as he climbed up to address the crowd through a power megaphone. "Southport's going crazy." He had to pause for breath between each sentence. "Earth's pulling back all the important people. They're packing them into the ships. They're leaving only colonials with no Earth rights. Those ships left when they decided the plague was coming from here. They won't let anybody back until the plague is licked. There won't be an Earth technician on Mars tomorrow."

"No bombs?" someone called.

"No bombs. The ships must have started before you rebelled, maybe meant honestly to save their own kind. But now it's a military action, and don't think it won't mean trouble. The poor devils in the city bet on the wrong horse. Now they can't run their food factories or anything else for long. Not without technicians. They've got to whip you now. Up to this time, they've been fighting for the Lobbies. Now they'll fight you for their own bellies to get your supplies. And they've still got shuttle rockets and fuel for them. Now beat it. I gotta confer with Jake."

Doc started after the judge, but Dr. Harkness caught his arm and drew him aside. Chris followed.

"I've found another epidemic," Harkness told them. "Over at Marconi. It's kept me on the run all night, and now half the village is down with it. Starts like a common cold, runs a fair fever, and the skin breaks out all over with bright red dots...."

He went on describing it. Chris began asking him about what medical supplies he had brought with him, pilfered from Northport hospital. She seemed to know what it was, but refused to say until she saw the cases. Doc also preferred to wait. Sometimes things weren't as bad as they seemed, though usually they were worse.

Marconi was dead to all outward appearances, with nobody on the streets. It had been a village of great hopes a week before, since this was where they had decided to experiment with switching the people back to Earth-normal. They'd had the best chance of survival of anyone on Mars until this came up.

Three people lay on the beds in the first house Harkness led them to. The room was darkened, and a man was stumbling around, trying to tend the others, though the little spots showed on his skin. He grinned weakly. "Hi, Doc. I guess we're making a lot of trouble, ain't we?"

Chris gave Doc no chance to answer. "Just as I thought. Measles! Plain old-fashioned measles."

"Figured so," the sick man said. "Like my brother back on Earth."

The others looked doubtful, but Doc reassured them. Chris should know; she'd worked in a swanky hospital where the patients were mostly Earth-normal. Measles was one of the diseases which was foiled by the metabolism switch. Well, at least they wouldn't have to be quarantined here.

Chris finished treating the family with impersonal efficiency, discussing the symptoms loudly with Harkness. "It's a good thing it isn't serious!"

"No," Harkness answered bitterly. "Not serious. It's only killed five children and three adults so far!"

"It would, here," Doc agreed unhappily. He led Chris out of the room on the pretext of washing his hands. "It's serious enough to force us to abandon the whole idea of going back to Earth-normal. Measles today, smallpox, tuberculosis, scarlet fever and everything else tomorrow. These people have lived Mars-normal so long their natural immunity has been destroyed. On Earth where the disease was everywhere, kids used to pick up some immunity with constant exposure, even without what might be called a case of the disease. Here, the blood has no reason to build antibodies. They can be killed by things people used to laugh at. How the disease got here, I don't know. But it's here. So we'll have to give up the idea of switching back to Earth-normal."

He gathered up one of the kits and started toward the other houses. "And Lord knows how long it will take to get the blood for the other treatment, even if it works."

They worked as a team for a while, with Harkness frowning as he watched Chris. Finally the young doctor stopped Chris outside the fifth house. "These are my patients, Dr. Ryan. I left the Lobby because I didn't believe colonials were mere livestock. I still feel the same. I appreciate your help in diagnosis and methods of treatment. But I can't let you handle my patients this way."

"Dan!" She swung around with eyes glazing. "Dan, are you going to stand for that?"

"I think you'd better wait in the tractor, Chris."

He was lucky enough to catch the kit she threw at him before its precious contents spilled. But it wasn't luck that guided his hand to the back of her skirt hard enough to leave it stinging.

Her face froze and she stormed out. A moment later they heard the tractor start off.

But Doc had no time to think of her. He and Harkness split up and began covering the streets, house by house, while he passed on the word to abandon the metabolism switch and go back to Mars-normal.

Jake sent two other doctors to relieve them late in the evening. Things were somewhat quieter at GHQ as Doc reported the events at Marconi.

"Where's Dr. Ryan?" Jake asked at last.

Doc exchanged glances with Harkness. "She isn't in the lab?"

"Wasn't there an hour ago."

Doc cursed himself for letting her go. With the knowledge that the radio in the mike was disabled, she'd obviously grabbed the first chance to report back. And with her had gone news of the only cure they had found.

Jake took it as philosophically as he could, though it was a heavy blow to his hopes. They spent half the night looking for her tractor, on the chance that she might have gotten lost or broken down, but there was no sign of it.

She was waiting in the laboratory when he returned at dawn. Her face was dirty and her uniform was a mess. But she was smiling. She got up to greet him, holding out two large bottles.

"Infant plasma—straight from Southport. And if you think I had it easy lying my way in and out of the hospital, you're a fool, Dan Feldman. If the man who took my place there hadn't been a native idiot, I never would have gotten away with it."

The things he had suspected could still be right, he realized. She could have reported everything to the Lobby. It was a better explanation than her vague account of bullying her way in and out. But she'd had a rough drive, and he wanted the plasma. Curiously, he was glad to have her back with him. He reached out a hand for the bottles.

She put the bottle on the table and grabbed up a short-bladed knife. "Not so fast," she cried. Her eyes were blazing now. "Dan Feldman, if you touch those bottles until you've crawled across the floor on your face and apologized for the way you treated me the last few days, I'll cut your damned heart out."

He shook his head, chuckling at the picture she made. There were times when he could almost see why he'd married her.

"All right, Chris," he gave in. "I'll be darned if I'll crawl, but you've earned an apology. Okay?"

She sighed uncertainly. Then she nodded and began changing for work.

XIV

Immunity

They worked through the day in what seemed to be armed truce. There was no coffee waiting for him when he awoke next, as he'd come to expect, but he didn't comment. He went to where she was already working, checking on the results of the plasma on the cultures.

The response had been slower than with the mouse blood, but now the bugs seemed to be dead. The filaments were destroyed, and there were no signs of the big cells. It seemed to be a cure, at least in the culture bottles.

"We'll need volunteers," he decided. "There should be animals, but we don't have any. At least this stuff isn't toxic. We need a natural immune and someone infected. Two of each, so one can be treated and the other used for a control. Makes four. Not enough to be sure, but it will have to do."

"Two," Chris corrected. "You're not infected, I am."

"Two others," he agreed. "I'll get them from Jake."

Most of GHQ was out on the street, but Doc found Jake inside the big schoolroom where he enjoyed his early morning bracky and coffee. The chief listened and agreed at once, turning to the others in the room.

"Who's had the jumping headache? Okay, Swanee. Who never had it?" He blinked in surprise as three men nodded out of the eight present. "I guess you go, Tom."

The two men stood up, tamping out their weeds, and went out with Doc.

Chris had everything set up. They matched coins to decide who would be treated. Doc noticed that Chris would get no plasma, while he was scheduled for everything. He watched her prepare the culture and add the accelerator that would speed development and make certain he and Tom were infected, then let her inject it.

That was all, except for the waiting. To keep conditions more closely alike, they were to stay there until the tests were finished, not even eating for fear of upsetting the conditions. Swanee dug out a pack of worn cards and began to deal while Doc dug out some large pills to use as chips.

It was an hour later when the pain began. Doc had just won the pot of fifty pills and opened his mouth for the expected gloating. He yelled as an explosion seemed to go off inside his head. Even closing his mouth was agony.

A moment later, Tom began to sweat. It got worse, spreading to the whole area of the back of the head and neck. Doc lay on the cot, envying Chris and Swanee who had already been infected naturally. He longed desperately for bracky, and had to keep reminding himself that no drugs must upset the tests. It was the longest day he had ever spent, and he began to doubt that he could get through it. He watched the little clock move from one minute to nine over to half a minute and hung breathless until it hit the nine. There was no question about whether the infection had taken. Now they could dull the agony.

Chris had the anodyne tablets already dissolved in water, and Swanee was passing out three lighted bracky weeds. It took a few minutes for the relief of the anodyne, and even that couldn't kill all the pain. But it didn't matter by comparison. He sucked the weed, mashed it out and began dealing the cards again.

They had a plentiful supply of the anodyne and used it liberally during the night. The test was a speeded-up simulation of the natural course of the disease, where painkiller would take time to get for most people here, but would then be used generously.

Precisely at nine in the morning, Chris began to inject Swanee and Doc with plasma.

Now there was no thought of cards. They waited, trying to talk, but with most of their attention on the clock. Doc had estimated that an hour should be enough to show results, but it was hard to remember that an hour was the guess as to the minimum time.

He winced as Chris took a tiny bit of flesh from his neck. She went to the other men, and then submitted to his work on herself. Then she began preparing the slides.

"Feldman," she read the name of the slide as she inserted it into the microscope. Then her breath caught sharply. "Only dead cells!"

It was the same for Swanee and Tom. Each had to look at his own slide and have it explained before the results could be believed. But at last Chris bent over her own slide. A minute later she glanced up, nodding. "What it should be. It checks."

Tom whooped and went out the door to notify Jake. There was only plasma for some two hundred injections, but that should yield sufficient proof. Once salvation was offered, there should be no trouble convincing the people that blood donations from their children were worthwhile.

Later, when the last of the plasma had been used, they could finally relax. Chris slipped off her smock and dropped onto the cot. A tired smile came onto her lips. "You're forgiven, Dan," she said. A moment later she was obviously asleep. Doc meant to join her, but it was too much effort. He leaned his head forward onto his arms, vaguely wondering why she was calling off the feud.

It was night outside when he awoke, and he was lying on the cot, though he still felt cramped and strained. He stirred, groaning, and finally realized that a hand was on his shoulder shaking him. He looked up to see Jake above him. Chris was busy with the coffee maker.

Jake slumped onto the cot beside Doc. "We took Southport," he announced.

That knocked the sleep out of Doc's system. "You what?"

"We took it, lock, stock and barrel. I figured the news of your cure would put guts into the men, and it did. But we'd probably have taken it anyhow. There wasn't anything to fight for there after Earth pulled out and the plague really hit. Wilson mistook last-minute panic for fighting spirit. The poor devils didn't have anything to fight about, once the Lobby stopped goading them."

Doc tried to assimilate the news. But once the surprise was gone, he found it meant very little. Maybe his revolutionary zeal had cooled, once the Lobby men had pulled out. "We'll need a lot more plasma than there is in Southport," he said.

"Not so much, maybe," Jake denied. "Doc, three of the men you injected were shot down as runners. Your plasma's no good."

"It takes time to work, Jake. I told you there might be a case or two that would be too close to the edge. Three is more than I expected; but it's not impossible."

"There was plenty of time. They blew after we got back from Southport." Jack dropped his hand on Doc's shoulder, and his face softened. "Harkness tested every man you injected. He finished half an hour ago. Five showed dead bugs. The rest of them weren't helped at all."

Doc fumbled for a weed, trying to think. But his thoughts refused to focus. "Five!"

"Five out of two hundred. That's about average. And what about Tom? He was jumping around after the test last night, telling how you'd cured him, how he'd seen the dead bugs; but he never had the jumping headache, and you never gave him the plasma! He's got dead bugs, though. Harkness tested him."

Doc let his realization of his own idiocy sink in until he could believe it. Jake was right. Tom had never been treated, yet Chris had reported dead bugs. They'd all been so ready to believe in miracles that no one had been able to think straight after the long wait.

"There was a bump on his neck —a small one," he said slowly. "Jake, he must have caught it, even if he seemed immune. If he was taking anodyne anyway for something-or unconscious —"

"He was up in Northport six years ago for a kidney operation," Jake admitted doubtfully. "We had to chip in to pay for it. But you still didn't treat him, and he's cured. Face it, Doc, that plasma is no good inside the body."

His hand tightened on Doc's shoulder again. "We're not blaming you. We don't judge a man here except by what he is. Maybe the stuff helps a little. We'll go on using it when we get it; tell everybody you were a mite optimistic, so they'll figure it's a gamble, but have a little hope left. And you keep trying. Something cured it in Tom. Now you find out what."

Doc watched him go out numbly, and turned to Chris.

"It can't be right," she said shakily. "You and Swanee were cured. Maybe it was the accelerator. It had to be something."

"You didn't have the accelerator," he accused.

"No, and I've still got live bugs. I was never supposed to be cured, so I expected to see just what I saw. How I missed the fact that Tom should have been like me, I don't know. Damn it, oh, damn it!"

He's never seen her cry before, except in fury. But she mastered it almost at once, shaking tears out of her eyes. "All right. Plasma works in a bottle but not in an adult body. Maybe something works in the body but not in a bottle."

"Maybe. And maybe some people are just naturally immune after it reaches a certain stage. Maybe we ran into coincidence."

But he didn't believe that, any more than she did. The answer had to be in the room. He'd taken a massive dose of the disease and been cured in a few hours.

Outside the room, the war went on, drawing toward a close. The supposed partial cure was good propaganda, if nothing else, and Jake was widening his territory steadily. There was only token resistance against him. He had the Southport shuttles now to cover huge areas in a hurry. But inside the room, the battle was less successful. It wasn't the accelerator. It wasn't the tablets of anodyne. They even tried sweeping the floor and using the dust without results.

Then another test in the room, made with four volunteers Jake selected, yielded complete cures after injections with plain salt water in place of plasma.

The plague speeded up again. About four people out of a hundred now seemed to have caught the disease and cured themselves. They accounted for what faith was left in Doc's plasma and gave some unfounded hope to the others.

Northport fell a week later, putting the whole planet in rebel hands.

Jake returned, wearier than ever. He'd proved to be one of the natural immunes, but the weight of the campaign that could only end in a defeat by the plague left him no room to rejoice in his personal fortune.

This time he looked completely defeated. And a moment later, Doc saw why as Jake flipped a flimsy sheet onto the table. It bore the seals of Space and Medical Lobbies.

Jake pointed upwards. "The war rockets are there, all right. We knew they'd come. Now all they want for calling them off is our surrender and your cure. If they don't get both, they'll blow the planet to bits. We have two days."

The rockets could be seen clearly with binoculars. There were more than enough to destroy all life on the planet. Maybe they'd be used eventually, anyhow, since the Lobbies wanted no more rebellion. But with a cure for the plague, he might have bought them off.

Chris stood beside him, looking as if it were a bitter pill for her, too. She'd risked herself in the hands of the enemy, had cooperated with him in everything she'd been taught to oppose, and had worked like a dog. Now the Lobbies seemed to forget her as a useless tool. They were falling back on a raw power play and forgetting any earlier schemes.

"Maybe they'd hold off for a while if I agreed to go to them and share all my ideas, specimens and notes," he said at last. "Do you think your Lobby would settle for that, Chris?"

"I don't know, Dan. I've stopped thinking their way." She seemed almost apologetic for the admission.

He dropped an arm over her shoulder and turned with her back to the laboratory. "Okay, then we've got to find a miracle. We've got two days ahead of us. At least we can try."

But he knew he was lying to himself. There wasn't anything he could think of to try.

XV
Decision

Two days was never enough time for a miracle. Doc decided as he packed his notes into a small bag and put it beside his bundle of personal belongings. He glanced around the room for the last time, and managed a grin at Jake's gloomy expression.

"Maybe I can bluff them, or maybe they'll string along for a while," he said. "Anyhow, now that they've agreed to take me and my notes in place of the cure we're fresh out of, I've got to be on that shuttle when it goes back to their men at orbital station."

Jake nodded. "I don't like selling friends down the river, Doc. But it wouldn't do you any more good to blow up with the planet, I reckon. They won't call off the war rockets when they do get you, of course. But maybe they won't use them, except as a threat to put the Lobbies back in, stronger than ever."

He stuck out one of his awkwardly shaped hands, clapped the aspirator over his face and hurried out. Doc picked up his bags and went toward the little tractor where Lou was waiting to drive him and Chris back toward Southport and the shuttle rocket that would be landing for them. They hadn't mentioned Chris in their demands, but her father must expect her to return.

After they had him, he'd be on his own. His best course was probably to insist on talking only to Ryan at Medical Lobby, and then being completely honest. The room here would be kept sealed, in case the Lobby wanted to investigate where he had failed. And his notes were honest, which was something that could usually be determined. Chris could testify to that, anyhow, since she'd kept a lot of them for him.

At best, there would be a chance for some compromise and perhaps some clue for them that might eventually end the plague. They had enough men to work on it, and billions in equipment. At worst, he should gain a little time.

"Cheer up, Chris," he told her as he climbed through the little airlock. "Maybe Harkness will turn up the cure before our negotiations break down. He has the whole of Northport Hospital to play with. They haven't tried to chase him out of there yet. After all, we almost found something with no equipment except wild imaginations."

She shook her head as the tractor began moving. "Shut up! I've got enough trouble without your coming down with logorrhea. Don't be a fool."

"Why change now?" he asked her. "Everything I've done has been because I am a fool. I guess my luck lasted longer than I could expect. And I'm still fool enough to think that the solution has to turn up eventually. We know it has to be in that room. Damn it, we must know it-if we could only think straight now."

She reached over and touched his hand, but made no comment. They had been over that statement of desperation too many times already. But it kept nagging at him-something in the room, something in the room! Something so common that nobody noticed it!

They passed a crowd chasing down a runner. Something in that room could have saved the unlucky man. It could have saved Mars, perhaps.

He growled for the hundredth time, cursing his fatigue-numbed mind. Too little sleep, too much coffee and bracky....

He reached for the package of weed, realizing that he would miss it on Earth, if he ever got there. Like everything here on the planet, he'd begun by detesting it and wound up finding it the thing he wanted to keep forever. He lighted the bracky and sat smoking, watching Lou drive. When the first was finished, he lighted another from the butt.

She put out a hand and took it away. "Please, Dan. I can stand the stuff, but I'll never like it, and the tractor's stuffy enough already. I've taken enough of it. And it keeps reminding me of our test-the three of you stinking up the place, puffing and blowing that out, while I couldn't even get a breath of air...."

She was getting logorrhea herself now and —

The answer finally hit him! He jerked around, making a grab for Lou's shoulder, motioning for the man to head back.

"Bracky-it has to be! Chris, that's it. Jake picked out the second group of men from his friends-and they are all cronies because they hang around so much in their so-called smoking room. The first time, it killed the bugs for all of us who smoked-and it didn't work for you because you never learned the habit."

Lou had the tractor turned and the rheostat all the way to the floor.

She was sitting up now, but she wasn't fully satisfied. "The percentage of immunes seems about right. But why do some of the smokers get the disease while some don't?"

"Why not? It depends on whether they pick up the habit before or after the disease gets started. Tom must have got his while he was in Northport. They wouldn't let him smoke there-if he had the habit before, for that matter."

She found no fault with that. He twisted it back and forth in his mind, trying to find a fault. There seemed to be none. The only trouble was that they couldn't send a message that bracky was the cure and hope that Earth would prove it true. No polite note of apology would do after that. They had to be sure. Too many other ideas had proved wrong already.

Jake saw them coming and came running toward the laboratory, but Lou stopped the tractor before it reached the building and let the older man in.

"Get me a dozen men who have the plague. I want the worst cases you have, and ones that Harkness tested himself," Doc ordered. "And then start praying that the cure we've got works fast."

Chris was at the electron mike at once, but one of her hands reached out for the weed. She began puffing valiantly, making sick faces. Now other men began coming in, their faces struggling to find hope, but not daring to believe yet. Jake followed them.

"We'll test at ten-minute intervals. That will be about two hours for the last from the group," Doc decided. One of the doctors Harkness had brought to the villages was busy cutting tiny sections from the lumps on the men's necks, while Chris ran them through the microscope to make sure the bugs were still alive. The regular optical mike was strong enough for that.

Doc handed each man a bracky weed, with instructions to keep smoking, no matter how sick it made him.

There were no results at the end of ten minutes when the first test was made. The second, at the end of twenty minutes, was still infected with live bugs. At the half-hour, Chris frowned.

"I can't be sure-take a look, Dan."

He bent over, moving the slide to examine another spot. "I think so. The next one should tell."

There was no doubt about the fourth test. The bugs were dead, without a single exception that they could find.

One by one, the men were tested and went storming out, shouting the news. For a minute, the gathering crowd was skeptical, remembering the other failures. Then, abruptly, men were screaming, crying and fighting for the precious bracky, like the legions of the damned grabbing for lottery tickets when the prize was a passport to paradise.

Jake swore as he moved toward the door. "We're low on bracky here. Have to get a supply from Edison, I guess, and cart it to the shuttle. Enough for a sample, and to make them want more. It'll be tough, but we'll get it there in time-by the time the shuttle should be picking you up. Doc, you've won our war! From now on, if Earth wants to keep her population up, we'll be a free planet!"

Chris turned slowly from the microscope, holding a slide in her hands. "My bugs," she said unbelievingly. "Dan, they're dead!"

Jake patted her shoulder. "That makes it perfect, girl. Now come on. We've got to start celebrating a victory!"

It was the general feeling of most of the heads of the villages when they met the next day in Southport, using the courtroom that had been presided over so long by Judge Ben Wilson. It was victory, and to the victor belonged the spoils. The bracky had gone out to Earth on a converted war rocket that could make the trip in less than two weeks, and one packet had been specially labeled for Captain Everts. But Earth had already confirmed the cure. The small amounts of the herb found in the botanical collections had been enough to satisfy all doubts.

Harkness, Chris and Doc had been fighting against the desire to rob Earth blind that filled most of the men here for hours now. Now they had the backing of Jake and Ben Wilson. And now finally they leaned back, sensing that the argument had been won.

Bargaining was all right in its place, but it had no place in affairs of life and death such as this. They had to see that Earth received all the bracky she needed. It was only right to charge a fair price for it, but they couldn't restrict it by withholding or overcharging. And they could still gain their ends without blackmail.

Martian alkaloids were tricky things, and bracky smoke contained a number of them. It would take Earth at least ten years to discover and synthesize the right one-and it would still probably cost more than it would to import the weed from Mars. As long as the source of that weed was here, and in the hands of the colonials, there would be no danger of Earth's bombing the planet.

Harkness got up to underscore a point Wilson had made. "The plague lived a million years, and it won't disappear now. The jumping headache, or Selznick's migraine, is unpleasant enough to make us reasonably sure that there will be a steady consumption of the weed. Our problem will be to keep the children from using too much of it, probably." He pulled a weed out and lighted it, puckering his face as the smoke bit his tongue. "I'm told that this gets to be an enjoyable habit. If I can believe that, surely you can believe me when I say we don't have to bargain with lives."

The village men were human, and most of them could remember the strain they had been under when they expected those they loved to die at any hour. It had made them crave vengeance, but now as they had a chance to reexamine it, they began to find it harder to impose the horror of any such threat on others. The final vote was almost unanimous.

Doc listened as they wrangled over the wording of the message to Earth, feeling disconnected from it. He passed Chris a bracky and lighted it for her. She took it automatically, smiling as the smoke hit her lungs. It was one thing they had in common now, at least.

Ben Wilson finally read the message.

"To the people of Earth, greetings!

"On behalf of the free people of Mars, I have the honor to announce that this planet hereby declares itself a sovereign and independent world. We shall continue to regard Earth as our mother, and to consider the health and welfare of her people in no way second to our own in matters which affect both planets. We trust that Earth will share this feeling of mutual friendship. We trust that all strains of hostility will be ended. The advantages to each from peaceful commerce make any course other than the most cordial of relations unthinkable.

"We shall consider proof of such friendship an order by Earth to all rockets circling this planet that they shall deliver themselves safely into our hands, in order that we may begin converting them to peaceful purposes for the trade that is to come. In turn, we pledge that all efforts will be made to ensure a prompt delivery of those products most in demand, including the curative bracky plant."

He turned to Doc then. "You want to sign it, Dr. Feldman? Make it as acting president or something, until we can get around to voting you into permanent office."

"You and Jake fight over the job," Doc told him. "No, Ben, I mean it."

He got up and moved out into the outer room, where he could avoid the stares of amazement that were turned to him. He'd never asked for the honor, and he didn't want it.

Chris came with him. Her face was shocked and something was slowly draining out of it as he looked at her.

"Forget it, Chris," he said. "You're going back to Earth. There is nothing for you here."

She hadn't quite given up. "There could be, Dan. You know that."

"No. No, Chris, I don't think there ever can be. You can't find a man strong enough to rule who'll be weak enough to let you rule in his place. It didn't work on Earth, and it won't work here. Forget the dreams you had of what could be done with a new planet. Those are the dreams that made a mess of the old one."

"I'll be back," she told him. "Some day I'll be back."

He shook his head again. "No. You wouldn't like what you find here. Freedom is heady stuff, but you have to have a taste for it. You can't acquire a fondness for it secondhand. And for a while, there's going to be freedom here. Besides, once you get back to Earth, you'll forget what happened here."

She sighed at last. For the first time since he had known her, she seemed to give in completely. And for that brief moment, he loved what she could have been, but never would be.

"All right, Dan," she said quietly. "I can't fight you. I never could, I see now. I'll take the rocket back. What are you going to do?"

He hadn't bothered to think, but he knew the answer. "Research. What else?"

There would be a lot of research done here. It had been suppressed too long, and had piled up a back-pressure that would have to be relieved. And from that research, he suspected, would come the end of the stable oligarchy of Earth. It could never stand against the changes that would be pouring out of Mars.

She put her hands on his shoulders and moved forward to kiss him. He bent down to meet her, and found her eyes were wet. Maybe his were, too. Then she broke free.

"You're a fool, Dan Feldman," she whispered, and began moving down the hallway and out of the council hall of Mars.

Doc Feldman nodded slowly as he let her go. He was a fool. He had always been a fool, and always would be. And that was why he could never take over leadership here. Fools and idealists should never govern a world. It took practical men such as Jake to do that.

But the practical men needed the foolish idealists, too. And maybe for a time here on Mars their kind of men and his kind of fools could make one more stab at the ancient puzzle of freedom.

Outside the war rockets of Earth began landing quietly on the free soil of Mars.

Police Your Planet

Chapter I
One Way Ticket

There were ten passengers in the little pressurized cabin of the electric bus that shuttled between the rocket field and Marsport. Ten men, the driver-and Bruce Gordon.

He sat apart from the others, as he had kept to himself on the ten-day trip between Earth and Mars, with the yellow stub of his ticket still stuck defiantly in the band of his hat, proclaiming that Earth had paid his passage without his permission being asked. His big, lean body was slumped slightly in the seat. There was no expression on his face.

He listened to the driver explaining to a couple of firsters that they were actually on what appeared to be one of the mysterious canals when viewed from Earth. Every book on Mars gave the fact that the canals were either an illusion or something which could not be detected on the surface of the planet.

He glanced back toward the rocket that still pointed skyward back on the field, and then forward toward the city of Marsport, sprawling out in a mess of slums beyond the edges of the dome that had been built to hold air over the central part. And at last he stirred and reached for the yellow stub.

He grimaced at the ONE WAY stamped on it, then tore it into bits and let the pieces scatter over the floor. He counted them as they fell; thirty pieces, one for each year of his life. Little ones for the two years he'd wasted as a cop. Shreds for the four years as a kid in the ring before that-he'd never made the top. Bigger bits for two years also wasted in trying his hand at professional gambling; and the six final pieces that spelled his rise from a special reporter helping out with a police shake-up coverage, through a regular leg-man turning up rackets, and on up like a meteor until....He'd made his big scoop, all right. He'd dug up enough about the Mercury scandals to double circulation.

And the government had explained what a fool he'd been for printing half of a story that was never supposed to be printed until all could be revealed. They'd given Bruce Gordon his final assignment.

He shrugged. He'd bought a suit of airtight coveralls and a helmet at the field; he had some cash, and a set of reader cards in his pocket. The supply house, Earthside, had assured him that this pattern had never been exported to Mars. With them and the knife he'd selected, he might get by.

The Solar Security office had given him the knife practice, to make sure he could use it, just as they'd made sure he hadn't taken extra money with him beyond the regulation amount.

"You're a traitor, and we'd like nothing better than seeing your guts spilled," the Security man had told him. "That paper you swiped was marked top secret. But we don't get many men with your background-cop, tinhorn, fighter-who have brains enough for our work. So you're bound for Mars, rather than the Mercury mines. If..."

It was a big *if*, and a vague one. They needed men on Mars who could act as links in their information bureau, and be ready to work on their side when the expected trouble came. They wanted men who could serve them loyally, even without orders. If he did them enough service, they might let him back to Earth. If he caused trouble enough, they could still ship him to Mercury.

"And suppose nothing happens?" he asked.

"Then who cares? You're just lucky enough to be alive."

"And what makes you think I'm going to be a spy for Security?"

The other had shrugged. "Why not, Gordon? You've been a spy for a yellow scandal sheet. Why not for us?"

Gordon had been smart enough to realize that perhaps Security was right.

They were in the slums around the city now. Marsport had been settled faster than it was ready to receive. Temporary buildings had been thrown up, and then had remained, decaying into deathtraps. It wasn't a pretty view that visitors got as they first reached Mars. But nobody except the romantic fools had ever thought frontiers were pretty.

The drummer who had watched Gordon tear up his yellow stub moved forward now. "First time?" he asked.

Gordon nodded, mentally cataloguing the drummer as the cockroach type, midway between the small-businessman slug and the petty-crook spider types that weren't worth bothering with. But the other took it as interest.

"Been here dozens of times, myself. Risking your life just to go into Marsport. Why Congress doesn't clean it up, *I'll* never know!"

Gordon's mind switched to the readers in his bag. The cards were plastic, and should be good for a week or so of use before they showed wear. During that time, by playing it carefully, he should have his stake. Then, if the gaming tables here were as crudely run as an oldtimer he'd known on Earth had said, he could try a coup.

"...be at Mother Corey's soon," the fat little drummer babbled on. "Notorious-worst place on Mars. Take it from me, brother, that's something! Even the cops are afraid to go in there. See it? There, to your left!"

The name was vaguely familiar as one of the sore spots of Marsport. Bruce Gordon looked, and spotted the ragged building, half a mile outside the dome. It had been a rocket-maintenance hangar once, then had been turned into temporary dwelling for the first deportees, when Earth began flooding Mars. Now, seeming to stand by habit alone, it radiated desolation and decay.

He stood up, grabbing for his bag, and spinning the drummer aside. He jerked forward, and caught the driver's shoulder. "Getting off!"

The driver shrugged his hand away. "Don't be crazy, mister! They —" He turned, saw it was Gordon, and his face turned blank. "It's your life, buster," he said, and reached for the brake. "I'll give you five minutes to get into coveralls and helmet and out through the airlock."

Gordon needed less than that; he'd practiced all the way from Earth. The transparent plastic of the coveralls went on easily enough, and his hands found the seals quickly. He slipped his few possessions into a bag at his belt, slid the knife into a spring holster above his wrist, and picked up the bowl-shaped helmet. It seated on a plastic seal, and the little air compressor at his back began to hum, ready to turn the thin wisp of Mars' atmosphere into a barely breathable pressure. He tested the Marspeaker-an amplifier and speaker in another pouch, designed to raise the volume of his voice to a level where it would carry through even the air of Mars.

The driver swore at the lash of sound, and grabbed for the airlock switch.

Gordon moved down unpaved streets that zig-zagged along, thick with the filth of garbage and poverty-the part of Mars never seen in the newsreels, outside the shock movies. Thin kids with big eyes and sullen mouths crowded the streets in their airsuits, yelling profanity. The street was filled with people watching with a numbed hunger for any kind of excitement.

It was late afternoon, obviously. Men were coming from the few bus routes, lugging tools and lunch baskets, slumped and beaten from labor in the atomic plants, the Martian conversion farms, and the industries that had come inevitably where inefficiency was better than the high prices of imports. The saloons were doing well enough, apparently, from the number that streamed in through their airlock entrances. But Gordon saw one of the bartenders paying money to a thickset person with an arrogant sneer; he knew then that the few profits from the cheap beer were never going home with the man. Storekeepers in the cheap little shops had the same lines on their faces as they saw on those of their customers.

Poverty and misery were the keynotes here, rather than the evil half-world the drummer had babbled about. But to Gordon's trained eyes, there was plenty of outright rottenness, too.

He grimaced, grateful that the supercharger on his airsuit filtered out some of the smell which the thin air carried. He'd thought he was familiar with human misery from his own Earth slum background. But there was no attempt to disguise it here.

Ahead, Mother Corey's reared up —a huge, ugly half-cylinder of pitted metal and native bricks, showing the patchwork of decades, before repairs had been abandoned. There were no windows, though once there had been; and the front was covered with a big sign that spelled out *Condemned*. The airseal was filthy, and there was no bell.

Gordon kicked against the side, waited, and kicked again. A slit opened and closed. He waited, then drew his knife and began prying at the worn cement around the airseal, looking for the lock that had been there.

The seal suddenly quivered, indicating that metal inside had been withdrawn. Gordon grinned tautly, stepped through, and pushed the blade against the inner plastic.

"All right, all right," a voice whined out of the darkness. "You don't have to puncture my seal. You're in."

"Then call them off!"

A wheezing chuckle answered him, and a phosphor bulb glowed weakly, shedding some light on a filthy hall. "Okay, boys," the voice said, "come on down. He's alone, anyhow. What's pushing, stranger?"

"A yellow ticket," Gordon told him, "and a government allotment that'll last me two weeks in the dome. I figure on making it last six here, and don't let my being a firster give you hot palms. My brother was Lanny Gordon!"

It happened to be true, though Bruce Gordon hadn't seen his brother from the time the man had left the family, as a young punk, to the day they finally convicted him on his twenty-first murder. But here, if it was like places he'd known on Earth, even second-hand contact with "muscle" was useful.

It seemed to work. A huge man oozed out of the shadows, his gray face contorting its doughy fat into a yellow-toothed grin, and a filthy hand waved back the others. There were a few wisps of long, gray hair on the head and face, and they quivered as he moved forward.

"Looking for a room?" he whined.

"I'm looking for Mother Corey."

"Then you're looking at him, cobber. Sleep on the floor, want a bunk, squat with four, or room and duchess to yourself?"

There was a period of haggling, followed by a wait as Mother Corey kicked four grumbling men out of a four-by-seven hole on the second floor. Gordon's money had carried more weight than his brother's reputation; for that, Corey humored his guest's wish for privacy. "All yours, cobber, while your crackle's blue."

It was a filthy, dark place. In one corner was an unsheeted bed. There was a rusty bucket for water, a hole kicked through the floor for waste water. Plumbing, and such luxuries, apparently hadn't existed for years-except for the small cistern and worn water-recovery plant in the basement, beside the tired-looking weeds in the hydroponic tanks that tried unsuccessfully to keep the air breathable.

"What about a lock on the door?" Gordon asked.

"What good would it do you? Got a different way here, we have. One credit a week, and you get Mother Corey's word nobody busts in. And it sticks, cobber-one way or the other."

Gordon paid, and tossed his pouch on the filthy bed. With a little work, the place could be cleaned enough.

He pulled the cards out of his pouch, trying to be casual. Mother Corey stood staring at the pack while Bruce Gordon changed out of his airsuit, gagging faintly as the full effluvium of the place hit him. "Where does a man eat around here?"

Mother Corey pried his eyes off the cards and ran a thick tongue over heavy lips. "Eh? Oh. Eat. There's a place about ten blocks back. Cobber, stop teasing me! With elections coming up, and the boys loaded with vote money back in town-with a deck of cheaters like that-you want to *eat*?"

He picked the deck up fondly, while a faraway look came into his clouded eyes. "Same ones-same identical ones I wore out nigh twenty years ago. Smuggled two decks up here. Set to clean up-and I did, for a while." He shook his head sadly, and handed the deck back to Gordon. "Come on down. For the sight of these, I'll give you the lay for your pitch. And when your luck's made or broken, remember Mother Corey was your friend first, and your old Mother can get longer use from them than you can."

He waddled off, telling of his plans to take Mars for a cleaning, once long ago. Gordon followed him, staring at the surrounding filth.

His thoughts were churning so busily that he didn't see the blonde girl until she had forced her way past them on the stairs. Then he turned back, but she had vanished into one of the rooms.

Chapter II
Honest Izzy

A lot could be done in ten days, when a man knew what he was after. It was exactly ten days later. Bruce Gordon stood in the motley crowd inside the barnlike room where Fats ran a bar along one wall, and filled the rest of the space with assorted tables-all worn. Gordon was sweating slightly as he stood at the roulette table, where both zero and double-zero were reserved for the house.

The croupier was a little wizened man wanted on Earth. His eyes darted down to the point of the knife that showed under Gordon's sleeve, and he licked his lips, showing snaggled teeth. The wheel hesitated and came to a halt, with the ball trembling in a pocket.

"Twenty-one wins again." He pushed chips toward Gordon, as if every one of them came out of his own pay. "Place your bets."

Two others around the table watched narrowly as Gordon left his chips where they were; they then exchanged looks and shook their heads. In a Martian roulette game, numbers with that much riding just didn't turn up. The croupier shifted his weight, then caught the wheel and spun it savagely.

Gordon's leg ached from his strained position, but he shifted his weight onto it more heavily, and sweat popped out on the croupier's face. His eyes darted down, to where the full weight of Gordon seemed to rest on the heel that was grinding into his instep. He tried to pull his foot off the button that was concealed in the floor.

The heel ground harder, bringing a groan from him. And the ball hovered over Twenty-one and came to rest there once more.

Slowly, painfully, the little man counted stacks of chips and moved them across the table toward Gordon, his hands trembling.

Gordon straightened from his awkward position, drawing his foot back, and reached out for the pile of chips. Then he scooped it up and nodded. "Okay. I'm not greedy."

The strain of watching the games until he could spot the fix, and then holding the croupier down, had left him momentarily weak, but Gordon could still feel the tensing of the crowd. Now he let his eyes run over them-the night citizens of Marsport, lower-dome section. Spacemen who'd missed their ships; men who'd come here with dreams, and stayed without them-the shopkeepers who couldn't meet their graft and were here to try to win it on a last chance; street women and petty grifters. The air was thick with their unwashed bodies-all Mars smelled, since water was still too rare for frequent bathing-and their cheap perfume, and clouded with cheap Marsweed cigarettes.

Gordon swung where their eyes pointed, until he saw Fats Eller sidling through the groups, then let the knife slip into the palm of his hand as the crowd seemed to hold its breath. Fats plucked a sheaf of Martian bank notes from his pocket and tossed them to the croupier.

"Cash in his chips." Then his pouchy eyes turned to Gordon. "Get your money, punk, and get out! And stay out!"

For a moment, as he began pocketing the bills, Gordon thought he was going to get away that easily. Fats watched him dourly, then swung on his heel, just as a shrill, strangled cry went up from someone in the crowd.

The deportee let his glance jerk to it, then froze. His eyes caught the sight of a hand pointing behind him, and he knew it was too crude a trick to bother with. But he paused, shocked to see the girl he'd seen on Mother Corey's stairs gazing at him in well-feigned warning. In spite of his better judgment, she caught his eyes and drew them down over curves and swells that would always be right for arousing a man's passion.

He glanced back at Fats, who had started to turn again. Gordon took a step backwards, preparing to duck. Again the girl's finger motioned behind him; he disregarded it-and then realized it was a mistake.

It was the faintest swish in the air that caught his ear; he brought his shoulders up and his head down. Fast as his reaction was, it was almost too late. The weapon crunched against his shoulder and slammed over the back of his neck, almost knocking him out.

His heel lashed back and caught the shin of the man behind him. Gordon's other leg spun him around, still crouching; the knife in his hand started coming up, sharp edge leading, and aimed for the belly of the bruiser who confronted him. The pug saw the blade and tried to check his lunge.

Gordon felt the blade strike; but he was already pulling his swing, and it only gashed a long streak. The thug shrieked hoarsely and fell over. That left the way clear to the door; Bruce Gordon was through it and into the night in two soaring leaps. After only a few days on Mars, his legs were still hardened to Earth gravity, and he had more than a double advantage over the others.

Outside, it was the usual Martian night in the poorer section of the dome, which meant near-darkness. Most of the street lights had never been installed-graft had eaten up the appropriations, instead-and the nearest one was around the corner, leaving the side of Fats' Place in the shadow. Gordon checked his speed, threw himself flat, and rolled back against the building, just beyond the steps that led to the street.

Feet pounded out of the door above as Fats and the bouncer broke through. Gordon's hand had already knotted a couple of coins into his kerchief; he waited until the two turned uncertainly up the street and tossed it. It struck the wall near the corner, sailed on, and struck again at the edge of the unpaved street with a muffled sound.

Fats and the other swung, just in time to see a bit of dust where it had hit. "Around the corner!" Fats yelled. "After him, and shoot!"

In the shadows, Gordon jerked sharply. It was rare enough to have a gun here; but to use one inside the dome was unthinkable. His eyes shot up, to where the few dim lights were reflected off the great plastic sheet that was held up by air pressure and reinforced with heavy webbing. It was the biggest dome ever built-large enough to cover all of Marsport before the slums sprawled out beyond it; it still covered half the city, and made breathing possible here without a helmet. But the dome wasn't designed to stand stray bullets; and having firearms inside it-except for a few chosen men-was a crime punishable by death.

Fats had swung back, and was now herding the crowd inside his place. He might have been only a small gambling-house owner, but within his own circle his words carried weight.

Gordon got to his hands and knees and began crawling away from the corner. He came to a dark alley, smelling of decay where garbage had piled up without being carted away. Beyond lay a lighted street, and a sign that announced *Mooney's Amusement Palace-Drinks Free to Patrons!* He looked up and down the street, then walked briskly toward the somewhat plusher gambling hall there. Fats couldn't touch him in a competitor's place.

Inside Mooney's, he headed quickly for the dice table. He lost steadily on small bets for half an hour, admiring the skilled palming of the "odds" cubes. The loss was only a tiny dent in his new pile, but Gordon bemoaned it properly-as if he were broke-and moved over to the bar. This one had seats. The bartender had a consolation boilermaker waiting; he gulped half of it before he realized it had been needled with ether.

Beside him, a cop was drinking the same slowly, watching another policeman at a Canfield game. He was obviously winning, and now he got up and came over to cash in his chips.

"You'd think they'd lose count once in a while," he complained to his companion. "But nope-fifty even a night, no more ... Well, come on, Pete. We'd better get back to Fats and tell him the swindler got away."

Gordon followed them out and turned south, down the street toward the edge of the dome and the entrance where he'd parked his airsuit and helmet. He kept glancing back, whenever he was in the thicker shadows, but there seemed to be no one following him.

At the gate of the dome, he looked back again, then ducked into the locker building. He threaded through the maze of the lockers with his knife ready in his hand, trying not to attract suspicion. At this hour, though, most of the place was empty. The crowds of foremen and deliverymen who'd be going in and out through the day were lacking.

He found his suit and helmet and clamped them on quickly, transferring the knife to its spring sheath outside the suit. He checked the tiny batteries that were recharged by generators in the soles of the boots with every step. Then he paid his toll for the opening of the private slit and went through, into the darkness outside the dome.

Lights bobbed about-police in pairs, patrolling in the better streets, walking as far from the houses as they could; a few groups, depending on numbers for safety; some of the very poor, stumbling about and hoping for a drink somehow; and probably hoods from the gangs that ruled the nights here.

Gordon left his torch unlighted, and moved along; there was a little illumination from the phosphorescent markers at some of the corners, and from the stars. He could just make his way without marking himself with a light.

Damn it, he should have hired a few of the younger bums from Mother Corey's. Here he couldn't hear footsteps. He located a pair of patrolling cops, and followed them down one street, until they swung off. Then he was on his own again.

"Gov'nor!" The word barely reached him, and Bruce Gordon spun around, the knife twitching into his hand. It was a thin kid of perhaps eighteen behind him, carrying a torch that was filtered to bare visibility. It swung up, and he saw a pock-marked face that was twisted in a smile meant to be ingratiating.

"You've got a pad on your tail," the kid said, again as low as his amplifier would permit. "Need a convoy?"

Gordon studied him briefly, and grinned. Then his grin wiped out as the kid's arm flashed to his shoulder and back, a series of quick jerks that seemed almost a blur. Four knives stood buried in the ground at Gordon's feet, forming a square-and a fifth was in the kid's hand.

"How much?" he asked, as the kid scooped up the blades and shoved them expertly back into shoulder sheaths. The kid's hand shaped a C quickly, and Gordon slipped his arm through a self-sealing slit in the airsuit and brought out two of them.

"Thanks, gov'nor," the kid said, stowing them away. "You won't regret it." Gordon started to turn. Then the kid's voice rose sharply to a yell. "Okay, honey, he's the Joe!"

Out of the darkness, ten to a dozen figures loomed up. The kid had jumped aside with a lithe leap, and now stood between Gordon and the group moving in for the kill. Gordon swung to run, and found himself surrounded. His eyes flickered around, trying to spot something in the darkness that would give him shelter.

A bludgeon was suddenly hurtling toward him, and he ducked it, his blood thick in his throat and his ears ringing with the same pressure of fear he'd always known just before he was kayoed in the ring. Then he selected what he hoped was the thinnest section of the attackers and leaped forward. With luck, he might jump over them, using his Earth strength.

There was a flicker of dawnlight in the sky, now, however; and he made out others behind, ready for just such a move. He changed his lunge in mid-stride, and brought his arm back with the knife. It met a small round shield on the arm of the man he had chosen, and was deflected at once.

"Give 'em hell, gov'nor," the kid's voice yelled, and the little figure was beside him, a shower of blades seeming to leap from his hand in the glare of his bare torch. Shields caught them frantically, and then the kid was in with a heavy club he'd torn from someone's hand.

Gordon had no time to consider his sudden traitor-ally. He bent to the ground, seizing the first rocks he could find, and threw them. One of the hoods dropped his club in ducking; Gordon caught it up and swung in a single motion that stretched the other out.

Then it was a melée. The kid's open torch, stuck on his helmet, gave them light enough, until Gordon could switch on his own. Then the kid dropped behind him, fighting back-to-back. Here, in close quarters, the attackers were no longer using knives. One might be turned on its owner, and a slit suit meant death by asphyxiation.

Gordon saw the blonde girl on the outskirts, her face taut and glowing. He tried to reach her with a thrown club wrested from another man, but she leaped nimbly aside, shouting commands.

Two burly goons were suddenly working together. Gordon swung at one, ducked a blow from the other, and then saw the first swinging again. He tried to bring his club up-but knew it was too late. A dull weight hit the side of his head, and he felt himself falling.

It took only minutes for dawn to become day on Mars, and the sun was lighting up the messy section of back street when Bruce Gordon's eyes opened and the pain of sight struck his aching head. He groaned, then looked frantically for the puff of escaping air. But his suit was still sealed. Ahead of him, the kid lay sprawled out, blood trickling from an ugly bruise along his jaw.

Then Gordon felt something on his suit, and his eyes darted to hands just finishing an emergency patch. His eyes darted up and met those of the blonde vixen!

Amazement kept him motionless for a second. There were tears in the eyes of the girl, and a sniffling sound reached him through her Marspeaker. Apparently, she hadn't noticed that he had revived, though her eyes were on him. She finished the patch, and ran perma-sealer over it. Then she began putting her supplies away, tucking them into a bag that held notes that could only have been stolen from his pockets-her share of the loot, apparently.

He was still thinking clumsily as she got to her feet and turned to leave. She cast a glance back, hesitated, and then began to move off.

He got his feet under him slowly, but he was reviving enough to stand the pain in his head. He came to his feet, and leaped after her. In the thin air, his lunge was silent, and he was grabbing her before she knew he was up.

She swung with a single gasp, and her hand darted down for her knife, sweeping it up and toward him; he barely caught the wrist coming toward him. Then he had her firmly, bringing her arm back and up, until the knife fell from her fingers.

She screamed and began writhing, twisting her hard young body like a boa constrictor in his hands. But he was stronger. He bent her back over his knee, until a mangled moan was coming from her speaker; then his foot kicked out, knocking her feet out from under her. He let her hit the ground, caught both her wrists in his, and brought his knee down on her throat, applying more pressure until she lay still. Then he reached for the pouch.

"Damn you!" Her cry was more in anguish then it had been when he was threatening to break her back. "You damned firster, I'll kill you if it's the last thing I do. And after I saved your miserable life...."

"Thanks for that," he grunted. "Next time don't be a fool. When you kill a man for his money, he doesn't feel very grateful for your reviving him."

He started to count the money. About a tenth of what he had won-not even enough to open a cheap poker den, let alone bribe his way back to Earth.

The girl was out from under his knee at the first relaxation of pressure. Her hand scooped up the knife, and she came charging toward him, her mouth a taut slit across half-bared teeth. Gordon rolled out of her swing, and brought his foot up. It caught her squarely under the chin, and she went down and out.

He picked up the scattered money and her knife, then made sure she was still breathing. He ran his hands over her, looking for a hiding place for more money; there was none.

"Good work, gov'nor," the kid's thin voice approved, and Gordon swung to see the other getting up painfully. The kid grinned, rubbing his bruise. "No hard feelings, gov'nor, now! They paid me to stall you, so I did. You bonused me to protect you, and I bloody well tried. Honest Izzy, that's me. Gonna buy me a job as a cop. That's why I needed the scratch. Okay, gov'nor?"

Gordon hauled back his hand to knock the other from his feet, and then dropped it. A grin writhed onto his face, and broke into sudden grudging laughter.

"Okay, Izzy," he admitted. "For this stinking planet, I guess you're something of a saint. Come along, and we'll both apply for that job-after I get my stuff."

He might as well join the law. Security had wanted him to police their damned planet for them-and he might as well do it officially.

He tossed the girl's knife down beside her, motioned to Izzy, and began heading for Mother Corey's.

Chapter III
The Graft is Green

Izzy seemed surprised when he found that Gordon was turning in to the quasi-secret entrance to Mother Corey's. "Coming here myself," he explained. "Mother got ahold of a load of snow, and sent me out to contact a big pusher. Coming back, the goons picked me up and gave me the job on you. Hey, Mother!"

Bruce Gordon didn't ask how Mother Corey had acquired the dope. When Earth had deported all addicts two decades before, it had practically begged for dope smuggling.

The gross hulk of Mother Corey appeared almost at once. "Izzy and Bruce. Didn't know you'd met, cobbers. Contact, Izzy?"

"Ninety per cent for uncut," Izzy answered.

They went up to Gordon's hole-in-the-wall, with Mother Corey wheezing behind, while the rotten wood of the stairs groaned under his grotesque bulk. At his questions, Gordon told the story tersely.

Mother Corey nodded. "Same old angles, eh? Get enough to do the job, they mug you. Stop halfway, and the halls are closed to you. Pretty soon, they'll be trick-proof, anyhow; they're changing over to electric eyes. Eh, you haven't forgotten me, cobber?"

Gordon hadn't. The old wreck had demanded five per cent of his winnings for tipping him off. Mother Corey had too many cheap hoods among his friends to be fooled with. Gordon counted out the money reluctantly, while Izzy explained that they were going to be cops.

The old man shook his head, estimating what was left to Gordon. "Enough to buy a corporal's job, pay for your suit, and maybe get by," he decided. "Don't do it, cobber. You're the wrong kind. You take what you're doing serious. When you set out to tinhorn a living, you're a crook. Get you in a cop's outfit, and you'll turn honest. No place here for an honest cop-not with elections coming up, cobber. Well, I guess you gotta find out for yourself. Want a good room?"

Gordon's lips twitched. "Thanks, Mother, but I'll be staying inside the dome, I guess."

"So'll I," the old man gloated. "Setting in a chair all day, being an honest citizen. Cobber, I already own a joint there —a nice one, they tell me. Lights. Two water closets. Big rooms, six-by-ten —fifty of them, big enough for whole families. And strictly on the level, cobber. It's no hide-out, like this."

He rolled the money in his greasy fingers. "Now, with what I get from the pusher, I can buy off that hot spot on the police blotter. I can go in the dome and walk around, just like you." His eyes watered, and a tear went dripping down his nose. "I'm getting old. They'll be calling me 'Grandmother' pretty soon. So I'm turning my Chicken House over to my granddaughter and I'm going honest. Want a room?"

Gordon grinned, and nodded. Mother Corey knew the ropes, and could be trusted. "Didn't know you had a granddaughter."

Izzy snorted, and Mother Corey grinned wolfishly. "You met her, cobber. The blonde you shook down! Came up from Earth eight years ago, looking for me. I sold her to the head of the East Point gang. Since she killed him, she's been doing pretty well on her own. Mostly. Except when she makes a fool of herself, like she did with you. But she'll come around to where I'm proud of her, yet....If you two want to carry in the snow, collect, and turn it over to Commissioner Arliss for me —I can't pass the dome till he gets it —I'll give you both rooms for six months free. Except for the lights and water, of course."

Izzy nodded, and Gordon shrugged. On Mars, it didn't seem odd to begin applying for a police job by carrying in narcotics. He wondered how they'd go about contacting the commissioner.

But that turned out to be simple enough. After collecting, Izzy led the way into a section marked "Special Taxes" and whispered a few casual words. The man at the desk went into an office marked private, and came back a few minutes later.

"Your friend has no record with us," he said in a routine voice. "I've checked through his tax forms, and they're all in order. We'll confirm officially, of course."

In the Applications section of the big Municipal Building, at the center of the dome, there was a long form to fill out at the desk; but the captain there had already had answers typed in.

"Save time, boys," he said genially. "And time's valuable, ain't it? Ah, yes." He took the sums they had ready-there was a standard price-and stamped their forms. "And you'll want suits. Isaacs? Good, here's your receipt. And you, Corporal Gordon. Right. Get your suits one floor down, end of the hall. And report in eight tomorrow morning!"

It was as simple as that. Bruce Gordon was lucky enough to get a fair fit in his suit. He'd almost forgotten what it felt like to be in uniform.

Izzy was more businesslike. "Hope they don't give us too bad territory, gov'nor," he remarked. "Pickings are always a little lean on the first few beats, but you can work some fairly well."

Gordon's chest fell; this was Mars!

The room at the new Mother Corey's —an unkempt old building near the edge of the dome-proved to be livable, though it was a shock to see Mother Corey himself in a decent suit, and using perfume.

The beat was in a shabby section where clerks and skilled laborers worked. It wasn't poor enough to offer the universal desperation that gave the gang hoodlums protective coloring, nor rich enough to have major rackets of its own.

Izzy was disgusted. "Cripes! Hope they've got a few cheap pushers around that don't pay protection direct to the captain. You take that store; I'll go in this one!"

The proprietor was a druggist who ran his own fountain where the synthetics that replaced honest Earth foods were compounded into sweet and sticky messes for the neighborhood kids. He looked up as Gordon came in; then his face fell. "New cop, eh? No wonder Gable collected yesterday, ahead of time. All right, you can look at my books. I've been paying fifty, but you'll have to wait until Friday."

Gordon nodded and swung on his heel, surprised to find that his stomach was turning. The man obviously couldn't afford fifty credits a week. But it was the same all along the street. Even Izzy admitted finally that they'd have to wait.

"That damned cop before us! He really tapped them! And we can't take less, so I guess we gotta wait until Friday."

The next day, Bruce Gordon made his first arrest. It was near the end of his shift, just as darkness was falling and the few lights were going on. He turned a corner and came to a short, heavy hoodlum backing out of a small liquor store with a knife in throwing position. The crook grunted as he started to turn and stumbled onto Gordon. His knife flashed up.

Without the need to worry about an airsuit, Gordon moved in, his arm jerking forward. He clipped the crook on the inside of the elbow, while grabbing the wrist with his other hand. The man went sailing over Gordon's head, to crash into the side of the building. He let out a yell.

Gordon rifled the hood's pockets, and located a roll of bills stuffed in. He dragged them out, before snapping cuffs on the man. Then he pulled the crook inside the store.

A woman stood there, moaning over a pale man on the floor; blood oozed from a welt on the back of his head. There was both gratitude and resentment as she looked up at Gordon.

"You'd better call the hospital," he told her sharply. "He may have a concussion. I've got the man who held you up."

"Hospital?" Her voice broke into another wail. "And who can afford hospitals? All week we work, all hours. He's old, he can't handle the cases. I do that. Me! And then you come, and you get your money. And *he* comes for his protection. Papa is sick. Sick, do you hear? He sees a doctor, he buys medicine. Then Gable comes. This man comes. We can't pay him! So what do we get-we get knifes in the faces, saps on the head —a concussion, you tell me! And all the money-the money we had to pay to get stocks to sell to pay off from the profits we don't make-all of it, he wants! Hospitals! You think they give away at the hospitals free?"

She fell to her knees, crying over the injured man.

Gordon tossed the roll of bills onto the floor beside her; the injury seemed only a scalp wound, and the old man was already beginning to groan. He opened his eyes and saw the bills in front of him, at which the woman was staring unbelievingly. His hand darted out, clutching it. "God!" he moaned softly, and his eyes turned up slowly to Gordon.

"In there!" It was a shout from outside. Gordon had just time to straighten up before the doorway was filled with two knife-men and a heavier one behind them.

His hands dropped to the handcuffed man on the floor, and he caught him up with a jerk, slapping his body back against the counter. He took a step forward, jerking his hands up and putting his Earth-adapted shoulders behind it. The hood sailed up and struck the two knife-men squarely.

There was a scream as their automatic attempts to save themselves buried both knives in the body of their friend. Then they went crashing down, and Gordon was over them.

The desk captain at the precinct house groaned as they came in, then shook his head. "Damn it," he said. "I suppose it can't be helped, though; you're new, Gordon. Hennessy, get the corpse to the morgue, and mark it down as a robbery attempt. I'm going to have to book you and your men, Mr. Jurgens!"

The heavy leader of the two angry knife-men grinned. "Okay, Captain. But it's going to slow down the work I'm doing on the Mayor's campaign for re-election! Damn that Maxie —I told him to be discreet. Hey, you know what you've got, though —a real considerate man! He gave the old guy his money back!"

They took Bruce Gordon's testimony, and sent him home.

Jurgens was waiting for him when he came on the beat. From his look of having slept well, he must have been out almost as soon as he was booked. Two other men stood behind Gordon, while Jurgens explained that he didn't like being interrupted on business calls "about the Mayor's campaign, or anything else," and that next time there'd be real hard feelings. Gordon was surprised when he wasn't beaten, but not when the racketeer suggested that any money found at a crime was evidence and should go to the police. The captain had told him the same.

By Friday, he had learned. He made his collections early. Gable had sold him the list of what was expected, and he used it, though he cut down the figures in a few cases. There was no sense in killing the geese that laid the eggs.

The couple at the liquor store had their payment waiting, and they handed it over, looking embarrassed. It wasn't until he was gone that he found a small bottle of fairly good whiskey tucked into his pouch. He started to throw it away, and then lifted it to his lips. Maybe they'd known how he felt better than he had. Mother Corey's words about his change of attitude came back. Damn it, he had to dig up enough money to get back to Earth.

He collected, down to the last account. It was a nice haul; at that rate, he'd have to stand it only for a few months. Then Gordon's lips twisted, as he realized it wasn't all gravy. There were angles, or the price of a corporalcy would have been higher.

One of the older men answered his questions. "Fifty per cent of the take to the Orphan's and Widow's fund. Better make it more than Gable turned in, if you want to get a better beat."

The envelopes were lying on a table marked "Voluntary Donations"; Gordon filled his out, with a figure a bit higher than half of Gable's take, and dropped it in the box. The captain, who had been watching him carefully, settled back and smiled.

"Widows and Orphans sure appreciate a good man," he said. "I was kind of worried about you, Gordon, but you got a nice touch. One of my new boys-Isaacs, you know him-was out checking up after you, and the dopes seem to like you."

Gordon had wondered why Izzy had been pulled off the beat. As he turned to leave, the captain held up a hand. "Special meeting tomorrow. We gotta see about getting out a good vote. Election only three weeks away."

Gordon went home. He'd learned by now that the native Martians-those who'd been here for at least thirty years, or had been born here-were backing a reform candidate and new ticket. But Mayor Wayne had all of the rest of the town in his hand. He'd been in twice, and had lifted the graft take by a truly remarkable figure. From where Gordon stood, it looked like a clear victory for the reformer, Nolan.

He went into the meeting willing to agree to anything. He applauded all the speeches about how much Mayor Wayne had done for them, and signed the pledge expressing his confidence, along with the implied duty he had to make his beat vote right. Then he stopped, as the captain stood up.

"We gotta be neutral, boys," he boomed. "But it don't mean we can't show how well we like the Mayor. Just remember, he got us our jobs! Now I figure we can all kick in a little to help his campaign. I'm going to start it off with five thousand credits, two thousand of them right now."

They fell in line, though there was no cheering. The price might have been fixed in advance. A thousand for a plain cop, fifteen hundred for a corporal, and so on, each contributing a third of it now. Gordon grimaced; he had six hundred left. This would take nearly all of it.

A man named Fell shook his head, fearfully. "Can't do a thing now. My wife had a baby and an operation, and — —"

"Okay, Fell," the captain said, without a sign of disapproval. "Freitag, what about you? Fine, fine!"

Gordon's name came, and he shook his head. "I'm new-and I'm strapped now. I'd like — —"

"Quite all right, Gordon," the captain boomed. "Harwick!"

He finished the roll, and settled back, smiling. "I guess that's all, boys. Thanks from the Mayor. And go on home....Oh, Fell, Gordon, Lativsky-stick around. I've got some overtime for you, since you need extra money. The boys out in Ward Three are shorthanded. Afraid I'll have to order you out there!"

Ward Three was the hangout of a cheap gang of hoodlums, numbering some four hundred, who went in for small crimes mostly. But they had recently declared war on the cops.

After eight hours of overtime, Gordon reported in with every bone sore from small missiles, and his suit filthy from assorted muck. He had a beautiful shiner where a stone had clipped him.

The captain smiled. "Rough, eh? But I hear robbery went down on your beat last night. Fine work, Gordon. We need men like you. Hate to do it, but I'm afraid you'll have to take the next shift at Main and Broad, directing traffic. The usual man is sick, and you're the only one I can trust with the job!"

Gordon stuck it out, somehow, but it wasn't worth it. He reported back to the precinct with the five hundred in his hand, and his pen itching for the donation agreement.

The captain took it, and nodded. "I wasn't kidding about your being a good man, Gordon. Go home and get some sleep, take the next day off. After that, we've got a new job for you!"

Chapter IV
Captain Murdoch

The new assignment was to the roughest section in all Marsport-the slum area beyond the dome, out near the rocket field. Here all the riffraff that had been unable to establish itself in better quarters had found some sort of a haven. At one time, there had been a small dome and a tiny city devoted to the rocket field. But Marsport had flourished enough to kill it off. The dome had failed from neglect, and the buildings inside had grown shabbier.

Bruce Gordon was trapped; he couldn't break his job with the police-if he did, he'd be brought back as a criminal. Some of Mars' laws dated from the time when law enforcement had been hampered by lack of men, rather than by the type of men.

The Stonewall gang numbered perhaps five hundred. They hired out members to other gangs, during the frequent wars. Between times, they picked up what they could by mugging and theft, with a reasonable amount of murder thrown in at a modest price.

Even derelicts and failures had to eat; there were stores and shops throughout the district which eked out some kind of a marginal living. They were safe from protection racketeers there-none bothered to come so far out. And police had been taken off the beats there after it grew unsafe even for men in pairs to patrol the area.

The shopkeepers, and some of the less unfortunate people there, had protested loud enough to reach clear back to Earth. Marsport had hired a man from Earth to come in and act as chief of the section. Captain Murdoch was an unknown factor, and now was asking for more men. The pressure was enough to get them for him.

Gordon reported for work with a sense of the bottom falling out, mixed with a vague relief.

"You're going to be busy," Murdoch announced shortly in the dilapidated building that had been hastily converted to a precinct house. "Damn it, you're men, not sharks. I've got a free hand, and we're going to run this the way we would on Earth. Your job is to protect the citizens here-and that means everyone not breaking the laws-whether you feel like it or not. No graft. The first man making a shakedown will get the same treatment we're going to use on the Stonewall boys. You'll get double pay here, and you can live on it!"

He opened up a box on his desk and pulled out six heavy wooden sticks, each thirty inches long and nearly two inches in diameter. There was a shaped grip on each, with a thong of leather to hold it over the wrist.

He picked out five of the men, including Gordon "You five will come with me. I'm going to show how we operate. The rest of you can team up any way you want tonight, pick any route that's open. Okay, men, let's go."

Bruce Gordon grinned slowly as he swung the stick, and Murdoch's eyes fell on him. "Earth cop!"

"Two years," Gordon admitted.

"Then you should be ashamed to be in this mess. But whatever your reasons, you'll be useful. Take those two and give them some lessons, while I do the same with these."

For a second, Gordon cursed himself. Murdoch had fixed it so he'd be a squad leader, and that meant he'd be unable to step out of line. At double standard pay, with normal Mars expenses, he might be able to pay for passage back to Earth in three years-if Security let him. Otherwise, it would take thirty.

He began wondering about Security, then. Nobody had tried to get in touch with him. Were they waiting for him to get up on a soapbox?

There was a crude lighting system here, put up by the citizens. At the front of each building, a dim phosphor bulb glowed; when darkness fell, they would have nothing else to see by.

Murdoch bunched them together. "A good clubbing beats hanging," he told them. "But it has to be *good*. Go in for business, and don't stop just because the other guy quits. Give them hell!"

Moving in two groups of threes, at opposite sides of the street, they began their beat. They were covering an area of six blocks one way, and two the other.

They had traveled the six blocks and were turning down a side street when they found their first case; it was still daylight. Two of the Stonewall boys were working over a tall man in a newer airsuit. As the police swung around, one of the thugs casually ripped the airsuit open.

A thin screech like a whistle came from Murdoch's Marspeaker, and the captain went forward, with Gordon at his heels. The hoodlums tossed the man aside easily, and let out a yell. From the buildings around, an assortment of toughs came at the double, swinging knives, picks, and bludgeons.

There was no chance to save the citizen, who was dying from lack of air. Gordon felt the solid pleasure of the finely turned club in his hands. It was light enough for speed, but heavy enough to break bones where it hit. A skilled man could knock a knife, or even a heavy club, out of another's hand with a single flick of the wrist. And he'd had practice.

He saw Murdoch's club dart in and take out two of the gang, one on the forward swing, one on the recover. Gordon's eyes popped at that. The man was totally unlike a Martian captain, and a knot of homesickness for Earth ran through his stomach.

He swallowed the sentiment; his own club was moving now. Standing beside Murdoch, they were moving forward. The other four cops had come in reluctantly.

"Knock them out and kick them down!" Murdoch yelled. "And don't let them get away!"

Gordon was after a thug who was attempting to run away. He brought him to the ground with a single blow across the kidneys.

It was soon over. They rounded up the men of the gang, and one of the cops started off. Murdoch called, "Where are you going?"

"To find a phone and call the wagon."

"We're not using wagons," Murdoch told him. "Line them up."

When the hoods came to, they found themselves helpless, and facing police with clubs. If they tried to run, they were hit from behind; if they stood still, they were clubbed carefully. If they fought back, the pugnaciousness was knocked out of them at once.

Murdoch indicated one who stood with his shoulders shaking and tears running down his cheeks. The captain's face was as sick as Gordon felt. "Take him aside. Names."

Gordon found a section away from the others. "I want the name of every man in the gang you can remember," he told the man.

Horror shot over the other's bruised features. "Colonel, they'd kill me! I don't know."

His screams were almost worse than the beating but names began to come. Gordon took them down, and then returned with the man to the others.

Murdoch took his nod as evidence enough, and turned to the wretched toughs. "He squealed," he announced. "If he should turn up dead, I'll know you boys are responsible, and I'll find you. Now get out of this district, or get honest jobs! Because every time one of my men sees one of you, this will happen again. And you can pass the word along that the Stonewall gang is dead!"

He turned and moved off down the street, the others at his side. Gordon nodded. "I've heard the theory, but never saw it in practice. Suppose the whole gang jumps us at once?"

Murdoch shrugged. "Then we're taken. The old book I got the idea from didn't mention that."

Trouble began brewing shortly after, though. Men stood outside, studying the cops on their beat. Murdoch sent one of the men to pick up a second squad of six, and then a third. After that, the watchers began to melt away.

"We'd better shift to another territory," Murdoch decided. Gordon realized that the gang had figured that concentrating the police here meant other territories would be safe.

Two more groups were given the treatment. In the third one, Bruce Gordon spotted one of the men who'd been beaten before. He was a sick-looking spectacle.

Murdoch nodded. "Object lesson!"

The one good thing about the captain, Gordon decided, was that he believed in doing his own dirtiest work. When he was finished, he turned to two of the other captives.

"Get a stretcher, and take him wherever he belongs," he ordered. "I'm leaving you two able to walk for that. But if *you* get caught again, you'll get still worse."

The squad went in, tired and sore; all had taken a severe beating in the brawls. But there was little grumbling. Gordon saw grudging admiration in their eyes for Murdoch, who had taken more punishment than they had.

Gordon rode back in the official car with Murdoch and both were silent most of the way. But the captain stirred finally, sighing. "Poor devils!"

Gordon jerked up in surprise. "The gang?"

"No, the cops they're giving me. We're covered, Gordon. But the Stonewall gang is backing Wayne. He's let me come in because he figures it will get him more votes. But afterwards, he'll have me out; and then the boys with me will be marks for the gang when it comes back. Besides, it'll show on the books that they didn't kick into his fund. I can always go back to Earth, and I'll try to take you along. But it's going to be tough on them."

Bruce Gordon grimaced. "I've got a yellow ticket, from Security."

Murdoch blinked. He dropped his eyes slowly. "So you're *that* Gordon? But you're still a good cop."

They rode on further in silence, until Gordon broke the ice to ease the tension. He found himself liking the other.

"What makes you think Wayne will be re-elected? Nobody wants him, except a gang of crooks and those in power."

Murdoch grinned bitterly. "Ever see a Martian election? No, you're a firster. He can't lose! And then hell is going to pop, and this whole planet may be blown wide open!"

It fitted with the dire predictions of Security, and with the spying Gordon was going to do—according to them.

He discussed it with Mother Corey, who agreed that Wayne would be re-elected.

"Can't lose," the old man said. He was getting even fatter, now that he was eating better food from the fair restaurant around the corner.

"He'll win," Mother Corey repeated. "And you'll turn honest all over, now you're in uniform. Take me, cobber. I figured on laying low for a while, then opening up a few rooms for a good pusher or two, maybe a high-class duchess. Cost 'em more, but they'd be respectable. Only now I'm respectable myself, they don't look so good. But this honesty stuff, it's like dope. You start out on a little, and you have to go all the way."

"It didn't affect Honest Izzy," Gordon pointed out.

"Nope. Because Izzy is always honest, according to how he sees it. But you got Earth ideas of the stuff, like I had once. Too bad." He sighed ponderously.

The week moved on. The groups grew more experienced, and Murdoch was training a new squad every night. Gordon's own squad was equipped with shields now, and they were doing better. The number of muggings and holdups in the section was going down. They seldom saw a man after he'd been treated.

One of the squads was jumped by a gang of about forty, and two of the men were killed before the nearest other squad could pull a rear attack. That day the whole force worked overtime hunting for the men who had escaped; and by evening the Stonewall boys had received proof that it didn't pay to go against the police in large numbers.

After that, they began to go hunting for the members of the gang. They had the names of nearly all of them, and some pretty good ideas of their hide-outs.

It wasn't exactly legal; but nothing was, here. If a doctor's job was to prevent illness, instead of merely curing it, then why shouldn't it be a policeman's job to prevent crime? Here, that was best done by wiping out the Stonewall gang to the last member.

This could lead to abuses, as he'd seen on Earth. But there probably wouldn't be time for it if Mayor Wayne was re-elected.

The gang had begun to break up, but the nucleus would be the last to go. The police had orders to beat any member on sight, now. Citizens were appearing on the streets at night for the first time in years. And there were smiles-hungry, beaten smiles, but still genuine ones-for the cops.

Chapter V
Recall

It was night outside, and the phosphor bulbs at the corners glowed dimly, giving him barely enough light by which to locate the way to the extemporized precinct house. Bruce Gordon reached the outskirts of the miserable business section, noticing that a couple of the shops were still open. It had probably been years since any had dared risk it after the sun went down. And the slow, doubtful respect on the faces of the citizens as they nodded to him was even more proof that Haley's system was working. Gordon nodded to a couple, and they grinned faintly at him. Damn it, Mars could be cleaned up....

He grinned at himself, then something needled at his mind, until he swung back. The man who had just passed was carrying a lunch basket, and was wearing the coveralls of one of the crop-prospector crews; but the expression on his face had been wrong.

Red hair, too heavily built, a lighter section where a mustache had been shaved and the skin not quite perfectly powdered....Gordon moved forward quickly, until he could make out the thin scar showing through the make-up over the man's eyes. He'd been right-this was O'Neill, head of the Stonewall gang.

Gordon hit the signal switch, and the Marspeaker let out a shrill whistle. O'Neill had turned to run, and then seemed to think better of it. His hand darted down to his belt, just as Gordon reached him.

The heavy locust stick met the man's wrist before the weapon was half drawn-another gun! Guns suddenly seemed to be flourishing everywhere. The gun dropped from O'Neill's hand as the wrist snapped, and the Stonewall chief let out a high-pitched cry of pain. Then another cop came around a corner at a run.

"You can't do it to me! I'm reformed; I'm going straight! You damned cops can't...." O'Neill was blubbering. The small crowd that was collecting was all to the good, Gordon knew, and he let O'Neill go on. Nothing could help break up the gangs more than having a leader break down in public.

The other cop had yanked out O'Neill's wallet, and now tossed it to Gordon. One look was enough-the work papers had the telltale over-thickening of the signature that had showed up on other papers, obviously forgeries. The cops had been passing them on the hope of finding one of the leaders.

Some turned away as Gordon and the other cop went to work, but most of them weren't squeamish. When it was over, the two picked up their whimpering captive. Gordon pocketed the revolver with his free hand. "Walk, O'Neill!" he ordered. "Your legs are still whole. Use them!"

The man staggered between them, whimpering at each step. If any members of the gang were around, they made no attempt to rescue him.

Jenkins, the other cop, had been holding the wallet. Now he held it out toward Gordon. "The gee was heeled, Corporal. Must of been making a big contact in something. Fifty-fifty?"

"Turn it in to Murdoch," Gordon said, and then cursed himself. There must have been over two thousand credits in the wallet.

The captain's face had been buried in a pile of papers, but now Murdoch came around to stare at the gang leader. He inspected the forged work papers, and jerked his thumb toward one of the hastily built cells where a doctor would look O'Neill over-eventually. When Gordon and Jenkins came back, Murdoch tossed the money to them. "Split it. You guys earned it by keeping your hands off it. Anyhow, you're as entitled to it as he was-or the grafters back at Police Headquarters. I never saw it. Gordon, you've got a visitor!"

His voice was bitter, but he made no opening for them to question him as he picked up the papers and began going through them again. Gordon went down the passage to the end of the hall, in the direction Murdoch had indicated. Waiting for him was the lean, cynical little figure of Honest Izzy, complete with uniform and sergeant's stripes.

"Hi, gov'nor," the little man greeted him. "Long time no see. With you out here and me busy nights doing a bit of convoy work on the side, we might as well not both live at Mother's."

Bruce Gordon nodded, grinning in spite of himself. "Convoy duty, Izzy? Or dope running?"

"Whatever comes to hand, gov'nor. The Force pays for my time during the day, and I figure my time's my own at night. Of course, if I ever catch myself doing anything shady during the day, I'll have to turn myself in. But it ain't likely." He grinned in satisfaction. "Now that I've dug up the scratch to buy these stripes and get made sergeant-and that takes the real crackle —I'm figuring on taking it easy."

"Like this social call?" Gordon asked him.

The little man shook his head, his ancient eighteen-year-old face turning sober. "Nope. I've been meaning to see you, so I volunteered to run out some red tape for your captain. You owe me some bills, gov'nor. Eleven hundred fifty credits. You didn't pay up your pledge to the campaign fund, so I hadda fill in. A thousand, interest at ten per cent a week, standard. Right?"

Gordon had heard of the friendly interest charged on the side here, but he shook his head. "Wrong, Izzy. If they want to collect that dratted pledge of theirs, let them put me where I can make it. There's no graft out here."

"Huh?" Izzy turned it over, and shook his head. Finally he shrugged. "Don't matter, gov'nor. Nothing about that in the pledge, and when you sign something, you gotta pay it. You *gotta*."

"All right," Gordon admitted. He was suddenly in no mood to quibble with Izzy's personal code. "So you paid it. Now show me where I signed any agreement saying I'd pay *you* back!"

For a second, Izzy's face went blank; then he chuckled. "Jet me! You're right, gov'nor. I sure asked for that one. Okay; I'm bloody well suckered, so forget it."

Gordon shrugged and gave up. He pulled out the bills and handed them over. "Thanks, Izzy."

"Thanks, yourself." The kid pocketed the money cheerfully, nodding. "Buy you a beer. Anyhow, you won't miss it. I came out to tell you I got the sweetest beat in Marsport-over a dozen gambling joints on it-and I need a right gee to work it with me. So you're it!"

For a moment, Gordon wondered what Izzy had done to earn that beat, but he could guess. The little guy knew Mars as few others did, apparently, from all sides. And if any of the other cops had private rackets of their own, Izzy was undoubtedly the man to find it out, and use the information. With a beat such as that, even going halves, and with all the graft to the upper brackets, he'd still be able to make his pile in a matter of months.

But he shook his head. "I'm assigned here, Izzy, at least for another week, until after elections...."

"Better take him up, Gordon," Murdoch told him bitterly. The captain looked completely beaten as he came into the room and dropped onto the bench. "Go on, accept, damn it. You're not assigned here any more. None of us are. Mayor Wayne found an old clause in the charter and got a rigged decision, pulling me back under his full authority. I thought I had full responsibility to Earth, but he's got me. Wearing their uniform makes me a temporary citizen! So we're being smothered back into the Force, and they'll have their patsies out here, setting things up for the Stonewall boys to come back by election time. So grab while the grabbing's good, because by tomorrow morning I'll have this all closed down!"

He shook off Gordon's hand and stood up roughly, to head back up the hallway. Then he stopped and looked back. "One thing, though, I've still got enough authority to make you a sergeant. It's been a pleasure working with you, Sergeant Gordon!"

He swung out of view abruptly, leaving Gordon with a heavy weight in his stomach. Izzy whistled, and began picking up his helmet, preparing to go outside. "So that's the dope I brought out, eh? Takes it kind of hard, doesn't he?"

"Yeah," Gordon answered. There was no use trying to explain it to Izzy. "Yeah, we do. Come on."

Outside, Gordon saw other cops moving from house to house, and he realized that Murdoch must be sending out warnings to the citizens that things would soon be rough again.

Izzy held out a hand to Gordon. "Let's get a beer, gov'nor-on me!"

It was as good an idea as any he had, Gordon decided. He might as well enjoy what life he still had while he could. The Stonewall gang-what was left of it-and all its friends would be gunning for him now. The Force wouldn't have been fooled when Izzy paid his pledge, and they'd mark him down as disloyal-if they didn't automatically mark down all who'd served under Murdoch. And he didn't have the ghost of an idea as to what Security wanted of him, or where they were hiding themselves.

"Make it two beers, Izzy," he said. "Needled!"

Chapter VI
Sealed Letter

In the few days at the short-lived Nineteenth Precinct, Bruce Gordon had begun to feel like a cop again, but the feeling disappeared as he reported in at Captain Isaiah Trench's Seventh Precinct. Trench had once been a colonel in the Marines, before a court-martial and sundry unpleasantnesses had driven him off Earth. His dark, scowling face and lean body still bore a military air.

He looked Bruce Gordon over sourly. "I've been reading your record. It stinks. Making trouble for Jurgens-could have been charged as false arrest. No co-operation with your captain until he forced it; out in the sticks beating up helpless men. Now you come crawling back to your only friend, Isaacs. Well, I'll give it a try. But step out of line and I'll have you cleaning streets with your bare hands. All right, *Corporal* Gordon. Dismissed. Get to your beat."

Gordon grinned wryly at the emphasis on his title. No need to ask what had happened to Murdoch's recommendation. He joined Izzy in the locker room, summing up the situation.

"Yeah." Izzy looked worried, his thin face pinched in. "Maybe I didn't do you a favor, gov'nor, pulling you here. I dunno. I got some pics of Trench from a guy I know. That's how I got my beat so fast in the Seventh. But Trench ain't married, and I guess I've used up the touch. Maybe I could try it, though."

"Forget it," Gordon told him. "I'll work it out somehow."

The beat was a gold mine. It lay through the section where Gordon had first tried his luck on Mars. There were a dozen or so gambling joints, half a dozen cheap saloons, and a fair number of places listed as rooming houses, though they made no bones about the fact that all their permanent inhabitants were female. Then the beat swung off, past a row of small businesses and genuine rooming houses, before turning back to the main section.

They began in the poorer section. It wasn't the day to collect the "tips" for good service, which had been an honest attempt to promote good police service before it became a racket. But they were met everywhere by sullen faces. Izzy explained it. The city had passed a new poll tax-to pay for election booths, supposedly-and had made the police collect it. Murdoch must have disregarded the order, but the rest of the force had been busy helping the administration.

But once they hit the main stem, things were mere routine. The gambling joints took it for granted that beat cops had to be paid, and considered it part of their operating expense. The only problem was that Fats' Place was the first one on the list. Gordon didn't expect to be too welcome there.

There was no sign of the thug, but Fats came out of his back office just as Gordon reached the little bar. He came over, nodded, picked up a cup and dice and began shaking them.

"High man for sixty," he said automatically, and expertly rolled bull's-eyes for a two. "Izzy said you'd be around. Sorry my man drew that *knife* on you the last time, Corporal."

Gordon rolled an eight, pocketed the bills, and shrugged. "Accidents will happen, Fats."

"Yeah." The other picked up the dice and began rolling sevens absently. "How come you're walking beat, anyhow? With what you pulled here, you should have bought a captaincy."

Gordon told him briefly. The man chuckled grimly. "Well, that's Mars," he said, and turned back to his private quarters.

Mostly, it was routine work. They came on a drunk later, collapsed in an alley. But the muggers had apparently given up before Izzy and Gordon arrived, since the man had his wallet clutched in his hand. Gordon reached for it, twisting his lips.

Izzy stopped him. "It ain't honest, gov'nor. If the gees in the wagon clean him, or the desk man gets it, that's their business. But I'm going to run a straight beat, or else!"

That was followed by a call to remove a berserk spaceman from one of the so-called rooming houses. Gordon noticed that workmen were busy setting up a heavy wooden gate in front of the entrance to the place. There were a lot of such preparations going on for the forthcoming elections.

Then the shift was over. But Gordon wasn't too surprised when his relief showed up two hours late; he'd half-expected some such nastiness from Trench. But he was surprised at the look on his tardy relief's face.

The man seemed to avoid facing him, muttered, "Captain says report in person at once," and swung out of the scooter and onto his beat without further words.

Gordon was met there by blank faces and averted looks, but someone nodded toward Trench's office, and he went inside. Trench sat chewing on a cigar. "Gordon, what does Security want with you?"

"Security? Not a damned thing, if I can help it. They kicked me off Earth on a yellow ticket, if that's what you mean."

"Yeah." Trench shoved a letter forward; it bore the "official business" seal of Solar Security, and was addressed to Corporal Bruce Gordon, Nineteenth Police Precinct, Marsport. Trench kept his eyes on it, his face filled with suspicion and the vague fear most men had for Security.

"Yeah," he said again. "Okay, probably routine. Only next time, Gordon, put the *facts* on your record with the Force. If you're a deportee, it should show up. That's all!"

Bruce Gordon went out, holding the envelope. The warning in Trench's voice wasn't for any omission on his record, he knew. He shoved the envelope into his belt pocket and waited until he was in his own room before opening it.

It was terse, and unsigned.

> Report expected, overdue. Failure to observe duty will result in permanent resettlement to Mercury.

He swore, coldly and methodically, while his stomach dug knots in itself. The damned, stupid, blundering fools! That was all Trench and the police gang had to see; it was obvious that the letter had been opened. Sure, report at once. Drop a letter in the mailbox, and the next morning it would be turned over to Commissioner Arliss' office. Report or be kicked off to a planet that Security felt enough worse than Mars to use as punishment! Report *and* find Mars a worse place than Mercury could ever be.

He felt sick as he stood up to find paper and pen and write a terse, factual account of his own personal doings-minus any hint of anything wrong with the system here. Security might think it was enough for the moment, and the local men might possibly decide it a mere required formality. At least it would stall things off for a while....

But Gordon knew now that he could never hope to get back to Earth legally. That vague promise by Security was so much hogwash; yet it was surprising how much he had counted on it.

He tore the envelope from Security into tiny shreds, too small for Mother Corey to make sense of, and went out to mail the letter, feeling the few bills in his pocket. As usual, less than a hundred credits.

He passed a sound truck blatting out a campaign speech by candidate Nolan, filled with too-obvious facts about the present administration, together with hints that Wayne had paid to have Nolan assassinated. Gordon saw a crowd around it and was surprised, until he recognized them as Rafters-men from the biggest of the gangs supporting Wayne. The few citizens on the street who drifted toward the truck took a good look at them and moved on hastily.

It seemed incredible that Wayne could be re-elected, though, even with the power of the gangs. Nolan was probably a grafter, too; but he'd at least be a change, and certainly the citizens were aching for that.

The next day his relief was later. Gordon waited, trying to swallow their petty punishments, but it went against the grain. Finally, he began making the rounds, acting as his own night man. The owners of the joints didn't care whether they paid the second daily dole to the same man or another, but they wouldn't pay it again that same night. He'd managed to tap most of the places before his relief showed. He made no comment, but dutifully filled out the proper portion of both takes for the Voluntary Donation box. It wouldn't do his record any good with Trench, but it should put an end to the overtime.

Trench, however, had other ideas. The overtime continued, but it was dull after that—which made it even more tiring. But the time he took a special release out to the spaceport was the worst. Seeing the big ship readying for take-off back to Earth....

Then it was the day before election. The street was already bristling with barricades around the entrances, and everything ran with a last desperate restlessness, as if there would be no tomorrow. The operators all swore that Wayne would be elected, but seemed to fear a miracle. On the poorer section of the beat, there was a spiritless hope that Nolan might come in with his reform program. Men who would normally have been punctilious about their payments were avoiding Bruce Gordon, if in hope that, by putting it off a day or so, they could run into a period where no such payment would ever be asked—or a smaller one, at least. And he was too tired to chase them down. His collections had been falling off already, and he knew that he'd be on the carpet for that, if he didn't do better. It was a rich territory, and required careful mining; even as the week had gone, he still had more money in his wallet than he had expected.

But there had to be still more before night.

He was lucky; he came on a pusher working one of the better houses—long after his collections should have been over. He knew by the man's face that no protection had been paid higher up. The pusher was well-heeled; Gordon confiscated the money.

This time, Izzy made no protest. Lifting the roll of anyone outside the enforced part of Mars' laws was apparently honest, in his eyes. He nodded, and pointed to the man's belt. "Pick up the snow, too."

The pusher's face paled. He must have had his total capital with him, because stark ruin shone in his eyes. "Good God, Sergeant," he pleaded, "leave me something! I'll make it right. I'll cut you in. I gotta have some of that for myself!"

Gordon grimaced. He couldn't work up any great sympathy for anyone who made a living out of drugs.

They cleaned the pusher, and left him sitting on the steps, a picture of slumped misery. Izzy nodded approval. "Let him feel it a while. No sense jailing him yet. Bloody fool had no business starting without lining the groove. Anyhow, we'll get a bunch of credits for the stuff when we turn it in."

"Credits?" Gordon asked.

"Sure." Izzy patted the little package. "We get a quarter value. Captain probably gets fifty per cent from one of the pushers who's lined with him. Everybody's happy."

"Why not push it ourselves?" Gordon asked in disgust.

"Wouldn't be honest, gov'nor. Cops are supposed to turn it in."

Trench was almost jovial when he weighed the package and examined it to find how much it had been cut. He issued them slips, which they added as part of the contributions. "Good work—you, too, Gordon. Best week in the territory for a couple of months. I guess the citizens like you, the way they treat you." He laughed at his stale joke, and Gordon was willing to laugh with him. The credit on the dope had paid for most of the contributions. For once, he had money to show for the week.

Then Trench motioned Bruce Gordon forward, and dismissed Izzy with a nod of his head. "Something to discuss, Gordon. Isaacs, we're holding a little meeting, so wait around. You're a sergeant already. But, Gordon, I'm offering you a chance. There aren't enough openings for all the good men, but....Oh, bother the soft soap. We're still short on election funds, so there's a raffle. The two men holding winning tickets get bucked up to sergeants. A hundred credits a ticket. How many?"

He frowned suddenly as Gordon counted out three bills. "You have a better chance with more tickets. A *much* better chance!"

The hint was hardly veiled. Gordon stuck the tickets into his wallet. Mars was a fine planet for picking up easy money—but holding it was another matter.

Trench counted the money and put it away. "Thanks, Gordon. That fills *my* quota. Look, you've been on overtime all week. Why not skip the meeting? Isaacs can brief you, later. Go out and get drunk, or something."

The comparative friendliness of the peace offering was probably the ultimate in graciousness from Trench. Idly, Gordon wondered what kind of pressures the captains were under; it must be pretty stiff, judging by the relief the man was showing at making quota.

"Thanks," he said, but his voice was bitter in his ears. "I'll go home and rest. Drinking costs too much for what I make. It's a good thing you don't have income tax here."

"We do," Trench said flatly; "forty per cent. Better make out a form next week, and start paying it regularly. But you can deduct your contributions here."

Gordon got out before he learned more good news.

Chapter VII
Electioneering

As Bruce Gordon came out from the precinct house, he noticed the sounds first. Under the huge dome that enclosed the main part of the city, the heavier air pressure permitted normal travel of sound; and he'd become sensitive to the voice of the city after the relative quiet of the Nineteenth Precinct. But now the normal noise was different. There was an undertone of hushed waiting, with the sharp bursts of hammering and last-minute work standing out sharply through it. Voting booths were being finished here and there, and at one a small truck was delivering ballots. Voting by machine had never been established here. Wherever the booths were being thrown up, the nearby establishments were rushing gates and barricades in front of the buildings.

Most of the shops were already closed-even some of the saloons. To make up for it, stands were being placed along the streets, carrying banners that proclaimed free beer for all loyal administration friends. The few bars that were still open had been blessed with the sign of some mob, and obviously were well staffed with hoodlums ready to protect the proprietor. Private houses were boarded up. The scattering of last-minute shoppers along the streets showed that most of the citizens were laying in supplies to last until after election.

Gordon passed the First Marsport Bank and saw that it was surrounded by barbed wires, with other strands still being strung, and with a sign proclaiming that there was high voltage in the wires. Watching the operation was Jurgens; it was obvious that his hoodlums had been hired for the job.

Toward the edge of the dome, where Mother Corey's place was, the narrower streets were filling with the gangs, already half-drunk and marching about with their banners and printed signs. Curiously enough, all the gangs weren't working for Wayne's re-election. The big Star Point gang had apparently grown tired of the increasing cost of protection from the government, and was actively campaigning for Nolan. Their home territory reached nearly to Mother Corey's, before it ran into the no man's land separating it from the gang of Nick the Croop. The Croopsters were loyal to Wayne.

Gordon turned into his usual short-cut, past a rambling plastics plant and through the yard where their trucks were parked. He had half expected to find it barricaded, but apparently the rumors that Nick the Croop owned it were true; it would be protected in other ways, with the trucks used for street fighting, if needed. He threaded his way between two of the trucks.

Then a yell reached his ears, and something swished at him. An egg-sized rock hit the truck behind him and bounced back, just as he spotted a hoodlum drawing back a sling for a second shot.

Gordon was on his knees between heartbeats, darting under one of the trucks. He rolled to his feet, letting out a yell of his own, and plunged forward. His fist hit the thug in the elbow, just as the man's hand reached for his knife. His other hand chopped around, and the edge of his palm connected with the other's nose. Cartilage crunched, and a shrill cry of agony lanced out.

But the hoodlum wasn't alone. Another came out from the rear of one of the trucks. Gordon ducked as a knife sailed for his head; they were stupid enough not to aim for his stomach, at least. He bent down to locate some of the rubble on the ground, cursing his folly in carrying his knife under his uniform. The new beat had given him a false sense of security.

He found a couple of rocks and a bottle and let them fly, then bent for more.

Something landed on his back, and fingernails were gouging into his face, searching for his eyes!

Instinct carried him forward, jerking down sharply and twisting. The figure on his back sailed over his head, to land with a harsh thump on the ground. Brassy yellow hair spilled over a girl's face, and her breath slammed out of her throat as she hit. But the fall hadn't been enough to do serious damage.

Bruce Gordon jumped forward, bringing his foot up in a savage swing, but she'd rolled, and the blow only glanced against her ribs. She jerked her hand down for a knife, and came to her knees, her lips drawn back against her teeth. "Get him!" she yelled. Then he recognized her-Sheila Corey.

The two thugs had held back, but now they began edging in. Gordon slipped back behind another truck, listening for the sound of their feet. He'd half-expected another encounter with the Mother's granddaughter.

They tried to outmaneuver him; he stepped back to his former spot, catching his breath and digging frantically for his knife. It came out, just as they realized he'd tricked them.

Sheila was still on her knees, fumbling with something, and apparently paying no attention to him. But now she jerked to her feet, her hand going back and forward.

It was a six-inch section of pipe, with a thin wisp of smoke, and the throw was toward Gordon's feet. The hoodlums yelled, and ducked, while Sheila broke into a run away from him. The little homemade bomb landed, bounced, and lay still, with its fuse almost burned down.

Gordon's heart froze in his throat, but he was already in action. He spat savagely into his hand, and jumped for the bomb. If the fuse was powder-soaked, he had no chance. He brought his palm down against it, and heard a faint hissing. Then he held his breath, waiting.

No explosion came. It had been a crude job, with only a wick for a fuse.

Sheila Corey had stopped at a safe distance; now she grabbed at her helpers, and swung them with her. The three came back, Sheila in the lead with her knife flashing.

Gordon side-stepped her rush, and met the other two head-on, his knife swinging back. His foot hit some of the rubble on the ground at the last second, and he skidded. The leading mobster saw the chance and jumped for him. Gordon bent his head sharply, and dropped, falling onto his shoulders and somersaulting over. He twisted at the last second, jerking his arms down to come up facing the other.

Then a new voice cut into the fracas, and there was the sound of something landing against a skull with a hollow thud. Gordon got his head up just in time to see a man in police uniform kick aside the first hoodlum and lunge for the other. There was a confused flurry; then the second went up into the air and came down in the newcomer's hands, to land with a sickening jar and lie still. Behind, Sheila Corey lay crumpled in a heap, clutching one wrist in the other hand and crying silently.

Bruce Gordon came to his feet and started for her. She saw him coming, cast a single glance at the knife that had been knocked from her hands, then sprang aside and darted back through the parked trucks. In the street, she could lose herself in the swarm of Nick's Croopsters; Gordon turned back.

The iron-gray hair caught his eyes first. Then, as the solidly built figure turned, he grunted. It was Captain Murdoch-now dressed in the uniform of a regular beat cop, without even a corporal's stripes. And the face was filled with lines of strain that hadn't been there before.

Murdoch threw the second gangster up into a truck after the first one and slammed the door shut, locking it with the metal bar which had apparently been his weapon. Then he grinned wryly, and came back toward Gordon.

"You seem to have friends here," he commented. "A good thing I was trying to catch up with you. Just missed you at the Precinct House, came after you, and saw you turn in here. Then I heard the rumpus. A good thing for me, too, maybe."

Gordon blinked, accepting the other's hand. "How so? And what happened?" He indicated the bare sleeve.

"One's the result of the other," Murdoch told him. "They've got me sewed up, and they're throwing the book at me. The old laws make me a citizen while I wear the uniform-and a citizen can't quit the Force. That puts me out of Earth's jurisdiction. I can't even cable for funds, and I guess I'm too old to start squeezing money out of citizens. I was coming to ask whether you had room in your diggings for a guest-and I'm hoping now that my part here cinches it."

Murdoch had tried to treat it lightly, but Gordon saw the red creeping up into the man's face. "Forget that part. There's room enough for two in my place-and I guess Mother Corey won't mind. I'm damned glad you were following me."

"So'm I, Gordon. What'll we do with the prisoners?"

"Leave 'em; we couldn't get a Croopster locked up tonight for anything."

He started ahead, leading the way through the remaining trucks and back to the street that led to Mother Corey's. Murdoch fell in step with him. "This is the first time I've had to look you up," he said. "I've been going out nights to help the citizens organize against the Stonewall gang. But that's over now-they gave me hell for inciting vigilante action, and confined me inside the dome. The way they hate a decent cop here, you'd think honesty was contagious."

"Yeah." Gordon preferred to let it drop. Murdoch was being given the business for going too far on the Stonewall gang, not for refusing to take normal graft.

They came to the gray three-story building that Mother Corey now owned. Gordon stopped, realizing for the first time that there was no trace of efforts to protect it against the coming night and day. The entrance was unprotected. Then his eyes caught the bright chalk marks around it-notices to the gangs to keep hands off. Mother Corey evidently had pull enough to get every mob in the neighborhood to affix its seal.

As he drew near, though, two men edged across the street from a clump watching the beginning excitement. Then, as they identified Gordon, they moved back again. Some of the Mother's old lodgers from the ruin outside the dome were inside now-obviously posted where it would do the most good.

Corey stuck his head out of the door at the back of the hall as Gordon entered, and started to retire again-until he spotted Murdoch. Gordon explained the situation hastily.

"It's your room, cobber," the old man wheezed. He waddled back, to come out with a towel and key, which he handed to Murdoch. "Number forty-two."

His heavy hand rested on Gordon's arm, holding the younger man back. Murdoch gave Gordon a brief, tired smile, and started for the stairs. "Thanks, Gordon. I'm turning in right now."

Mother Corey shook his head, shaking the few hairs on his head and face, and the wrinkles in his doughy skin deepened. "Hasn't changed, that one. Must be thirty years, but I'd know Asa Murdoch anywhere. Took me to the spaceport, handed me my yellow ticket, and sent me off for Mars. A nice, clean kid-just like my own boy was. But Murdoch wasn't like the rest of the neighborhood. He still called me 'sir,' when my boy was walking across the street, so the lad wouldn't know they were sending me away. Oh well, that was a long time ago, cobber. A long time."

He rubbed a pasty hand over his chin, shaking his head and wheezing heavily. Gordon chuckled. "Well, how —?"

Something banged heavily against the entrance seal, and there was the sound of a hot argument, followed by a commotion of some sort. Corey seemed to prick up his ears, and began to waddle rapidly toward the entrance.

It broke open before he could reach it, the seal snapping back to show a giant of a man outside holding the two guards from across the street, while a scar-faced, dark man shoved through briskly. Corey snapped out a quick word, and the two guards ceased struggling and started back across the street. The giant pushed in after the smaller thug.

"I'm from the Ajax Householders Protection Group," the dark man announced officially. "We're selling election protection. And brother, do you need it, if you're counting on those mugs. We're assessing you —"

"Not long on Mars, are you?" Mother Corey asked. The whine was entirely missing from his voice now, though his face seemed as expressionless as ever. "What does your boss Jurgens figure on doing, punk? Taking over *all* the rackets for the whole city?"

The dark face snarled, while the giant moved a step forward. Then he shrugged. "Okay, Fatty. So Jurgens is behind it. So now you know. And I'm doubling your assessment, right now. To you, it's —"

A heavy hand fell on the man's shoulder, and Mother Corey leaned forward slightly. Even in Mars' gravity, his bulk made the other buckle at the knees. The hand that had been reaching for the knife yanked the weapon out and brought it up sharply.

Gordon started to step in, then, but there was no time. Mother Corey's free hand came around in an open-palmed slap that lifted the collector up from the floor and sent him reeling back against a wall. The knife fell from the crook's hand, and the dark face turned pale. He sagged down the wall, limply.

The giant opened his mouth, and took half a step forward; but the only sound he made was a choking gobble. Mother Corey moved without seeming haste, but before the other could make up his mind. There was a series of motions that seemed to have no pattern. The giant was spun around, somehow; one arm was jerked back behind him, then the other was forced up to it. Mother Corey held the wrists in one hand, put his other under the giant's crotch, and lifted. Carrying the big figure off the floor, the old man moved toward the seal. His foot found the button, snapping the entrance open. He pitched the giant out overhanded; holding the entrance, he reached for the dark man with one hand and tossed him on top of the giant.

"To me, it's nothing," he called out. "Take these two back to young Jurgens, boys, and tell him to keep his punks out of my house."

The entrance snapped shut then, and Corey turned back to Gordon, wiping the wisps of hair from his face. He was still wheezing asthmatically, but there seemed to be no change in the rhythm of his breathing. "As I was going to say, cobber," he said, "we've got a little social game going upstairs-the room with the window. Fine view of the parades. We need a fourth."

Gordon started to protest that he was tired and needed his sleep; then he shrugged. Corey's house was one of the few that had kept some relation to Earth styles by installing a couple of windows in the second story, and it would give a perfect view of the street. He followed the old man up the stairs.

Two other men were already in the surprisingly well-furnished room, at the little table set up near the window. Bruce Gordon recognized one as Randolph, the publisher of the little opposition paper. The man's pale blondness, weak eyes, and generally rabbity expression totally belied the courage that had permitted him to keep going at his hopeless task of trying to clean up Marsport. The *Crusader* was strictly a one-man weekly, against Mayor Wayne's *Chronicle*, with its Earth-comics and daily circulation of over a hundred thousand. Wayne apparently let the paper stay in business to give himself a talking point about fair play; but Randolph walked with a limp from the last working over he had received.

"Hi, Gordon," he said. His thin, high voice was cool and reserved, in keeping with the opinion he had expressed publicly of the police as a body. But he did not protest Corey's selection of a partner. "This is Ed Praeger. He's an engineer on our railroad."

Gordon acknowledged the introduction automatically. He'd almost forgotten that Marsport was the center of a thinly populated area, stretching for a thousand miles in all directions beyond the city, connected by the winding link of the electric monorail. "So there really is a surrounding countryside," he said.

Praeger nodded. He was a big, open-faced man, just turning bald. His handshake was firm and friendly. "There are even cities out there, Gordon. Nothing like Marsport, but that's no loss. That's where the real population of Mars is-decent people, men who are going to turn this into a real planet some day."

"There are plenty like that here, too," Randolph said. He picked up the cards. "First ace deals. Damn it, Mother, sit down-wind from me, won't you? Or else take a bath."

Mother Corey chuckled, and wheezed his way up out of the chair, exchanging places with Gordon. "I got a surprise for you, cobber," he said, and there was only amusement in his voice. "I got me in fifty gallons of water today, and tomorrow I do just that. Made up my mind there was going to be a cleanup in Marsport, even if Wayne does win. And stop examining the cards, Bruce. I don't cheat my friends. The readers are put away for old-times' sake."

Randolph shrugged, and went on as if he hadn't interrupted himself. "Ninety per cent of Marsport is decent. They have to be. It takes at least nine honest men to support a crook. They come up here to start over-maybe spent half their life saving up for the trip. They hear a man can make fifty credits a day in the factories, or strike it rich crop prospecting. What they don't realize is that things cost ten times as much here, too. They plan, maybe, on getting rich and going back to Earth...."

"Nobody goes back," Mother Corey wheezed. "*I* know." His eyes rested on Gordon.

"A lot don't want to," Praeger said. "I never meant to go back. I've got me a farm up north. Another ten years, and I retire to it. My kids are up there now-grandkids, that is. They're Martians; maybe you won't believe me, but they can breathe the air here without a helmet."

The others nodded. Gordon had learned that a fair number of third-generation people got that way. Their chests were only a trifle larger, and their heartbeat only a few points higher; it was an internal adaptation, like the one that had occurred in test animals reared at a simulated forty-thousand-feet altitude on Earth, before Mars was ever settled.

"They'll take the planet away from Earth yet," Randolph agreed. "Marsport is strictly artificial. It's kept going only because it's the only place where Earth will set down her ships. If Security doesn't do anything, time will."

"Security!" Gordon muttered bitterly. Security was good at getting people in trouble, but he had seen no other sign of it.

Randolph frowned over his cards. "Yeah, I know. The government set them up, gave them a mixture of powers, and has been trying to keep them from working ever since. But somehow they did clean up Venus; and every crook here is scared to death of the name. How come a muckraking newspaperman like you never turned up anything on them, Gordon?"

Gordon shrugged. It was the first reference he'd heard to his background, and he preferred to let it drop.

But Mother Corey cut in, his voice older and hoarser, and the skin on his jowls even grayer than usual. "Don't sell them short, cobber. I did-once....You forget them, here, after a while. But they're around...."

Bruce Gordon felt something run down his armpit, and a chill creep up his back....

Out on the street, a sudden whooping began, and he glanced down. The parade was on, the Croopsters in full swing, already mostly drunk. The main body went down the street, waving fluorescent signs, while side-guards preceded them, armed with axes, knocking aside the flimsier barricades as they went. He watched a group break into a small grocery store to come out with bundles. They dragged out the storekeeper, his wife, and young daughter, and pressed them into the middle of the parade.

"If Security's so damned powerful, why doesn't it stop that?" he asked bitterly.

Randolph grinned at him. "They might do it, Gordon. They just might. But are you sure you want it stopped?"

"All right," Mother Corey said suddenly. "This is a social game, cobbers."

Outside, the parade picked up enthusiasm as smaller gangs joined behind the main one. There were a fair number of plain citizens who had been impressed into it, too, judging by the appearance of little frightened groups in the middle of the mobsters.

Gordon couldn't understand why the police hadn't at least been kept on duty, until Honest Izzy came into the room. The little man found a chair and bought chips silently; he looked tired.

"Vacation?" Mother Corey asked.

Izzy nodded. "Trench took forever giving it to us, Mother. But it's the same old deal; all the police gees get tomorrow off-you, too, gov'nor. No cops to influence the vote, that's the word. We even gotta wear civvies when we go out to vote for Wayne."

Gordon looked down at the rioters, who were now only keeping up a pretense of a parade. It would be worse tomorrow, he supposed; and there would be no cops. The image of the old woman and her husband in the little liquor store where he'd had his first experience came back to him. He wondered how well barricaded they were.

He felt the curious eyes of Mother Corey dancing from him to Izzy and back, and heard the old man's chuckle. "Put a uniform on some men and they begin to believe they're cops, eh, cobber?"

He shoved up from the table abruptly and headed for his room, swearing to himself.

Chapter VIII
Vote Early and Often

Izzy was up first the next morning, urging them to hurry before things began to hum. From somewhere, he dug up a suit of clothes that Murdoch could wear. He found the gun that Gordon had confiscated from O'Neill and filled it from a box of ammunition he'd apparently purchased.

"I picked up some special permits," he said. "I knew you had this cannon, gov'nor, and I figured it'd come in handy. Wouldn't be caught dead with one myself. Knives, that's my specialty. Come on, Cap'n, we gotta get out the vote."

Murdoch shook his head. "In the first place, I'm not registered."

Izzy grinned. "Every cop's registered in his own precinct; Wayne got the honor system fixed for us. Show your papers and go into any booth in your territory. That's all. And you'd better be seen voting often, too, Cap'n. What's your precinct?"

"Eleventh, but I'm not voting. I'd like to come along with you to observe, but I wouldn't make any choice between Wayne and Nolan."

Downstairs, the rear room was locked, with one of Mother Corey's guards at the door. From inside came the rare sound of water splashing, mixed with a wheezing, off-key caterwauling. Mother Corey was apparently making good on his promise to take a bath. As they reached the hall, one of Trench's lieutenants came through the entrance, waving his badge at the protesting man outside.

He spotted the three, and jerked his thumb. "Come on, you. We're late. And I ain't staying on the streets when it gets going."

A small police car was waiting outside, and they headed for it. Bruce Gordon looked at the debacle left behind the drunken, looting mob. Most of the barricades were down. Here and there, a few citizens were rushing about trying to restore them, keeping wary eyes on the mobsters who had passed out on the streets.

Suddenly a siren blasted out in sharp bursts, and the lieutenant jumped. "Come on, you gees. I gotta be back in half an hour."

They piled inside, and the little electric car took off at its top speed. But now the quietness had been broken. There were trucks coming out of the plastics plant, and mobsters were gathering up their drunks, and chasing the citizens back into their houses. Some of them were wearing the forbidden guns, but it wouldn't matter on a day when no police were on duty.

In the Ninth Precinct, the Planters were the biggest gang, and all the others were temporarily enrolled under them. Here, there were less signs of trouble. The joints had been better barricaded, and the looting had been kept to a minimum.

The three got off. A scooter pulled up alongside them almost at once, with a gun-carrying mobster riding it. "You mugs get the hell out of–Oh, cops! Okay, better pin these on."

He handed out gaudy arm bands, and the three fastened them in place. Nearly everyone else already had them showing. The Planters were moving efficiently. They were grouped around the booths, and they had begun to line up their men, putting them in position to begin voting at once.

Then the siren hooted again, a long, steady blast. The bunting in front of the booths was pulled off, and the lines began to move. Izzy led the way to the one at the rich end of their beat, and moved toward the head of the line. "Cops," he said to the six mobsters who surrounded the booth. "We got territory to cover."

A thumb indicated that they could go in. Murdoch remained outside, and one of the thugs reached for him. Izzy cut him off. "Just a friend on the way to his own route. Eleventh Precinct."

There were scowls, but they let it go. Then Gordon was in the little booth. It seemed to be in order. There were the books of registration, with a checker for Wayne, one for Nolan, and a third, supposedly neutral, behind the plank that served as a desk. The Nolan man was protesting.

"He's been dead for ten years. I know him. He's my uncle."

"There's a Mike Thaler registered, and this guy says he's Thaler," the Wayne man said decisively. "He votes."

One of the Planters passed his gun to the inspector for the Wayne side. The Nolan man gulped, and nodded. "Heh-heh, yes, just a mix-up. He's registered, so he votes."

The next man Gordon recognized as being from one of the small shops on his beat. The fellow's eyes were desperate, but he was forcing himself to go through with it. "Murtagh," he said, and his voice broke on the second syllable. "Owen Murtagh."

"Murtang....No registration!" The Wayne checker shrugged. "Next!"

"It's Murtagh. M-U-R-T-A-G-H. Owen Murtagh, of 738 Morrisy —"

"Protest!" The Wayne man cut off the frantic wriggling of the Nolan checker's finger toward the line in the book. "When a man can't get the name straight the first time, it's suspicious."

The supposedly neutral checker nodded. "Better check the name off, unless the real Murtagh shows up. Any objections, Yeoman?"

The Nolan man had no objections-outwardly. He was sweating, and the surprise in his eyes indicated that this was all new to him.

Bruce Gordon came next, showing his badge. He was passed with a nod, and headed for the little closed-off polling place. But the Wayne man touched his arm and indicated a ballot. There were two piles, and this pile was already filled out for Wayne. "Saves trouble, unless you want to do it yourself," he suggested.

Gordon shrugged, and shoved it into the slot. He went outside and waited for Izzy to follow. It was raw beyond anything he'd expected-but at least it saved any doubt about the votes.

The procedure was the same at the next booth, though they had more trouble. The Nolan man there was a fool-neither green nor agreeable. He protested vigorously, in spite of a suspicious bruise along his temple, and finally made some of the protests stick.

Gordon began to wonder how it could be anything but a clear unanimous vote, at that rate. Izzy shook his head. "Wayne'll win, but not that easy. The sticks don't have strong mobs, and they'll pile up a heavy Nolan vote. And you'll see things hum soon!"

Gordon had voted three times under the "honor system," before he saw. They were just nearing a polling place when a heavy truck came careening around a corner. Men began piling out of the back before it stopped-men armed with clubs and stones. They were in the middle of the Planters at once, striking without science, but with ferocity. The line waiting to vote broke up, but the citizens had apparently organized with care. A good number of the men in the line were with the attackers.

There was the sound of a shot, and a horrified cry. For a second, the citizens broke; then a wave of fury seemed to wash over them at the needless risk to the safety of all. The horror of rupturing the dome was strongly ingrained in every citizen of Marsport. They drew back, then made a concerted rush. There was a trample of bodies, but no more shots.

In a minute, the citizens' group was inside, ripping the fixed ballots to shreds, filling out and dropping their own. They ignored the registration clerks.

A whistle had been shrilling for minutes. Now another group came onto the scene, and the Planters' men began getting out rapidly. Some of the citizens looked up and yelled, but it was too late. From the approaching cars, pipes projected forward. Streams of liquid jetted out, and their agonized cries followed.

Even where he stood, Gordon could smell the fumes of ammonia. Izzy's face tensed, and he swore. "Inside the dome! They're poisoning the air."

But the trick worked. In no time, men in crude masks were clearing out the booth, driving the last struggling citizens away, and getting ready for business as usual.

Murdoch turned on his heel. "I've had enough. I've made up my mind," he said. "The cable offices must be open for the doctored reports on the election to Earth. Where's the nearest?"

Izzy frowned, but supplied the information. Bruce Gordon pulled Murdoch aside. "Come off the head-cop role; it won't work. They must have had reports on elections before this."

"Damn the trouble. It's never been this raw before. Look at Izzy's face, Gordon. Even he's shocked. Something has to be done about this, before worse happens. I've still got connections back there —"

"Okay," Gordon said bitterly. He'd liked Asa Murdoch, had begun to respect him. It hurt to see that what he'd considered hardheadedness was just another case of a fool fighting dragons with a paper sword.

"Okay, it's your death certificate," he said, and turned back toward Izzy. "Go send your sob stories, Murdoch."

They taught a bunch of pretty maxims in school-even slum kids learned that honesty was the best policy, while their honest parents rotted in unheated holes, and the racketeers rode around in fancy cars. It had got him once. He'd refused to take a dive as a boxer; he'd tried to play honest cards; he'd tried honesty on his beat back on Earth. He'd tried to help the suckers in his column, and here he was.

And Gordon had been proud to serve under Murdoch.

"Come on, Izzy," he said. "Let's vote!"

Izzy shook his head. "It ain't right, gov'nor."

"Let him do what he damn pleases," Gordon told him.

Izzy's small face puckered up in lines of worry. "No, I don't mean him. I mean this business of using ammonia. I know some of the gees trying to vote. They been paying me off-and that's a retainer, you might say. Now this gang tries to poison them. I'm still running an honest beat, and I bloody well can't vote for that! Uniform or no uniform, I'm walking beat today. And the first gee that gives trouble to the men who pay me gets a knife where he eats. When I get paid for a job, I do the job."

Gordon watched him head down the block, and started after the little man. Then he grimaced. Rule books! Even Izzy had one.

He went down the row, voting regularly. The Planters had things in order. The mess had already been cleaned up when he arrived at the cheaper end of the beat. It was the last place where he'd be expected to do his duty by Wayne's administration; he waited in line.

Then a voice hit at his ears, and he looked up to see Sheila Corey only two places in front of him. "Mrs. Mary Edelstein," she was saying. The Wayne man nodded, and there was no protest. She picked up a Wayne ballot, and dropped it in the box.

Then her eyes fell on Gordon. She hesitated for a second, bit her lips, and finally moved out into the crowd.

He could see no sign of her as he stepped out a minute later, but the back of his neck prickled.

He started out of the crowd, trying to act normal, but glancing down to make sure the gun was in its proper position. Satisfied, he wheeled suddenly and spotted her behind him, before she could slip out of sight.

Then a shout went up, yanking his eyes around with the rest of those standing near. The eyes had centered on the alleys along the street, and men were beginning to run wildly, while others were jerking out their weapons. He saw a big gray car coming up the street; on its side was painted the colors of the Planters. Now it swerved, hitting a siren button.

But it was too late. Trucks shot out of the little alleys, jamming forward through the people; there must have been fifty of them. One hit the big gray car, tossing it aside. It was Trench himself who leaped out, together with the driver. The trucks paid no attention, but bore down on the crowd. From one of them, a machine gun opened fire.

Gordon dropped and began crawling in the only direction that was open, straight toward the alleys from which the trucks had come. A few others had tried that, but most were darting back as they saw the colors of Nolan's Star Point gang on the trucks.

Other guns began firing; men were leaping from the trucks and pouring into the mob of Planters, forcing their way toward the booth in the center of the mess.

It was a beautifully timed surprise attack, and a well-armed one, even though guns were supposed to be so rare here. Gordon stumbled into someone ahead of him, and saw it was Trench. He looked up, and straight into the swinging muzzle of the machine gun that had started the commotion.

Trench was reaching for his revolver, but he was going to be too late. Gordon brought his up the extra half inch, aiming by the feel, and pulled the trigger. The man behind the machine gun dropped.

Trench had his gun out now, and was firing, after a single surprised glance at Gordon. He waved back toward the crowd.

But Gordon had spotted the open trunk of the gray car. He shook his head and tried to indicate it. Trench jerked his thumb and leaped to his feet, rushing back.

Gordon saw another truck go by, and felt a bullet miss him by inches. Then his legs were under him, and he was sliding into the big luggage compartment, where the metal would shield him.

Something soft under his feet threw him down. He felt a body under him, and coldness washed over him before he could get his eyes down. The cold went away, to be replaced by shock. Between his spread knees lay Murdoch, bound and gagged, his face a bloody mess.

Gordon reached for the gag, but the other held up his hands and pointed to the gun. It made sense. The knots were tight, but Gordon managed to get his knife under the rope around Murdoch's wrists and slice through it. The older man's hands went out for the gun; his eyes swung toward the street, while Gordon attacked the rope around his ankles.

The Star Point men were winning, though it was tough going. They had fought their way almost to the booth, but there a V of Planters' cars had been gotten into position somehow, and gunfire was coming from behind them. As he watched, a huge man reached over one of the cars, picked up a Star Point man, and lifted him behind the barricade.

The gag had just come out when the Star Point man jumped into view again, waving a rag over his head and yelling. Captain Trench followed him out, and began pointing toward the gray car.

"They want me," Murdoch gasped thickly. "Get out, Gordon, before they gang up on us!"

Gordon jerked his eyes back toward the alley on the other side. It went at an angle and would offer some protection.

He looked back, just as bullets began to land against the metal of the car. Murdoch held up one finger and put himself into a position to make a run for it. Then he brought the finger down sharply, and the two leaped out.

Trench's ex-Marine bellow carried over the fighting. "Get the old man!"

Bruce Gordon had no time to look back. He hit the alley in five heart-ripping leaps and was around the bend. Then he swung, just as Murdoch made it. Bullets spatted against the walls, and he saw blood pumping from under Murdoch's right shoulder.

"Keep going!" Murdoch ordered.

A fresh cry from the street cut into his order, however. Gordon risked a quick look, then stepped farther out to make sure.

The surprise raid by the Star Pointers hadn't been quite as much of a surprise as expected. Coming down the street, with no regard for men trying to get out of their way, the trucks of the Croopsters were battering aside the few who could not reach safety. There were no machine guns this time.

They smacked into the tangle of Star Point trucks, and came to a grinding halt, men piling out ready for battle. Gordon nodded. In a few minutes, Wayne's supporters would have the booth again; there'd be a delay before any organized search could be made for the fugitives. He looked down at Murdoch's shoulder.

"Come on," he said finally. "Or should I carry you?"

Murdoch shook his head. "I'll walk. Get me to a place where we can talk-and be damned to this. Gordon, I've got to talk-but I don't have to live. I mean that!"

Gordon started off, disregarding the words; a place of safety had to come first. He picked his way down alleys and small streets. The older man kept trying to stop to speak, but Gordon gave him no opportunity. There was one chance....

It was farther than he'd thought, and Gordon began to suspect he'd missed the way, until he saw the drugstore. Now it all fell into place-the first beat he'd had with Izzy.

He ducked down back alleys until he reached the right section. He scanned the street, jumped to the door of the little liquor store and began banging on it. There was no answer, though he was sure the old couple lived just over the store.

He began banging again. Finally, a feeble voice sounded from inside. "Who is it?"

"A man in distress!" he yelled back. There was no way to identify himself; he could only hope she would look.

The entrance seal opened briefly; then it flashed open all the way. He motioned to Murdoch, and jumped to help the failing man to the entrance. The old lady looked, then moved quickly to the other side.

"*Ach, Gott,*" she breathed. Her hands trembled as she relocked the seal. Then she brushed the thin hair off her face, and pointed. Gordon followed her up the stairs, carrying Murdoch on his back. She opened a door, passed through a tiny kitchen, and threw open another door to a bedroom.

The old man lay on the bed, and this time there was no question of concussion. The woman nodded. "Yes. Pappa is dead, God forbid it. He *would* try to vote. I told him and told him-and then ... With my own hands, I carried him here."

Gordon felt sick. He started to turn, but she shook her head quickly. "No. Pappa is dead. He needs no beds now, and your friend is suffering; put him here."

She lifted the frail body of the old man and lowered him onto the floor with a strength that seemed impossible. Then her hands were gentle as she helped lower Murdoch where the corpse had been. "I'll get alcohol from below-and bandages and hot water."

Asa Murdoch opened his eyes, breathing stertoriously. His face was blanched, his clothes a mess. But he protested as Gordon tried to strip them. "Let them go, kid. There's no way to save me now. And listen!"

"I'm listening!"

"With your *mind*, Gordon, not your ears. You've heard a lot about Security. Well, I'm Security. Top level-policy for Mars. We never got a top man here without his being discovered and killed-That's why we've had to work under all the cover-and against our own government. Nobody knew I was here-Trench was our man-Sold us out! We've got junior men-down to your level, clerks, such things. We've got a dozen plans. But we're not ready for an emergency, and it's here-now!

"Gordon, you're a self-made louse, but you're a man underneath it somewhere. That's why we rate you higher than you think you are. That's why I'm going to trust you-because I have to."

He swallowed, and the thin hand of the woman lifted brandy to his lips. "Pappa," she said slowly. "He was a clerk once for Security. But nobody came, nobody called...."

She went back to trying to bandage the bleeding bluish hole in his chest. Murdoch nodded faintly.

"Probably what happened to a lot-men like Trench, supposed to build an organization, just leaving the loose ends hanging." He groaned; sweat popped out on his forehead, but his eyes never left Gordon's. "Hell's going to pop. The government's just waiting to step in; Earth *wants* to take over."

"It should," Gordon said.

"No! We've studied these things. Mars won't give up-and Earth wants a plum, not responsibility. You'll have civil war and the whole planetary development ruined. Security's the only hope, Gordon-the only chance Mars had, has, or will have! Believe me, I know. Security has to be notified. There's a code message I had ready —a message to a friend-even you can send it. And they'll be watching. I've got the basic plans in the book here."

He slumped back. Gordon frowned, then found the book and pulled it out as gently as he could. It was a small black memo book, covered with pages of shorthand. The back was an address book, filled with names-many crossed out. A sheet of paper in normal writing fell out.

"The message ..." Murdoch took another swallow of brandy. "Take it. You're head of Security on Mars now. It's all authorized in the plans there. You'll need the brains and knowledge of the others-but they can't act. You can-we know about you."

The old woman sighed. She put down the hot water and picked up the bottle of brandy, starting down the stairs.

"Gordon!" Murdoch said faintly.

He turned to put his head down. From the stairs, a sudden cry and thump sounded, and something hit the floor. Gordon jumped toward the sound, to find the old lady bending over the inert figure of Sheila Corey.

"I heard someone," the woman said. She stared at the brandy bottle sickly. "*Gott in Himmel*, look at me. Am I a killer, too, that I should strike a young and beautiful girl. She comes into my house, and I sneak behind her ...It is an evil time, young man. Here, you carry her inside. I'll get some twine to tie her up. The idea, spying on you!"

Gordon picked the girl up roughly. That capped it, he thought. There was no way of knowing how much she'd heard, or whether she'd tipped others off. He dropped her near the bed, and went over to Murdoch. The man was dying now.

"So Security wants me to contact the others in the book and organize things?"

"Yes." Murdoch swallowed. "Not a good chance, then-but a chance. Still time —I think. Gordon?"

"What else can I do?" Bruce Gordon asked.

He knew it was no answer, but Asa Murdoch apparently accepted it as a promise. The gray-speckled head relaxed and rolled sideways on the bloody pillow.

"Dead," Gordon said to the woman, as she came up with the twine. "Dead, fighting windmills. And maybe winning. I don't know."

He turned toward Sheila —a split second too late. The girl came up from the floor with a single push of her arm. She pivoted on her heel, hit the door, and her heels were clattering on the stairs. Before Gordon could reach the entrance, she was whipping around into an alley.

He watched her go, sick inside, and the last he saw was the hand she held up, waving the little black book at him!

He turned back into the liquor shop; the woman seemed to read his face. "I should have watched her. It is a bad day for me, young man. I failed Pappa; I failed the poor man who died-and now I have failed you. It is better..."

He caught her as she fell toward him. She relaxed after a second. "Upstairs, please," she whispered, "beside Pappa. There was nothing else. And these Martian poisons-they are so sure, they don't hurt. Five minutes more, I think. Stay with me, I'll tell you how Pappa and I got married. I want somebody should know how it was with us once, together."

He stayed, then picked the two bodies up and moved them from the floor onto the bed where he had first seen the old man. He moved Murdoch's body aside, and covered the two gently. Finally, he went down the stairs, carrying Murdoch with him. The man's weight was a stiff load, even on Mars; but, somehow, he couldn't leave his body with the old couple.

He stopped finally ten blocks of narrow alleys away, and put Murdoch down.

Now he had no witnesses, except Sheila Corey. He had no book, no clues as to whom to see and what to do.

He heard the sound of a mobile amplifier, and strained his ears toward it. He got enough to know that Wayne had won a thumping victory, better than three to two.

Isaiah Trench was still captain of the Seventh Precinct.

Chapter IX
Contraband

Elections were over, but the few dim lights along the street showed only boarded-up and darkened buildings. There were sounds of stirring, but no one was trusting that the election-day brawls were completely ended yet.

Gordon hesitated, then swung glumly toward a corner where he could find a police call box. He heard a tiny patrol car turn the corner and ducked back into another alley to wait for it to go by. But they weren't looking for him. Their spotlight caught a running boy, clutching a few thin copies of the *Crusader* under a scrawny arm.

After the cops had dumped the unconscious kid into the back of the small squad car, and gone looking for more game, Gordon went over to look at the tattered scraps left of the opposition paper.

Randolph wasn't preaching this time, but was content to report the facts he'd seen. There had been at least ninety known killings; mobs had fought citizens outside the main market for three hours.

Yet in spite of all the ballot-stuffing and intimidations, Wayne had barely squeaked through, by a four per cent majority. It was obvious that the current administration could never win another election.

Bruce Gordon lifted the cradled phone from the box. "Gordon reporting," he announced.

A startled grunt came from the instrument, followed by the clicks of hasty switching. In less than fifteen seconds, Trench's voice barked out of the phone. "Gordon? Where the hell you been?"

"Up an alley between McCutcheon and Miles," Gordon told him. "With a corpse. Murdoch's corpse. Better send out the wagon."

Trench hesitated only a fraction of a second. "Okay, *I'll* be out in ten minutes."

Gordon clumped back to the alley and bent for a final inspection of Murdoch's body, to make sure nothing would prove the flaws in his weakly built story.

Isaiah Trench was better than his word. He swung his gray car up to the alley in seven minutes.

The door slammed behind him, a beam snapped out from his flashlight into the alley, and then he was beside Murdoch's body. He threw the light to Gordon and stooped to run expert hands over the corpse and through the pockets.

Finally, he stood up, frowning. "He's dead, all right. I don't get it. If you hadn't reported in ... Gordon, did he try to make you think he was —"

"Security?" Gordon filled in. "Yeah. Claimed he was head of it here, and wanted me to send a message to Earth for him."

Trench nodded, a touch of relief on his face. "Crazy!"

Gordon grimaced faintly.

"Crazy," Trench repeated. "He must have been to spin that story ... By the way, thanks for killing that sniper. You're a good shot. I'd be dead if you weren't, I guess."

Gordon made no comment, and Trench said, "I could start a nasty investigation, I guess. But I heard him raving, too. Give me a hand, and I'll take care of all this ... Want me to drop you off?"

They wangled the body into the trunk of the car. Then it was good to relax while Trench drove along the rubble-piled and nearly deserted streets. Gordon heard a sigh from beside him; Trench must have been under tension, too.

They didn't speak until Trench stopped in front of Mother Corey's place. Then the captain turned and stuck out his hand. "Congratulations, by the way. I forgot to tell you, but you won the lottery. You're a sergeant from now on."

Inside, a thick effluvium hit his nose, and Gordon turned to see Mother Corey's huge bulk waddling down the hall. The old man nodded. "We thought you'd gone on the lam, cobber. But I guess, since Trench brought you back, you've cooled. Good, good. As a respectable man now, I couldn't have stashed you from the cops-though I might have been tempted-mighty tempted." His face was melancholy. "Tell me, lad, did they get Murdoch?"

Bruce Gordon nodded, and the old man sighed. Something suspiciously like a tear glistened in his eyes.

"I thought you were taking a bath," Gordon commented.

The old man chuckled. "Fate's against me, cobber. With all the shooting, some punk put a bullet clean through the wall and the plastic of the tub. Fifty gallons of water, all wasted!"

He turned back toward the end of the hall, sighing again. Gordon went up the stairs, noticing that Izzy's door was open. The little man was stretched out on the bunk in his clothes, filthy; one side of his face swollen.

"Hi, gov'nor," he called out, his voice still cheerful. "I had odds you'd beat the ticket, though the Mother and me were worried there for a while. How'd you grease the fix?"

Gordon sketched it in, without mentioning Security. "What happened to you, Izzy?"

"Price of being honest. But the gees who paid me protection didn't get hurt, gov'nor." He winced, then grinned. "So they pay double tomorrow. Honesty pays, gov'nor, if you squeeze it once in a while ... Funny, you making sergeant; I thought two other gees won the lottery."

So the promotion *had* come from Trench! It bothered him. When a turkey sees corn on the menu, it's time to wonder about Thanksgiving.

Collections were good all week-probably as a result of Izzy's actions. Even after he arranged to pay his income tax, and turned over his "donation" to the fund, Gordon was well ahead for the first time since he'd landed here.

He had become almost superstitious about the way he was always left with no more than a hundred credits in his pockets. This time, he stripped himself to that sum at once, depositing the rest in the First Marsport Bank. Maybe it would break the jinx.

They were one of the few teams in the Seventh Precinct to make full quota. Trench was lavish in his praise. He was playing more than fair with Bruce Gordon now, but there was a basic suspicion in his eyes.

The next day, he drafted Izzy and Gordon for a trip outside the dome. "It's easy enough, and you'll get plenty of credit in the fund for it. I need two men who can keep their mouths shut."

They idled around the station through the morning. In the late afternoon, they left in a big truck capable of hauling what would have been fifty tons on Earth. Trench drove. Outside the dome, the electric motor carried them along at a steady twenty miles an hour, almost silently.

It was Gordon's first look at the real Mars. He saw small villages where crop prospectors and hydroponic farmers lived, with a few small industrial sections scattered over the desert. As they moved out, he saw the slow change from the beaten appearance of Marsport to something that seemed no worse than would be found among the share-croppers back on Earth. It was obvious that Marsport was the poison center here.

Some of the younger children were running around without helmets, confirming Praeger's claim that third-generation Martians somehow learned to adapt to the atmosphere.

Darkness fell sharply, as it always did in Mars' thin air, but they went on, heading out into the dunes of the desert. When they finally stopped, they were beside a small, battered space ship. Boxes were piled all around it, and others were being tossed out. Trent leaped from the truck, motioning them to follow, and they began loading the crates hastily. It took about an hour of hard work to load the last of them, and Trench was working harder than they were. Finished, he went up to one of the men from the ship, handed over an envelope, and came back to start the truck back toward Marsport. As the dunes dwindled behind them, Gordon could see the brief flare of the little rocket taking off.

They drove back through the night as rapidly as the truck could manage. Finally, they rolled into City Hall, down a ramp, and onto an elevator that took them three levels down. Trench climbed out and nodded in satisfaction. "That's it. Take tomorrow off, if you want, and I'll fix credit for you. But just remember you haven't seen anything. You don't know any more than our old friend Murdoch!"

He led them to another elevator, then swung back to the truck.

"Guns," Gordon said slowly. "Guns and contraband ammunition for the administration from Earth. And they must have paid half the graft they've taken for that. What the hell do they want it for?"

Izzy jerked a shoulder upwards and a twist ran across his pock-marked face. "War, what else? Gov'nor, Earth must be boiling about the election. Maybe Security's getting set to spring."

The idea of Marsport rebelling against Earth seemed ridiculous. Even with guns, they wouldn't have a chance if Earth sent a force of any strength to back Security. But it was the only explanation.

Gordon took the next day off to look for Sheila Corey, but nobody would admit having seen her.

He had seen crowds beginning to assemble all afternoon, but had paid no attention to them. Now he found the way back to Corey's blocked by a mob. Then he saw that the object of it all was the First Marsport Bank. It was only toward that that the shaking fists were raised. Gordon managed to get onto a pile of rubble where he could see over the crowd. The doors of the bank were locked shut, but men were attacking it with an improvised battering ram. As he watched, a pompous little man came to the upper window over the door and began motioning for attention. The crowd quieted almost at once, except for a single yell. "When do we get our money?"

"Please. Please." The voice reached back thinly as the bank president got his silence. "Please. It won't do you any good. Not a bit. We're broke. Not a cent left! And don't go blaming me. *I* didn't start the rush. Your friends did that. They took all the money, and now we're cleaned out. You can't —"

A rope rose from the crowd and settled around him. In a second, he was pulled down, and the crowd surged forward.

Gordon dropped from the rubble, staring at the bank. He'd played it safe this time-he'd put his money away, to make sure he'd have it!

A heavy hand fell on his shoulder, and he turned to see Mother Corey. "That's the way a panic is, cobber," the man said. "There's a run, then everything is ruined. I tried to get you when I first heard the rumor, but you were gone. And when this starts, a man has to get there first." He patted his side, where a bulge showed. "And I just made it, too."

The mob was beginning to break up now, but it was still in an ugly mood. "But what started it?"

"Rumors that Mayor Wayne got a big loan from the bank-and why not, seeing it was his bank! Nobody had to guess that he'd never pay it back, so —"

Gordon found Izzy organizing the bouncers from the joints and some of the citizens into a squad. Every joint was closed down tightly already. Gordon began organizing his own squad.

Izzy slipped over as he began to get them organized. "If we hold past midnight, we'll be set, gov'nor," he said. "They go crazy for a while, but give 'em a few hours and they stop most of it. I figure you know where all the scratch went?"

"Sure-guns from Earth! The damned fools!"

"Yeah. But not fools. Just bloody well-informed, gov'nor. Earth's sending a fleet-got official word of it. No way of telling how big, but it's coming."

It gave Gordon something to think about while they patrolled the beat. But he had enough for a time without that. The mobs left the section alone, apparently scared off by the organized group ready and waiting for them. But every street and alley had to be kept under constant surveillance to drive out the angry, desperate men who were trying to get something to hang onto before everything collapsed. He saw stores being broken into, beyond his beat; and brawls as one drunken, crazed crowd met another. But he kept to his own territory, knowing that there was nothing he could do beyond it.

By midnight, as Izzy had promised, the people had begun to quiet down, however. The anger and hysteria were giving way to a sullen, beaten hopelessness.

Honest Izzy finally seemed satisfied to turn things over to the regular night men. Gordon waited around a while longer, but finally headed back to Mother Corey's place.

Mother Corey put a cup of steaming coffee into his hands. "You look worse than I do, cobber. Worse than even that granddaughter of mine. She was looking for you!"

"Sheila?" Gordon jerked the word out.

"Yeah. She left a note for you. I put it up in your room." Mother Corey chuckled. "Why don't you two get married and make your fighting legal?"

"Thanks for the coffee," Gordon threw back at him. He was already mounting the stairs.

He tossed his door open and found the letter on his bed.

"I'd rather go to Wayne," it said, "but I need money. If you want the rest of this, you've got until three tonight to make an offer. If you can find me, maybe I'll listen."

The torn-off front cover of the notebook accompanied the letter. But it was a quarter after three already, he was practically broke-and he had no idea where she could be found.

Chapter X
Marriage of Convenience

Bruce Gordon jerked the door open to yell for Izzy while he tucked the bit of notebook cover into his pocket. Then he stopped as something nibbled at his mind; the odor Gordon had smelled before registered. He yanked out the bit of notebook and sniffed. It hadn't been close enough for any length of time to be contaminated by Mother Corey, so the smell could only come from one place.

He checked the batteries on his suit and put it on quickly. There was no point in wearing the helmet inside the dome, but it was better than trying to rent one at the lockers. He buckled it to a strap. The knife slid into its sheath, and the gun holster snapped onto the suit. As a final thought, he picked up the stout locust stick he'd used under Murdoch.

There were no cabs outside tonight, of course. The streets were almost deserted, except for some prowler or desperation-driven drug addict. He proceeded cautiously, however, realizing that it would be just like Sheila to ambush him. But he reached the exit from the dome with no trouble.

"Special pass to leave at this hour," the guard there reminded him. "Of course, if it's urgent, pal..."

Gordon was in no mood to try bribes. He let his hand drop to the gun. "Police Sergeant Gordon, on official business," he said curtly. "Get the hell out of my way."

The guard thought it over, and reached for the release. Gordon swung back as he passed through. "And you'd better be ready to open when I come back."

He was in comparative darkness almost at once, and tonight there was no sign of the lights of patrolling cops. Then three specks of glaring blue light suddenly appeared in the sky, jerking his eyes up. They were dropping rapidly.

Rockets that flamed bright blue-military rockets! Earth was finally taking a hand!

He crouched in a hollow that had once been some kind of a basement until the ships had landed and cut off their jets. Then he stood up, blinking his eyes until they could again make out the pattern of the dim bulbs. He'd seen enough by the rocket glare to know that he was headed right. And finally the ugly half-cylinder of patched brick and metal that was the old Mother Corey's Chicken Coop showed up against the faint light.

He moved in cautiously, as silently as he could, and located the semi-secret entrance to the building without meeting anyone. Once in the tunnel that led to the building, he felt a little safer.

He removed his helmet, and strapped it to the back of his suit, out of the way. The old hall was in worse shape than before. Mother Corey had run a somewhat orderly place, with constant vigilance; Bruce Gordon could never have come into the hallway without being seen in the old days.

Then a pounding sound came from the second floor, and Gordon drew back into the denser shadows, staring upwards. A heavy voice picked up the exchange of shouts.

"You, Sheila, you come outa there! You come right out or I'm gonna blast that there door down. You open up."

Gordon was already moving up the stairs when a second voice reached him, and this one was familiar. "Jurgens don't want *you*; all he wants is this place-we got use for it. It don't belong to you, anyhow! Come out now, and we'll let you go peaceful. Or stay in there and we'll blast you out-in pieces."

It was the voice of Jurgens' henchman who had called on Mother Corey before elections. The thick voice must belong to the big ape who'd been with him.

"Come on out," the little man cried again. "You don't have a chance. We've already chased all your boarders out!"

Gordon tried to remember which steps had creaked the worst, but he wasn't too worried, if there were only two of them. Then his head projected above the top step, and he hesitated.

Only the rat and the ape were standing near a heavy, closed door. But four others were lounging in the background. He lifted his foot to put it back down to a lower step, just as Sheila's muffled voice shrilled out a fog of profanity. He grinned, and then saw that he'd lifted his foot to a higher step.

There was a sharp yell from one of the men in the background and a knife sailed for him, but the aim was poor. Gordon's gun came out. Two of the men were dropping before the others could reach for their own weapons, and while the rat-faced man was just turning. The third dropped without firing, and the fourth's shot went wild. Gordon was firing rapidly, but not with such a stupid attempt at speed that he couldn't aim each shot. And at that distance, it was hard to miss.

Rat-face jerked back behind the big hulk of his partner, trying to pull a gun that seemed to be stuck; a scared man's ability to get his gun stuck in a simple holster was always amazing. The big guy simply lunged, with his hands out.

Gordon side-stepped and caught one of the arms, swinging the huge body over one hip. It sailed over the broken railing, to land on the floor below and crash through the rotten planking. He heard the man hit the basement, even while he was swinging the club in his hand toward the rat-faced man.

There was a thin, high-pitched scream as a collarbone broke. He slumped onto the floor, and began to try hitching his way down the steps. Gordon picked up the gun that had fallen out of the holster as the man fell and put it into his pouch. He considered the two, and decided they would be no menace.

"Okay, Sheila," he called out, trying to muffle his voice. "We got them all."

"Pie-Face?" Her voice was doubtful.

He considered what a man out here who went under that name might be like. "Sure, baby. Open up!"

"Wait a minute. I've got this nailed shut." There was the sound of an effort of some kind going on as she talked. "Though I ought to let you stay out there and rot. Damn it ...uh!"

The door heaved open then, and she appeared in it; then she saw him, and her jaw dropped open slackly. "You!"

"Me," he agreed. "And lucky for you, Cuddles."

Her hand streaked to a gun in her belt. "Kill him!"

This time, he didn't wait to be attacked. He went for the door, knocking her aside. His knee caught the outside of her hip as she spun; she fell over, dropping the gun.

The two men in the room were both holding knives, but in the ridiculous overhand position that seems to be an ingrained stupidity of the human race, until it's taught better. A single flip of his locust club against their wrists accounted for both of the knives. He grabbed them by the hair of their heads, then, and brought the two skulls together savagely.

Sheila lay stretched out on the floor, where her head had apparently struck against the leg of a bed. Gordon shoved the bodies of the two men aside and looked down at the wreck of a man who lay on the dirty blanket. "Hello, O'Neill," he said.

The former leader of the Stonewall gang stared up at the club swinging from Gordon's wrist. "You ain't gonna beat me this time? I'm a sick man. Sick. Can't hurt nobody. Don't beat me again."

Gordon's stomach knotted sickly. Doing something under the pressure of necessity was one thing; but to see the sorry results of it later was another. "All right," he said. "Just stay there until I get away from this rat's nest and I won't hit you. I won't even touch you."

He was sure enough that it was no act on O'Neill's part; he wasn't so sure about Sheila. He checked the two men on the floor, who were still out cold. Then he stepped through the door carefully, to make sure that the big bruiser hadn't come back.

His ears barely detected the sound Sheila made as she reached for the knife of one of the men. Then it came—the faintest catch of breath. Gordon threw himself flat to the floor. She let out a scream as he saw her momentum carry her over him; she was at the edge of the rail, and starting to fall.

He caught her feet in his hands and yanked her back. There was nothing phony this time as she hit the floor.

"Just a matter of co-ordination, Cuddles," he told her. "Little girls shouldn't play with knives; they'll grow up to be old maids that way."

Fury blackened her face, but she still couldn't function. He picked her up and tossed her back into the room. From the broken mattress on the bed, he dug out a coil of wire and bound her hands and feet with it.

"Can't say I think much of your choice of companions these days," he commented, looking toward the bed where O'Neill was cowering. "It looks as if your grandfather picks them better for you."

"You filthy-minded hog! D'you think I'd —I'd —One room in the place with a decent door, and you can't see why I'd choose that room to keep Jurgens' devils back. You-You —"

He'd been searching the room, but there was no sign of the notebook there. He checked again to see that the wire was tight, and then picked up the two henchmen who were showing some signs of reviving.

"I'll watch them," a voice said from the door. Gordon snapped his head up to see Izzy standing there. He realized he'd been a lot less cautious than he'd thought.

Izzy grinned at his confusion. "I got enough out of the Mother to case the pitch," he said. "I knew I was right when I spotted the apeman carrying a guy with a bad shoulder away from here. Jurgens' punks, eh?"

"Thanks for coming. What's it going to cost me?"

"Wouldn't be honest to charge unless you asked me to convoy you, gov'nor. And if you're looking for the vixen's room, it's where you bunked before. I got around after I spotted you here."

Sheila Corey forced herself to a sitting position and spat at Izzy. "Traitor! Crooked little traitor!"

"Shut up, Sheila," Izzy said. "Your retainer ran out."

Surprisingly, she did shut up. Gordon went to the little space-and saw that Izzy was right; there was a nearly used-up lipstick, a comb, and a cracked mirror. There was also a small cloth bag containing a few scraps of clothes.

He turned the room upside down, but there was no sign of the notebook or papers from it.

He located her helmet and carried it down with him. "You're going bye-bye, Cuddles," he told her. "I'm going to put this on you and then unfasten your arms and legs. But if you start to so much as wiggle your big toe, you won't sit down for a month."

She pursed her lips hotly, but made no reply. He screwed the helmet on, and unfastened her arms. For a second, she tensed, while he waited, grinning down at her. Then she slumped back and lay quiet as he unfastened her legs.

He tossed her over his shoulder, and started down the rickety stairs.

There was a little light in the sky. Five minutes later, it was full daylight, which should have been a signal for the workers to start for their jobs. But today they were drifting out unhappily, as if already sure there would be no jobs by nightfall.

A few stared at Gordon and his burden, but most of them didn't even look up. The two men trudged along silently.

"Prisoner," he announced crisply to the guard, but there was no protest this time. They went through, and he was lucky enough to locate a broken-down tricycle cab.

Mother Corey let them in, without flickering an eyelash as he saw his granddaughter. Bruce Gordon dropped her onto her legs. "Behave yourself," he warned her as he took off his helmet, and then unfastened hers.

Mother Corey chuckled. "Very touching, cobber. You have a way with women, it seems. Too bad she had to wear a helmet, or you might have dragged her here by her hair. Ah, well, let's not talk about it here. My room is more comfortable-and private."

Inside, Sheila sat woodenly on the little sofa, pretending to see none of them. Mother Corey looked from one to the other, and then back to Gordon. "Well? You must have had some reason for bringing her here, cobber."

"I want her out of my hair, Mother," Gordon tried to explain. "I can lock her up-carrying a gun without a permit is reason enough. But I'd rather you kept her here, if you'll take the responsibility. After all, she's your granddaughter."

"So she is. That's why I wash my hands of her. I couldn't control myself at her age, couldn't control my son, and I don't intend to handle a female of my line. It looks as if you'll have to arrest her."

"Okay. Suppose I rent a room and put a good lock on it. You've got the one that connects with mine vacant."

"I run a respectable house now, Gordon," Mother Corey stated flatly. "What you do outside my place is your own business. But no women, except married ones. Can't trust 'em."

Gordon stared at the old man, but he apparently meant just what he said. "All right, Mother," he said finally. "How in hell do I marry her without any rigmarole?"

Izzy's face seemed to drop toward the floor. Sheila came up off the couch with a choking cry and leaped for the door. Mother Corey's immense arm moved out casually, sweeping her back onto the couch.

"Very convenient," the old man said. "The two of you simply fill out a form —I've got a few left from the last time-and get Izzy and me to witness it. Drop it in the mail, and you're married."

"If you think I'd marry you, you filthy —" Sheila began.

Mother Corey listened attentively. "Rich, but not very imaginative," he said thoughtfully. "But she'll learn. Izzy, I have a feeling we should let them settle their differences."

As the door shut behind them, Gordon yanked Sheila back to the couch. "Shut up!" he told her. "This isn't a game. Hell's popping here-you know that better than most people. And I'm up to my neck in it. If I've got to marry you to keep you out of my hair, I will."

Her face was pasty-white, but she bent her head, and fluttered her eyelashes up at him. "So romantic," she sighed. "You sweep me off my feet. You-Why, you —"

"Me or Trench! I can take you to him and tell him you're mixed up in Security, and that you either have papers on you or out at the Chicken Coop to prove it. He won't believe *you* if I take you in. Well?"

She looked at him a long time in silence, and there was surprise in her eyes. "You'd do it! You really would....All right; I'll sign your damned papers!"

Ten minutes later, he stood in what was now a connecting double room, watching Mother Corey nail up the hall door to the room that was to be hers. There were no windows here, and his own room had an excellent lock on it already-one he'd put on himself. Izzy came back as Mother Corey finished the door and began knocking a small panel out of the connecting door. The old man was surprisingly adept with his hands as he fitted hinges and a catch to the panel, and re-installed it so that Sheila could swing it open.

"They're married," Izzy said. "It's in the mail to the register, along with the twenty credits. Gov'nor, we're about due to report in."

Gordon nodded. "Be with you in a minute," he said as he paid Mother Corey for the materials and work. He jerked his head and the two men went out, leaving him alone with Sheila.

"I'll bring you some food tonight. And you may not have a private bath, but it beats the Chicken Coop. Here." He handed her the key to the connecting door. "It's the only key there is."

Chapter XI
The Sky's the Limit

All that day, the three rocket ships sat out on the field. Nobody went up to them, and nobody came from them; surprisingly, Wayne had found the courage to ignore them. But rumors were circulating wildly. Bruce Gordon felt his nerves creeping out of his skin and beginning to stand on end to test each breeze for danger.

With the credit they'd accumulated in the fund, nearly all their collection was theirs. Gordon went out to do some shopping. He stopped when his money was down to a hundred credits, hardly realizing what he was doing. When he went out, the street was going crazy.

Izzy had been waiting, and filled him in. At exactly sundown, the rocket ships had thrown down ramps, and a stream of jeeps had ridden down them and toward the south entrance to the dome. They had presented some sort of paper and forced the guard to let them through. There were about two hundred men, some of them armed. They had driven straight to the huge, barnlike Employment Bureau, had chased out the few people remaining there, and had simply taken over. Now there was a sign in front which simply said MARSPORT LEGAL POLICE FORCE HEADQUARTERS. Then the jeeps had driven back to the rockets, gone on board, and the ships had taken off.

Gordon glanced at his watch, finding it hard to believe it could have been done so quickly. But it was two hours after sundown.

Now a car with a loudspeaker on top rolled into view —a completely armored car. It stopped, and the speaker began operating.

"Citizens of Marsport! In order to protect your interests from the proven rapacity of the administration here, Earth has revoked the independent charter of Marsport. The past elections are hereby declared null and void. Your home world has appointed Marcus Gannett as mayor, with Philip Crane as chief of police. Other members of the council will be by appointment until legal elections can be held safely. The Municipal Police Force is disbanded, and the Legal Police Force is now being organized.

"All police and officers who remain loyal to the legal government will be accepted at their present grade or higher. To those who now leave the illegal Municipal Force and accept their duty with the Legal Force, there will be no question of past conduct. Nor will they suffer financially from the change!

"Banks will be reopened as rapidly as the Legal Government can extend its control, and all deposits previously made will be honored in full."

That brought a cheer from the crowd, as the sound truck moved on. Gordon saw two of the police officers nearby fingering their badges thoughtfully.

Then another truck rolled into view, and the Mayor's canned voice came over it, panting as if he'd had to rush to make the recording. He began directly:

"Martians! Earth has declared war on us. She has denied us our right to rule ourselves —a right guaranteed in our charter. We admit there have been abuses; all young civilizations make mistakes. But we've developed and grown.

"This is an old pattern, fellow Martians! England tried it on her colonies three hundred years ago. And the people rose up and demanded their right to rule themselves. They had troubles with their governments, too-and they had panics. But they won their freedom, and it made them great-so great that now that *one* nation-not all Earth, but that single nation! —is trying to do to us what she wouldn't permit to herself.

"Well, we don't have an army. But neither do they. They know the people of this world wouldn't stand for the landing of foreign-that's right, *foreign* —troops. So they're trying to steal our police force from us and use it for their war.

"Fellow Martians, they aren't going to bribe us into that! Mars has had enough. I declare us to be in a state of revolution. And since they have chosen the weapons, I declare our loyal and functioning Municipal Police Force to be *our* army. Any man who deserts will be considered a traitor. But any man who sticks will be rewarded more than he ever expected. We're going to protect our freedom.

"Let them open their banks-our banks-again. And when they have established your accounts, go in and collect the money! If they give it to you, Mars is that much richer. If they don't, you'll know they're lying.

"Let them bribe us if they like. We're going to win this war."

Gordon felt the crowd's reaction twist again, and he had to admit that Wayne had played his cards well.

But it didn't make the question of where he belonged, or what he should do, any easier. He waited until the crowd had thinned out a little and began heading toward Corey's, with Izzy moving along silently beside him, carrying half the packages.

He remembered the promise of forgiveness for all sins on joining the new Legal Force; but he'd read enough history to know that it was fine-as long as the struggle continued. Afterwards, promises grew dim....

He had no use for the present administration, but Earth had no right to take over without a formal investigation, and a chance for the people to state their choice.

Then he grimaced at himself. He was in no position to move according to right and wrong. The only question that counted was how he had the best chance to ride out the storm, and to get back to Earth and a normal life.

He was still in a brown study as he took the bundles from Izzy and dropped them on his bed. Izzy went out, and Gordon stood staring at the wall. Trench? Or the new Commissioner Crane? If Earth should win-and they had most of the power, after all-and Bruce Gordon had fought against Security, the mines of Mercury were waiting.

He picked up the stuff from his bed and started to sweep it aside before he lay down. Then he remembered at last; he knocked on the panel, until it finally opened a crack.

"Here," he told her. "Food, and some other stuff. There are some refuse bags, too. Yell when you want them removed."

She took the bundles woodenly until she came to a plastic can. Then she gasped. "Water! Two gallons!"

"There are heat tablets, and a skin tub." The salesgirl had explained how one gallon was enough in the plastic bag that served as a tub; he had his doubts. "Detergent. The whole works."

She hauled the stuff in and started to close the panel. Then she hesitated. "I suppose I should thank you, but I don't like to be told I stink so much you can't stand me in the next room!"

"Hell, I've gotten so I can stand your grandfather," he answered. "It wasn't that." The panel slammed shut.

He still hadn't solved his problem in the morning; out of habit, he put on his uniform and went across to Izzy's room. But Izzy was already gone.

Gordon fished into the pocket of his uniform for paper and a pencil to leave a note in case Izzy came back. His fingers found the half notebook cover instead. He drew it out, scowling at it, and started to crumple it. Then he stopped, staring at the piece of imitation leather and paper that wouldn't bend.

His fingers were still stiff as he began tearing off the thin covering with his knife; the paper backing peeled away easily.

Under it lay a thin metal plate that glowed faintly even in the dim light of Izzy's room! Gordon nearly dropped it. He'd seen such an identification plate once before.

The printing on it leaped at him: "This will identify the bearer, BRUCE IRVING GORDON, as a PRIME agent of the Office of Solar Security, empowered to make and execute any and all directives under the powers of this office." The printing in capitals was obviously done by hand, but with the same catalytic "ink" as the rest of the badge. Murdoch must have prepared it, hidden it in the notebook, then died before the secret could be revealed.

A knock sounded from across the hall. Gordon thrust the damning badge as deep into his pouch as he could cram it and looked out. It was Mother Corey.

"You've got a visitor-outside," he announced. "Trench. And I don't like the stench of that kind of cop in my place. Get him away, cobber, get him away!"

Gordon found Trench pacing up and down in front of the house, scowling up at it. But the ex-Marine smiled as he saw Bruce Gordon in uniform. "Good. At least some men are loyal. Had breakfast, Gordon?"

Gordon shook his head, and realized suddenly that the decision seemed to have been taken out of his hands. They crossed the street and went down half a block. "All right," he said, when the coffee began waking him. "What's the angle?"

Trench dropped the eyes that had been boring into him. "I'll have to trust you, Gordon. I've never been sure. But either you're loyal now or I can't depend on anyone being loyal."

During the night, it seemed, the Legal Force had been recruiting. Wayne, Arliss, and the rest of the administration had counted on self-interest holding most of the cops loyal to them. They'd been wrong. Legal forces already controlled about half the city.

"So?" Gordon asked. He could have told Trench that the fund was good-enough reason for most police deserting.

Trench put his coffee down and yelled for more. It was obvious he'd spent the night without sleep. "So we're going to need men with guts. Gordon, you had training under Murdoch-who knew his business. And you aren't a coward, as most of these fat fools are. I've got a proposition, straight from Wayne."

"I'm listening."

"Here." Trench threw across a platinum badge. "Take that-captain at large-and conscript any of the Municipal Force you want, up to a hundred. Pick out any place you want, train them to handle those damned Legals the way Murdoch handled the Stonewall boys. In return, the sky's the limit. Name your own salary, once you've done the job. And no kickbacks, either!"

Gordon picked up the badge slowly and buckled it on, while a grim, satisfied smile spread over Trench's features. The problem seemed to have been solved. Gordon should have been satisfied, but he felt like Judas picking up the thirty pieces of silver. He tried to swallow them with the dregs of his coffee, and they stuck in his throat.

Comes the revolution and we'll all eat strawberries and scream!

A hubbub sounded outside, and Trench grimaced as a police whistle sounded, and a Municipal cop ran by. "We're in enemy territory," he said. "The Legals got this precinct last night. Captain Hendrix and some of his men wanted to come back with full battle equipment and chase them out. I had a hell of a time getting them to take it easy. I suppose that was some damned fool who tried to go back to his beat."

"Then you'd better look again," Gordon told him. He'd gone to the door and was peering out. Up the narrow little street was rolling a group of about seventy Municipal police and half a dozen small trucks. The men were wearing guns. And up the street a man in bright green uniform was pounding his fist up and down in emphasis as he called in over the precinct box.

"The idiot!" Trench grabbed Gordon and spun out, running toward the advancing men. "We've got to stop this. Get my car-up the street-call Arliss on the phone-under the dash. Or Wayne. I'll bring Hendrix."

Trench's system made some sense, and this business of marching as to war made none at all. Gordon grabbed the phone from under the dash. A sleepy voice answered to say that Commissioner Arliss and Mayor Wayne were sleeping. They'd had a hard night, and...

"Damn it, there's a rebellion going on!" Gordon told the man. Rebellion, rebellion! He'd meant to say revolution, but...

Trench was arguing frantically with the pompous figure of Captain Hendrix. From the other end of the street, a group of small cars appeared; and men began piling out, all in shiny green.

"Who's this?" the phone asked. When Gordon identified himself, there was a snort of disgust. "Yes, yes, congratulations. Trench was quite right; you're fully authorized. Did you call me out of bed just to check on that, young man?"

"No, I—" Then he hung up. Hendrix had dropped to his knees and fired before Trench could knock the gun from his hands.

There was no answering fire. The Legals simply came boiling down the street, equipped with long pikes with lead-weighted ends. And Hendrix came charging up, his men straggling behind him. Gordon was squarely in the middle. He considered staying in Trench's car and letting it roll past him. But he'd taken the damned badge.

"Hell," he said in disgust. He climbed out, just as the two groups met. It all had a curious feeling of unreality.

Then a man jumped for him, swinging a pike, and the feeling was suddenly gone. His hand snapped down sharply for a rock on the street. The pike whistled over his head, barely missing, and he was up, squashing the big stone into the face of the other. He jerked the pike away, kicked the man in the neck as he fell, and unsheathed his knife with the other hand.

Trench was a few feet away. The man might be a louse, but he was also a fighting machine of first order, still. He'd already captured one of the pikes. Now he grinned tightly at Gordon and began moving toward him. Gordon nodded-in a brawl such as this, two working together had a distinct advantage.

Then a yell sounded as more Legals poured down the street. One of them was obviously Izzy, wearing the same green as the others!

Gordon felt something hit his back, and instinctively fell, soaking up the blow. He managed to bend his neck and roll, coming to his feet. His knife slashed upwards, and the Legal fell-almost on top of the Security badge that had dropped from Gordon's pouch.

He jerked himself down and scooped it up, his eyes darting for Trench. He stuffed it back, ducking a blow. Then his glance fell on the entrance to Mother Corey's house-with Sheila Corey coming out of the seal!

Gordon threw himself back; he had to get to her.

He hadn't been watching as closely as he should. He saw the pike coming down and tried to duck...

He was vaguely conscious later of looking up, to see Sheila dragging him into some entrance, while Trench ran toward them. Sheila and Trench together-and the Security badge was still in his pouch!

Chapter XII
Wife or Prisoner?

Something cold and damp against his forehead brought Gordon part way out of his unconsciousness finally. There was the softness of a bed under him and the bitter aftertaste of Migrainol on his tongue. He tried to move, but nothing happened. The drug killed pain, but only at the expense of a temporary paralysis of all voluntary motion.

There was a sudden withdrawal of the cooling touch on his forehead, and then hasty steps that went away from him, and the sound of a door closing.

Steps sounded from outside; his door opened, and there was the sound of two men crossing the room, one with the heavy shuffle of Mother Corey.

"No wonder the boys couldn't find where you'd stashed him, Mother. Must be a bloody big false section you've got in that trick mattress of yours!"

"Big enough for him and for Trench, Izzy," Mother Corey's wheezing voice agreed. "Had to be big to fit me."

"You mean you hid Trench out, too?" Izzy asked.

There was a thick chuckle and the sound of hands being rubbed together. "A respectable landlord has to protect himself, Izzy. For hiding and a convoy back, our Captain Trench gave me a paper with immunity from the Municipal Force. Used that, with a bit of my old reputation, to get your Mayor Gannett to give me the same from the Legals. Gannett didn't want Mother Corey to think the Municipals were kinder than the Legals, so you're in the only neutral territory in Marsport. Not that you deserve it."

"Lay off, Mother," Izzy said sharply. "I told you I had to do it. I take care of the side that pays my cut, and the bloody administration pulled the plug on my beat twice. Only honest thing to do was to join the Legals."

"And get your rating upped to a lieutenant," Mother Corey observed. "Without telling cobber Gordon!"

"Like I say, honesty pays, Mother-when you know how to collect. Hell, I figured Bruce would do the same. He's a right gee."

Mother Corey chuckled. "Yeah, when he forgets he's a machine. How about a game of shanks?"

The steps moved away; the door closed again. Bruce Gordon got both eyes open and managed to sit up. The effects of the drug were almost gone, but it took a straining of every nerve to reach his uniform pouch. His fingers, clumsy and uncertain, groped back and forth for a badge that wasn't there!

He heard the door open softly, but made no effort to look up. The reaction from his effort had drained him.

Fingers touched his head carefully, brushing the hair back delicately from the side of his skull. Then there was the biting sting of antiseptic, sharp enough to bring a groan from his lips. Sheila's hair fell over her face as she bent to replace his bandages.

Her eyes wandered toward his, and the scissors and bandages on her lap hit the floor as she jumped to her feet. She turned toward her room, then hesitated as he grinned crookedly at her. "Hi, Cuddles," he said flatly.

She bit her lips and turned back, while a slow flush ran over her face. Her voice was uncertain. "Hello, Bruce. You okay?"

"How long have I been like this?"

"Fifteen hours, I guess. It's almost midnight." She bent over to pick up the bandages and to finish with his head. "Are you hungry? There's some canned soup —I took the money from your pocket. Or coffee..."

"Coffee." He forced himself up again; Sheila propped the flimsy pillow behind him, then went into her room to come back with a plastic cup filled with brown liquid that passed for coffee here. It was loaded with caffeine, at least.

"Why'd you come back?" he asked suddenly. "You were anxious enough to pick the lock and get out."

"I didn't pick it-you forgot to lock it."

He couldn't remember what he'd done after he found the badge. "Okay, my mistake. But why the change of heart?"

"Because I needed a meal ticket!" she said harshly. "When I saw that Legal cop ready to take you, I had to go running out to save you. Because I don't have the iron guts to starve like a Martian!"

It rocked him back on his mental heels. He'd thought that she had been attacking him on the street; but it made more sense this way, at that.

"You're a fool!" he told her bitterly. "You bought a punched meal ticket. Right now, I probably have six death warrants out on me, and about as much chance of making a living as —"

"I'll stick to my chances. I don't have any others now." She grimaced. "You get things done. Now that you've got a wife to support, you'll support her. Just remember, it was your idea."

He'd had a lot of ideas, it seemed. "I've got a wife who's holding onto a notebook that belongs to me, then. Where is it?"

She shook her head. "I'm keeping the notebook for insurance. Blackmail, Bruce. You should understand that! And you won't find it, so don't bother looking..." She went into the other room and shut the door. There was the sound of the lock being worked, and then silence.

He stared at the door foolishly, swearing at all women; then grimaced and turned back to the chair where his uniform still lay. He could stay here fighting with her, or he could face his troubles on the outside. The whole thing hinged on Trench; unless Trench had shown the badge to others, his problem boiled down to a single man.

Gordon found one tablet of painkiller left in the bottle and swallowed it with the dregs of the coffee. He made sure his knife was in its sheath and that the gun at his side was loaded. He found his police club, checked the loop at its end, and slipped it onto his wrist.

At the door to the hall, he hesitated, staring at Sheila's room. Wife or prisoner? He turned it over in his mind, knowing that her words couldn't change the facts. But in the end, he dropped the key and half his money beside her door, along with a spare knife and one of his guns.

He went by Izzy's room without stopping; technically, the boy was an enemy to all Municipals. This might be neutral territory, but there was no use pressing it. Gordon went down the stairs and out through the seal onto the street entrance, still in the shadows.

His eyes covered the street in two quick scans. Far up, a Legal cop was passing beyond the range of the single dim light. At the other end, a pair of figures skulked along, trying the door of each house they passed. With the cops busy fighting each other, this was better pickings than outside the dome.

He saw the Legal cop move out of sight and stepped onto the street, trying to look like another petty crook on the prowl. He headed for the nearest alley, which led through the truckyard of Nick the Croop.

The entrance was in nearly complete darkness. Gordon loosened his knife and tightened his grip on the locust stick.

Suddenly a whisper of sound caught his ears. He stopped, not too quickly, and listened, but everything was still. A hundred feet farther on, and within twenty yards of the trucks, a swishing rustle reached his ears and light slashed hotly into his eyes. Hands grabbed at his arms, and a club swung down toward his knife. But the warning had been enough. Gordon's arms jerked upwards to avoid the reaching hands. His boot lifted, and the flashlight spun aside, broken and dark. With a continuous motion, he switched the knife to his left hand in a thumb-up position and brought it back. There was a grunt of pain; he stepped backwards and twisted. His hands caught the man behind, lifted across a hip, and heaved, just before the front man reached him.

The two ambushers were down in a tangled mess. There was just enough light to make out faint outlines, and Gordon brought his locust club down twice, with the hollow thud of wood on skulls.

His head was swimming in a hot maelstrom of pain, but it was quieting as his breathing returned to normal. As long as his opponents were slower or less ruthless, he could take care of himself.

The trouble, though, was that Isaiah Trench was neither slow nor squeamish.

Gordon gathered the two hoodlums under his arms and dragged them with him. He came out in the truckyard and began searching. Nick the Croop had ridden his reputation long enough to be careless, and the third truck had its key still in the lock. He threw the two into the back and struck a cautious light.

One of them was Jurgens' apelike follower, his stupid face relaxed and vacant. The other was probably also one of Jurgens' growing mob of protection racketeers. Gordon yanked out the man's wallet, but there was no identification; it held only a small sheaf of bills.

He stripped out the money-and finally put half of it back into the wallet and dropped it beside the hoodlum. Even in jail, a man had to have smokes.

He stuck to the alleys, not using the headlights, after he had locked the two in and started the electric motor. He had no clear idea of how the battles were going, but it looked as if the Seventh Precinct was still in Municipal hands.

There was no one at the side entrance to Seventh Precinct Headquarters and only two corporals on duty inside; the rest were probably out fighting the Legals, or worrying about it. One of the corporals started to stand up and halt him, but wavered at the sight of the captain's star that was still pinned to his uniform.

"Special prisoners," Gordon told him sharply. "I've got to get information to Trench-and in private!"

The corporal stuttered. Gordon knocked him out of the way with his elbow, reached for the door to Trench's private office, and yanked it open. He stepped through, drawing it shut behind him, while his eyes checked the position of his gun at his hip. Then he looked up.

There was no sign of Trench. In his place, and in the uniform of a Municipal captain, sat the heavy figure of Jurgens. "Outside!" he snapped. Then his eyes narrowed, and a stiff smile came onto his lips as he laid the pen down. "Oh, it's you, Gordon?"

"Where's Captain Trench?"

The heavy features didn't change as Jurgens chuckled. "Commissioner Trench, Gordon. It seems Arliss decided to get rid of Mayor Wayne, but didn't count on Wayne's spies being better than his. So Trench got promoted-and I got his job for loyal service in helping the Force recruit. My boys always wanted to be cops, you know."

Gordon tried to grin in return as he moved closer, slipping the heavy locust club off his wrist.

"I sent Ape and Mullins out to get in touch with you," Jurgens said. "But I guess they didn't reach you before you left."

Gordon shook his head slightly, while the nerves bunched and tingled in his neck. "They hadn't arrived when I left the house," he said truthfully enough.

Jurgens reached out for tobacco and filled a pipe. He fumbled in his pockets, as if looking for a light. "Too bad. I knew you weren't in top shape, so I figured a convoy might be handy. Well, no matter. Trench left some instructions about you, and —"

His voice was perfectly normal, but Gordon saw the hand move suddenly toward the drawer that was half-open. And the cigarette lighter was attached to the other side of the desk.

The locust stick left Gordon's hand with a snap. It cut through the air a scant eight feet, jerked to a stop against Jurgens' forehead and clattered onto the top of the desk, while Jurgens folded over, his mouth still open, his hand slumping out of the drawer. The club rolled toward Gordon, who caught it before it could reach the floor.

But Jurgens was only momentarily out. As Gordon slipped the loop over his wrist again, one of the new captain's hands groped, seeking a button on the edge of the desk.

The two corporals were at the door when Gordon threw it open, but they drew back at the sight of his drawn gun. Feet were pounding below as he found the entrance that led to the truck. He hit the seat and rammed down the throttle with his foot before he could get his hands on the wheel.

It was a full minute before sirens sounded behind him, and Nick the Croop had fast trucks. He spotted the squad car far behind, ducked through a maze of alleys, and lost it for another few precious minutes. Then a barricade lay ahead.

The truck faltered as it hit the nearly finished obstacle, and Gordon felt his stomach squashing down onto the wheel. He kept his foot to the floor, strewing bits of the barricade behind him, until he was beyond the range of the Legal guns that were firing suddenly. Then he stopped and got out carefully, with his hands up.

"Captain Bruce Gordon, with two prisoners-bodyguards of Captain Jurgens," he reported to the three men in bright new Legal uniform who were approaching warily. "How do I sign up with you?"

Chapter XIII
Arrest Mayor Wayne!

The Legal forces were shorthanded and eager for recruits. They had struck quickly, according to plans made by experts on Earth, and now controlled about half of Marsport. But it was a sprawling crescent around the central section, harder to handle than the Municipal territory. Bruce Gordon was sworn in at once.

Then he cooled his heels while the florid, paunchy ex-politician Commissioner Crane worried about his rating and repeated how corrupt Mars was and how the collection system was over-absolutely over. In the end, he was given a captain's pay and the rank of sergeant. As a favor, he was allowed to share a beat with Honest Izzy under Captain Hendrix, who had simply switched sides after losing the morning's battle.

Gordon's credits were changed to Legal scrip, and he was issued a trim-fitting green uniform. Then a surprisingly competent doctor examined his wound, rebandaged it, and sent him home for the day. The change was finished-and he felt like a grown man playing with dolls.

He walked back, watching the dull-looking people closing off their homes, as they had done at elections. Here and there, houses had been broken into during the night. There were occasional buzzes of angry conversation that cut off as he approached.

Marsport had learned to hate all cops, and a change of uniform hadn't altered that; instead, the people seemed to resent the loss of the familiar symbol of hatred.

He found Izzy and Randolph at the restaurant across from Mother Corey's. Izzy grinned suddenly at the sight of the uniform. "I knew it, gov'nor-knew it the minute I heard Jurgens was a cop. Did you make 'em give you my beat?"

He seemed genuinely pleased as Gordon nodded, and then dropped it, to point to Randolph. "Guess what, gov'nor. The Legals bought Randy's *Crusader*. Traded him an old job press and a bag of scratch for his reputation."

"You'll be late, Izzy," Randolph said quietly. Gordon suddenly realized that Randolph, like everyone else, seemed to be Izzy's friend. He watched the little man leave, and reached out for the menu. Randolph picked it out of his hand. "You've got a wife home, muckraker. You don't have to eat this filth."

Gordon got up, grimacing at the obvious dismissal. But the publisher motioned him back again.

"Yeah, the Legals want the *Crusader* for their propaganda," he said wearily. "New slogans and new uniforms, and none of them mean anything. Here!" He drew a small golden band from his little finger. "My mother's wedding ring. Give it to her-and if you tell her it came from me, I'll rip out your guts!"

He got up suddenly and hobbled out, his pinched face working. Gordon turned the ring over, puzzled. Finally he got up and headed for his room, a little surprised to find the door unlocked. Sheila opened her eyes at his uniform, but made no comment. "Food ready in ten minutes," she told him.

She'd already been shopping, and had installed the tiny cooking equipment used in half Marsport. There was also a small iron lying beside a pile of his laundered clothes. He dropped onto the bed wearily, then jerked upright as she came over to remove his boots. But there was no mockery on her face-and oddly, it felt good to him. Maybe her idea of married life was different from his.

She was sanding the dishes and putting them away when he finally remembered the ring. He studied it again, then got up and dropped it beside her. He was surprised as she fumbled it on to see that it fitted-and more surprised at the sudden realization that she was entitled to it.

She studied it under the glare of the single bulb, and then turned to her room. She was back a few seconds later with a small purse. "I got a duplicate key. Yours is in there," she said thickly. "And-something else. I guess I was going to give it to you anyway. I was afraid someone else might find it —"

He cut her off brusquely, his eyes riveted on the Security badge he'd been sure Trench had taken. "Yeah, I know. Your meal ticket was in danger. Okay, you've done your nightly duty. Now get the hell out of my room, will you?"

The week went on mechanically, while he gradually adjusted to the new angles of being a Legal. The banks were open, and deposits honored, as promised. But it was in the printing-press scrip of Legal currency, useful only through Mayor Gannett's trick Exchanges. Water went up from fourteen credits to eighty credits for a gallon of pure distilled. Other things were worse. Resentment flared, but the scrip was the only money available, and it still bound the people to the new regime.

Supplies were scarce, salt and sugar almost unavailable. Earth had cut off all shipping until the affair was settled, and nobody in the outlands would deal in scrip.

He came home the third evening to find that Sheila had managed to find space for her bunk in his room, cut off by a heavy screen, and had closed the other room to save the rent. It led to some relaxation between them, and they began talking impersonally.

Gordon watched for a sign that Trench had passed on his evidence of the murder of Murdoch, but there was none. The pressure of the beat took his mind from it. Looting had stepped up.

Izzy had co-operated —reluctantly, until Gordon was able to convince him that it was the people who paid his salary. Then he nodded. "It's a helluva roundabout way of doing things, gov'nor, but if the gees pay for protection any old way, then they're gonna get it!"

They got it. Hoodlums began moving elsewhere, toward easier pickings.

Gordon turned his entire pay over to Sheila; at current prices, it would barely keep them in food for a week. "I told you you had a punched meal ticket," he said bitterly.

"We'll live," she answered him. "I got a job today-barmaid, on your beat, where being your wife helps."

He could think of nothing to say to it; but after supper, he went to Izzy's room to arrange for a raid on Municipal territory. Such small raids were nominally on the excuse of extending the boundaries, but actually they were out-and-out looting.

He came back to find her cleaning up, and shoved her away. "Go to bed. You look beat. I'll sand these."

She started to protest, then let him take over.

They never made the looting raid. The next morning, they arrived at the Precinct house to find men milling around the bulletin board, buzzing over an announcement there. Apparently, Chief Justice Arliss had broken with the Wayne administration, and the mimeographed form was a legal ruling that Wayne was no longer Mayor, since the charter had been voided. He was charged with inciting a riot, and a warrant had been issued for his arrest.

Hendrix appeared finally. "All right, men," he shouted. "You all see it. We're going to arrest Wayne. By jingo, they can't say we ain't legal now! Every odd-numbered shield goes from every precinct. Gordon, Isaacs-you two been talking big about law and order. Here's the warrant. Take it and arrest Wayne!"

It took nearly an hour to get the plans settled, but finally they headed for the trucks that had been arriving. Most of them belonged to Nick the Croop, who had apparently decided the Legals would win.

Gordon and Izzy found the lead truck and led the way. They neared the bar where Sheila was working, and Bruce Gordon swore. She was running toward the center of the street, frantically trying to flag him down, and he barely managed to swerve around her. "Damned fool!" he muttered.

Izzy's pock-marked face soured for a second as he stared at Gordon. "The princess? She sure is."

The crew at the barricade had been alerted, and now began clearing it aside hastily, while others kept up a covering fire against the few Municipals. The trucks wheeled through, and

Gordon dropped back to let scout trucks go ahead and pick off any rash enough to head for the call boxes. They couldn't prevent advance warning, but they could delay and minimize it.

They were near the big Municipal building when they came to the first real opposition, and it was obviously hastily assembled. The scouts took care of most of the trouble, though a few shots pinged against the truck Gordon was driving.

"Rifles!" Izzy commented in disgust. "They'll ruin the dome yet. Why can't they stick to knives?"

He was studying a map of the big building, picking their best entrance. Ahead, trucks formed a sort of V formation as they reached the grounds around it and began bulling their way through the groups that were trying to organize a defense. Gordon found his way cleared and shot through, emerging behind the defense and driving at full speed toward the entrance Izzy pointed out.

"Cut speed! Left sharp!" Izzy shouted. "Now, in there!"

They sliced into a small tunnel, scraping their sides where it was barely big enough for the truck. Then they reached a dead end, with just room for them to squeeze through the door of the truck and into an entrance marked with a big notice of privacy.

There was a guard beside an elevator, but Izzy's knife took care of him. They ducked around the elevator, unsure of whether it could be remotely controlled, and up a narrow flight of stairs, down a hallway, and up another flight. A Municipal corporal at the top grabbed for a warning whistle, but Gordon clipped him with a hasty rabbit punch and shoved him down the stairs. Then they were in front of an ornate door, with their weapons ready.

Izzy yanked the door open and dropped flat behind it. Bullets from a submachine gun clipped out, peppering the entrance and the door, and ricocheting down the hall. The yammering stopped, finally, and Izzy stuck his head and one arm out with a snap of his knife. Gordon leaped in, to see a Municipal dropping the machine gun.

There were about thirty cops inside, gathered around Mayor Wayne, with Trench standing at one side. The fools had obviously expected the machine gun to do all the work.

Izzy leaped for the machine gun and yanked it from dead hands, while the cops slowly began raising their arms. Wayne sat petrified, staring unbelievingly, and Gordon drew out the warrant. "Wayne, you're under arrest!"

Trench moved forward, his hands in the air, but with no mark of surprise or fear on his face. "So the bad pennies turn up. You damned fools, you should have stuck. I had big plans for you, Gordon. I've still got them, if you don't insist..."

His hands whipped down savagely toward his hips and came up sharply! Gordon spun, and the gun leaped in his hands, while the submachine gun jerked forward and clicked on an empty chamber. Trench was tumbling forward to avoid the shot, but he twitched as a bullet creased his shoulder. Then he was upright, waving empty hands at them, with the thin smile on his face deepening. He'd had no guns.

Gordon jerked around, but Wayne was already disappearing through a heavy door. And the cops were reaching for their guns. Gordon estimated the chances of escape and then leaped forward into their group, with Izzy at his side, seeking close quarters where guns wouldn't work.

Gun butts, elbows, fists, and clubs were pounding at him, while his own club lashed out savagely. In ten seconds, things began to haze over, but his arms went on mechanically, seeking the most damage they could work.

Then a heavy bellow sounded, and a seeming mountain of flesh thundered across the huge room. There was no shuffle to Mother Corey now. The huge legs pumped steadily, and the great arms were reaching out to flail aside clubs and knives. Men began spewing out of the brawl like straw from a thresher as the old man grabbed arms, legs, or whatever was handy. He had one cop in his left arm, using him as a flail against the others.

The Municipals broke. And at the first sign, Mother Corey leaped forward, dropping his flail and gathering Izzy and Gordon under his arms. He hit the heavy door with his shoulder and crashed through without breaking stride. Stairs lay there, and he took them three at a time.

He dropped them finally as they came to a side entrance. There was a sporadic firing going on there, and a knot of Municipals were clustered around a few Legals, busy with knives and clubs. Corey broke into a run again, driving straight into them and through, with Gordon and Izzy on his heels. The surprise element was enough to give them a few seconds.

Then they were around a small side building, out of danger. Sheila was holding the door of a large three-wheeler open. They ducked into it, while she grabbed the wheel.

They edged forward until they could make out the shape of the fight going on. The Legals had never quite reached the front of the building, obviously, and were now cut into sections. Corey tapped her shoulder, pointing out the rout, and she gunned the car.

They were through too fast to draw fire from the busy groups of battle-crazed men, leaping across the square and into the first side street they could find. Then she slowed, and headed for the main street back to Legal territory.

"Lucky we found a good car to steal," Mother Corey wheezed. He was puffing now, mopping rivulets of perspiration from his face. "I'm getting old, cobbers. Once I broke every strong-man record on Earth-still stand, too. But not now. Senile!"

"You didn't have to come," Izzy said.

"When my own granddaughter comes crying for help? When she finally admits she *needs* her old grandfather?"

Gordon was staring back at the straggling of trucks he could see beginning to break away. The raid was over, and the Legals had lost. Trench had tricked him.

Izzy grunted suddenly. "Gov'nor, if you're right, and the plain gees pay my salary, who's paying me to start fighting other cops? Or is it maybe that somebody isn't being exactly honest with the scratch they lift from the gees?"

"We still have to eat," Gordon said bitterly. "And to eat, we'll go on doing what we're told."

Chapter XIV
Full Circle

Hendrix had been wounded lightly, and was out when Gordon and Izzy reported. But the next day, they were switched to a new beat where trouble had been thickest and given twelve-hour duty—without special overtime.

Izzy considered it slowly and shook his head. "That does it, gov'nor. It ain't honest, treating us this way. If the crackle comes from the people, and these gees give everybody a skull cracking, then they're crooks. It ain't honest, and I'm too sick to work. And if that bloody doctor won't agree…"

He turned toward the dispensary. Gordon hesitated, and then swung off woodenly to take up his new beat. Apparently, his reputation had gone ahead of him, since most of the hoodlums had decided pickings would be easier on some beat where the cops had their own secret rackets to attend to, instead of head busting. But once they learned he was alone…

But the second day, two of the citizens fell into step behind him almost at once, armed with heavy clubs. Periodically during the shift, replacements took their place, making sure that he was never by himself. It surprised him even more when he saw that a couple of the men had come over from his old beat. Something began to burn inside him, but he held himself in, confining his talk to vague comments on the rumors going around.

There were enough of them, mostly based on truth. Part of Jurgens' old crowd had broken away from him and established a corner on most of the drugs available; they had secretly traded a supply to Wayne, who had become an addict, for a stock of weapons.

Gordon remembered the contraband shipment of guns, and compared it to the increase he'd noticed in weapons, and to the impossible prices the pushers were demanding. It made sense.

All kinds of supplies were low, and the outlands beyond Marsport had cut off all shipments. Scrip was useless to them, and the Legals were raiding all cargoes destined for Wayne's section. And the Municipals had imposed new taxes again.

He came back from what should have been his day off to find Izzy in uniform, waiting grimly. Behind the screen, there was a rustling of clothes, and a dress came sailing from behind it. While he stared, Sheila came out, finishing the zipping of her airsuit. She moved to a small bag and began drawing out the gun she had used and a knife. He caught her shoulders and shoved her back, pulling the weapons from her.

"Get out of my way, you damned Legal machine!" she spat.

"Easy, princess," Izzy said. "He hasn't seen it yet, I guess. Here, gov'nor!"

He picked up a copy of Randolph's new little *Truth* and pointed to the headline: SECURITY DENOUNCES RAPE OF MARSPORT!

The story was somewhat cooler than that, but not much. Randolph simply quoted what was supposed to be an official cable from Security on Earth, denouncing both governments and demanding that both immediately surrender. It listed the crimes of Wayne, then tore into the Legals as a bunch of dupes, sent by North America to foment trouble while they looted the city, and to give the Earth government an excuse for seizing military control of Marsport officially. Citizens were instructed not to co-operate; all members of either government were indicted for high treason to Security!

He crushed the paper slowly, tearing it to bits with his clenched hands; he'd swallowed the implication that the Legals *were* Security…

Then it hit him slowly, and he looked up. "Where's Randolph?"

"At his plant. At least he left for it, according to Sheila."

Gordon picked up Sheila's gun and buckled it on beside his own. She grabbed at it, but he shoved her back again. "You're staying here, Cuddles. You're supposed to be a woman now, remember!"

She was swearing hotly as they left, but made no attempt to follow. Gordon broke into a slow trot behind Izzy, until they could spot one of the few remaining cabs. He stopped it with his whistle, and dumped the passenger out unceremoniously, while Izzy gave the address.

"The damned fool opened up on the border-figured he'd circulate to both sections," Izzy said. "We'd better get out a block up and walk. And I hope we ain't *too* bloody late!"

The building was a wreck, outside; inside it was worse. Men in the Municipal uniform were working over the small job press and dumping the hand-set type from the boxes. On the floor, a single Legal cop lay under the wreckage, apparently having gotten there first and been taken care of by the later Municipals. Randolph had been sitting in a chair between two of the cops, but now he leaped up and tried to flee through the back door.

Izzy started forward, but Gordon pulled him back, as the cops reached for their weapons. The gun in his hand picked them out at quarters too close for a miss, starting with the cop who had jumped to catch Randolph. Izzy had ducked around the side, and now came back, leading the little man.

Randolph paid no attention to the dead men, nor to the bruises on his own body. He moved forward to the press, staring at it, and there were tears in his eyes as he ran his hands over the broken metal. Then he looked up at them. "Arrest or rescue?" he asked.

"Arrest!" a voice from the door said harshly, and Bruce Gordon swung to see six Legals filing in, headed by Hendrix himself. The captain nodded at Gordon. "Good work, Sergeant. By jinx, when I heard the Municipals were coming, I was scared they'd get him for sure. Crane wants to watch this guy shot in person!"

He grabbed Randolph by the arm.

"You're overlooking something, Hendrix," Gordon cut in. He had moved back toward the wall, to face the group. "If you ever look at my record, you'll find I'm an ex-newspaperman myself. This is a rescue. Tie them up, Izzy."

Hendrix was faster than Gordon had thought. He had his gun almost up before Gordon could fire. A bluish hole appeared on the man's forehead; he dropped slowly. The others made no trouble as Izzy bound them with baling wire.

"And I hope nobody finds them," he commented. "All right, Randy, I guess we're a bunch of refugees heading for the outside, and bloody lucky at that. Proves a man shouldn't have friends."

Randolph's face was still greenish-white, but he straightened and managed a feeble smile. "Not to me, Izzy. Right now I can appreciate friends. But you two better get going. I've got some unfinished business to tend to." He moved to one corner and began dragging out an old double-cylinder mimeograph. "Either of you know where I can buy stencils and ink and find some kind of a truck to haul this paper along?"

Izzy stopped and stared at the rabbity, pale little man. Then he let out a sudden yelp of laughter. "Okay, Randy, we'll find them. Gov'nor, you'd better tell my mother I'll be using the old sheets. Go on. You've got the princess to worry about. We'll be along later."

He grabbed Randolph's hand and ducked out the back before Gordon could protest.

Izzy could only have meant that they were going to hole up in Mother Corey's old Chicken Coop. Bruce Gordon had now managed to make a full circle, back to his beginnings on Mars. He'd started at the Coop with a deck of cards; now he was returning with a club.

He had counted on at least some regret from Mother Corey, however. But the old man only nodded after hearing that Randolph was safe. "Fanatics, crusaders and damned fools!" he said. He shook his head sadly and went shuffling back to his room, where two of his part-time henchmen were sitting.

Sheila had been sitting on the bunk, still in her airsuit. Now she jerked upright, then sank back with a slow flush. Her hands were trembling as she reached for a cup of coffee and handed it to him, listening to his quick report of Randolph's safety and the fact that he was going back outside the dome.

"I'm all packed," she said. "And I packed your things, too."

He shot his eyes around the room, realizing that it was practically bare, except for a few of her dresses. She followed his gaze, and shook her head. "I won't need them out there," she said. Her voice caught on that. "They'll be safe here."

"So will you, now that you've made up with the Mother," he told her. "Your meal ticket's ruined, Cuddles, and you made it clear a little while ago just where you stand. Remind me to tell you sometime how much fun it's been."

"Your mother was good with a soldering iron, wasn't she? You even look human." She bent to pick up a shoulder pack and a bag, and her face was normal when she stood up again. "You might guess that the cops would be happy to get hold of your wife now, though. Come on, it's a long walk."

He left the car beyond the gate, and they pushed through the locker room toward the smaller exit, stopping to fasten down their helmets. The guard halted them, but without any suspicion.

"Going hunting for those damned kids, eh?" he said. He stared at Sheila. "Lucky devil! All I got for a guide was an old bum. Okay, luck, Sergeant!"

It made no sense to Gordon, but he wasn't going to argue. They went through and out into the waste and slums beyond the domes, heading out until there were only the few phosphor bulbs to guide their way.

Gordon was moving cautiously, using his helmet light only occasionally, gun ready in his hand. But it was Sheila who caught the faint sound. He heard her cry out, and turned to see her crash into the stomach of a man with a half-raised stick. He went down with almost no resistance. Sheila shot the beam of her light on the thin, drawn face. "Rusty!"

"Hi, princess." He got up slowly, trying to grin. "Didn't know who it was. Sorry. Ever get that louse you were out for?"

She nodded. "Yeah, I got him. That's him-my husband! What's wrong with you, Rusty? You've lost fifty pounds, and —"

"Things are a mite tough out here, princess. No deliveries. Closed my bar, been living sort of hand to mouth, but not much mouth." His eyes bulged greedily as she dug into a bag and began to drag out the sandwiches she must have packed for the trip. But he shook his head. "I ain't so bad off. I ate something yesterday. But if you can spare something for the Kid-Hey, Kid!"

A thin boy of about sixteen crept out from behind some rubble, staring uncertainly. Then, at the sight of the food, he made a lunge, grabbed it, and hardly waited to get it through the slits of his suit before gulping it down. Rusty sat down, his lined old face breaking into a faint grin. He hesitated, but finally took some of the food.

"Shouldn't oughta. You'll need it. Umm." He swallowed slowly, as if tasting the food all the way down. "Kid can't talk. Cop caught him peddling one of Randolph's pamphlets, cut out part of his tongue. But he's all right now. Come on, Kid, hurry it up. We gotta convoy these people."

They were following a kind of road when headlights bore down on them. Gordon's hand was on his gun as they leaped for shelter, but there was no hostile move from the big truck. He studied it, trying to decide what a truck would be doing here. Then a Marspeaker-amplified voice shouted from it. "Any muckrakers there?"

"One," Gordon shouted back, and ran toward it, motioning the others to follow. He'd always objected to the nickname, but it made a good code. Randolph's frail hand came down to help them up, but a bigger paw did the actual lifting.

"Why didn't you two wait?" Mother Corey asked, his voice booming out of his Marspeaker. "I figured Izzy'd stop by first. Here, sit over there. Not much room, with my stuff and Randolph's, but it beats walking."

"What in hell brings you back?" Gordon asked.

The huge man shrugged ponderously. "A man gets tired of being respectable, cobber. And I'm getting old and sentimental about the Chicken Coop." He chuckled, rubbing his hands together. "But not so old that I can't handle a couple of guards that are stubborn about trucks, eh, Izzy?"

"Messy, but nice," Izzy agreed from the pile above them. "Tell those trained apes of yours to cut the lights, will you, Mother? Somebody must be using the Coop."

They stopped the truck before reaching the old wreck. In the few dim lights, the old building still gave off an air of mold and decay. Gordon shuddered faintly, then followed Izzy and the Mother into the semi-secret entrance.

Izzy went ahead, almost silent, with a thin strand of wire between his hands, his elbows weaving back and forth slowly to guide him. He was apparently as familiar with the garrote as the knife. But they found no guard. Izzy pressed the seal release and slid in cautiously, while the others followed.

In the beam of Gordon's torch, a single figure lay sprawled out on the floor halfway to the rickety stairs to the main house. Mother Corey grunted, and moved quickly to the coughing, battered old air machine. His fingers closed a valve equipped with a combination lock.

"They're all dead, cobbers," he wheezed. "Dead because a crook had to try his hand on a lock. Years ago, I had a flask of poison gas attached, in case a gang should ever squeeze me out."

In the filthy rooms above, Gordon found the corpses-about fifteen of them, and some former members of the Jurgens organization. He found the apelike bodyguard stretched out on a bunk, a vacant smile on his face.

A yell from the basement called him back down to where Izzy was busily going through piles of crates and boxes stacked along one wall. He was pointing to a lead-foil-covered box. "Dope! And all that other stuff's ammunition!"

He shivered, staring at the fortune in his hands. Then he grimaced and shoved the open can back in its case. He threw it back and began stacking ammunition cases in front of the dope. Gordon went out to get the others and start moving in the supplies and transferring the corpses to the truck for disposal. Randolph scurried off to start setting up his makeshift plant in the basement.

Mother Corey was staring about when they returned. "Filthy," he wailed. "A pigpen. They've ruined the Coop, cobber. Smell that air-even *I* can smell it!" He sniffed dolefully.

Mother Corey sighed again. "Well, it'll give the boys something to do," he decided. "When a man gets old, he likes a little comfort, cobber. Nice things around him..."

Gordon found what had been his old room and dumped his few things into it. Sheila watched him uncertainly, and then took possession of the next room. She came back a few minutes later, staring at the ages-old filth. "I'll be cleaning for a week," she said. "What are you going to do now, Bruce?"

He shook his head, and started back down the stairs. He hurried down into the basement where Randolph was arranging his mimeograph.

The printer listened only to the first sentence, and shook his head impatiently. "I was afraid you'd think of that, Gordon. Look, you never were a reporter-you ran a column. I've read the stuff you wrote. You killed and maimed with words. But you never dug up news that would help people, or tell them what they didn't suspect all along. And that's what I've got to have."

"Thanks!" Gordon said curtly. "Too bad Security didn't think I was as lousy a reporter as you do!"

"Okay. I'll give you a job, for one week. See what outer Marsport is like. Find what can be done, if anything, and do it if you can. Then come back and give me six columns on it. I'll pay Mother Corey for your food-and for your wife's —and if I can find one column's worth of news in it, maybe I'll give you a second week. I can't see a man's wife starve because he doesn't know how to make an honest living!"

———————————————————————

Rusty and one of Mother Corey's men were on guard, and the others had turned in. Gordon went up the stairs and threw himself onto the bed in disgust.

"Bruce!" Sheila stood outlined in the doorway against the dim glow of a phosphor bulb. Her robe was partly open, and hunger burned in him; then, before he could lift himself, she bent over and began unfastening his boots. "You all right, Bruce? I heard you tossing around."

"I'm fine," he told her mechanically. "Just making plans for tomorrow."

He watched her turn back slowly, then lay quietly, trying not to disturb her again. Tomorrow, he thought. Tomorrow he'd find some kind of an answer; and it wouldn't be Randolph's charity.

Chapter XV
Murdoch's Mantle

There were three men, each with a white circle painted on chest and left arm, talking to Mother Corey when Bruce Gordon came down the rickety steps. He stopped for a second, but there was no sign of trouble. Then the words of the thin man below reached him.

"So we figured when we found the stiffs maybe you'd come back, Mother. Damn good thing we were right. We can sure use that ammunition you found. Now, where's this Gordon fellow?"

"Here!" Gordon told the man. He'd recognized him finally as Schulberg, the little grocer from the Nineteenth Precinct.

The man swung suspiciously, then grinned weakly. There was hunger and strain on his face, but an odd authority and pride now. "I'll be doggoned. Whyn't you say he was with Murdoch?"

"They want someone to locate Ed Praeger and see about getting some food shipped in from outside, cobber," Mother Corey told him. "They got some money scraped together, but the hicks are doing no business with Marsport. You know Ed-just tell him I sent you. I'd go myself, but I'm getting too old to go chasing men out there."

"What's in it?" Gordon asked, reaching for his helmet.

There was a surprised exchange of glances from the others, but Mother Corey chuckled. "Heart like a steel trap, cobber," he said, almost approvingly. "Well, you'll be earning your keep here-yours and that granddaughter's, too. Here-you'll need directions for finding Praeger."

He handed the paper with his scrawled notes on it over to Gordon and went shuffling back. Gordon stuck it into his pouch, and followed the three. Outside, they had a truck waiting; Rusty and Corey's two henchmen were busy loading it with ammunition from the cellar.

Schulberg motioned him into the cab of the truck, and the other two climbed into the closed rear section. "All right," Gordon said, "what goes on?"

The other began explaining as he picked a way through the ruin and rubble. Murdoch had done better than Gordon had suspected; he'd laid out a program for a citizens' vigilante committee, and had drilled enough in the ruthless use of the club to keep the gangs down. Once the police were all busy inside the dome with their private war, the committee had been the only means of keeping order in the whole territory beyond. It was now extended to cover about half the area, as a voluntary police organization.

He pointed outside. It was changed; there were fewer people outside. Gordon had never seen group starvation before....

They passed a crowd around a crude gallows, and Schulberg stopped. A man was already dead and dangling. "Should turn 'em over to us cops," Schulberg said. "What's he hanged for?"

"Hoarding," a voice answered, and others supplied the few details. The dead man had been caught with a half bag of flour and part of a case of beans. Schulberg found a scrap of something and penciled the crime on it, together with a circle signature, and pinned it to the body.

"All food should be turned in," he explained to Gordon as they climbed back into the truck. "We figure community kitchens can stretch things a bit more. And we give a half extra ration to the guys who can find anything useful to do. We got enough so most people won't starve to death for another week, I guess. But you'd better get Praeger to send something, Gordon. Here, here's the scratch we scraped up."

He passed over a bag filled with a collection of small bills and coins. "We can trust you, I guess," he said dully. "Remember you with Murdoch, anyhow. And you can tell Praeger we got plenty of men looking for work, in case he can use 'em."

He pulled up to shout a report through the big Marspeaker as they passed the old building Murdoch had used as a precinct house. It now had a crude sign proclaiming it voluntary police HQ and outland government center. Then he went on until they came to a spur of the little electric monorail system, with three abandoned service engines parked at the end.

"Extra air inside, and the best we could do for food. Was gonna try myself, but I don't know Praeger," Schulberg said. He handed over a key, and nodded toward the first service engine.

"Good luck, Gordon-and damn it, we're-we gotta eat, don't we? You tell him that! It ain't much-but get what you can!"

He swung the truck, and was gone. Gordon climbed into the enclosed cab and pulled back questioningly on the only lever he could see. The engine backed briefly; he reversed the control. Then it moved forward, picking up speed. Apparently there was still power flowing in from the automatic atomic generators.

He got off to puzzle out a switch, using Mother Corey's scrawled instructions.

He had vaguely expected to see more of Mars, but for eight hours there was only the bare flatness and dunes of unending sandy surface and scraggly, useless native plants, opened out to the sun. Marsport had been located where the only vein of uranium had been found on Mars, and the growing section was closer to the equator.

Then he came to villages. Again there was the sight of children running around without helmets. He stopped once for directions, and a man stared at him suspiciously and finally threw a switch reluctantly.

He was finally forced to stop again, sure that he was near, now. This time, it was in what seemed to be a major shipping center in the heart of the lines that ran helter-skelter from village to village. Another suspicious-eyed man studied him. "You won't find Praeger on his farm-couldn't reach it in that, anyhow," he said finally. Then he turned up his Marspeaker. "Ed! Hey, Ed!"

Down the street, the seal of a building opened, and the big, bluff figure of Praeger came out. His eyes narrowed as he spotted Gordon; then he grinned and waved his visitor forward.

Inside, there was evidence of food, and a rather pretty girl brought out another platter and set it before Gordon. He ate while they exchanged uncertain, rambling information; finally, he got down to his errand.

Praeger seemed to read his mind. "I can get the stuff sent, Gordon. I'm head of the shipping committee for this quadrant. But why in hell should I? The last time, every car was looted in Outer Marsport. If they won't let us get the oil and chemicals we need, why should we feed them?"

"Ever see starvation?" Gordon asked, wishing again someone else who'd felt it could carry the message. He told about a man who'd committed suicide for his kids, not stopping as Praeger's face sickened slowly. "Hell, who wouldn't loot your trains if that's going on?"

"All right, if Mother Corey'll back up this volunteer police group. I've got kids of my own.... Look, you want food, we want to ship. Get your cops to give us an escort for every shipment through to the dome, and we'll drop off one car out of four for the outlands."

Gordon sat back weakly. "Done!" he said. "Provided the first shipment carries the most we can get for the credits I brought."

"It will-we've got some stuff that's about to spoil, and we can let you have a whole train of it." He took the sack of credits and tossed it toward a drawer, uncounted. "A damned good thing Security's sending a ship. Credits won't be worth much until they get this mess straightened out."

Gordon felt the hair at the base of his neck tingle. "What makes you think Security can do anything? They haven't shown a hand yet."

"They will," Praeger said. "You guys in Marsport feed yourselves so many lies you begin to believe them. But Security took Venus-and I'm not worried here, in the long run. Don't ask me how."

His voice was a mixture of bitterness and an odd certainty. "They set Security up as a nice little debating society, Gordon, to make it easy for North America to grab the planets by doing it through that Agency. Only they got better men on it than they wanted. So far, Security has played one nation against another enough to keep any from daring to swipe power on the planets. And this latest trick folded up, too. North America figured on Marsport folding up once they got a police war started, with a bunch of chiseling profiteers as their front; they expected the citizens to yell uncle all the way back to Earth. But out here, nobody thinks of Earth as a place to yell to for help, so they missed. And now Security's got Pan-Asia and United Africa balanced against North America, so the swipe won't work. We got the dope from our southern receiver. North America's called it all a mistaken emergency measure and turned it back to Security."

"Along with how many war rockets?" Gordon asked.

"None. They never gave any real power, never will. The only strength Security's ever had comes from the fact that it always wins, somehow. Forget the crooks and crooked cops, man! Ask the people who've been getting kicked around about Security, and you'll find that even most of Marsport doesn't hate it! It's the only hope we've got of not having all the planets turned into colonial empires! You staying over, or want me to give you an engineer and drag car so you can ride back in comfort?"

Gordon stared at the room, where almost everything was a product of the planet, at Praeger, and at the girl. Here was the real Mars-the men who liked it here, who were sure of their future. "I'll take the drag car."

He found Randolph waiting in a scooter outside the precinct house after he'd reported his results. He climbed in woodenly, leaving his helmet on as he saw the broken window. "A good job," the little man said. "And news for the paper, if I ever publish it again. I came over because I wasn't much use at the Coop, and everyone else was busy."

"Doing what?" Gordon asked.

Randolph grinned crookedly. "Running Outer Marsport. The Mother's the only man everybody knows, I guess-and his word has never been broken that anyone can remember. So he's helping Schulberg make agreements with the sections the volunteers don't handle. Place is lousy with people now. Heard about Mayor Wayne?"

Gordon shook his head, not caring, but the man went on. "He must have had his supply of drugs lifted somehow. He holed up one day, until it really hit him that he couldn't get any more. Then he went gunning for Trench, with some idea Trench had swiped the stuff-so Trench is now running the Municipals. And I hear the gangs are just about in control of both sections, lately."

The Chicken Coop was filled, as Randolph had said, but he slipped in and up the stairs, leaving the news to the publisher. The place had been cleaned up more than he had expected, and there must have been new plants installed beside the blower, since the air was somewhat fresher.

He found his own room, and turned in automatically...

"Bruce?" A dim light snapped on, and he stared down at Sheila. Then he blinked. His bunk had been changed to a wider one, and she lay under the thin covering on one side. Down the center, crude stitches of heavy cord showed where she had sewed the blanket to the mattress to divide it into two sections. And in one corner, a couple of blanket sections formed a rough screen.

She caught his stare and reddened slowly. "I had to, Bruce. The Coop is full, and they needed rooms-and I couldn't tell them that-that —"

"Forget it," he told her. He dropped to his own side, with barely enough room to slide between the bed and the wall, and began dragging off his boots and uniform. She started up to help him, then jerked back, and turned her head away. "Forget all you're thinking, Cuddles. I'm still not bothering unwilling women-and I'll even close my eyes when you dress."

She sighed, and relaxed. There was a faint touch of humor in her voice then. "They called it bundling once, I think. I —Bruce, I know you don't like me, so I guess it isn't too hard for you. But-sometimes ...Oh, damn it! Sometimes you're-nice!"

"Nice people don't get to Mars. They stay on Earth, being careful not to find out what it's like up here," he told her bitterly. For a second he hesitated, and then the account of the newsboy and his would-be killers came rushing out.

She dropped a hand onto his, nodding. "I know. The Kid-Rusty's friend-wrote down what they did to him."

Gordon grunted. He'd almost forgotten about the tongueless Kid. For a second, his thoughts churned on. Then he got up and began putting on his uniform again. Sheila frowned, staring at him, and began sliding from her side, reaching for her robe. She followed him down the creaking stairs, and to the room where Schulberg, Mother Corey, and a few others were still arguing some detail.

They looked up, and he moved forward, dragging a badge from his pouch. He slapped it down on the table in front of them. "I'm declaring myself in!" he told them coldly. "You know enough about Security badges to know they can't be forged. That one has my name on it, and rating as a Prime. Do you want to shoot me, or will you follow orders?"

Randolph picked it up, and fumbled in his pocket, drawing out a tiny badge and comparing them. He nodded. "I lost connection years ago, Gordon. But this makes you my boss."

"Then give it all the publicity you can, and tell them Security has just declared war on the whole damned dome section! Mother, I want all the dope we found!" With that-about the only supply of any size left-he could command unquestioning loyalty from every addict who hadn't already died from lack of it. Mother Corey nodded, instant understanding running over his puttylike face.

Schulberg shrugged. "After your deal with Praeger, we'd probably follow you anyhow. I don't cotton to Security, Gordon-but those devils in there are making our kids starve!"

Mother Corey heaved his bulk up slowly, wheezing, and indicated his chair at the head of the table. But Gordon shook his head. He'd made his decision. His head was emptied for the moment, and he wanted nothing more than a chance to hit the bed and forget the whole business until morning.

Sheila was staring at him as he shucked off his outer clothes mechanically and crawled under the blanket. She let the robe fall to the floor and slid into the bed without taking her eyes off him. "Is it true about Security sending a ship?" she asked at last. He nodded, and her breath caught. "What happens when they arrive, Bruce?"

She was shivering. He rolled over and patted her shoulder. "Who knows? Who cares? I'll see that they know you weren't guilty, though. Stop worrying about it."

She threw herself sideways, as far from him as she could get. Her voice was thick, muffled in the blanket. "Damn you, Bruce Gordon. I *should* have killed you!"

Chapter XVI
Get the Dome!

To Gordon's surprise, the publicity Randolph wrote about his being a Security Prime seemed to bring the other sections of Outer Marsport under the volunteer police control even faster. But he was too busy to worry about it. He left general co-ordination in the hands of Mother Corey, while Izzy and Schulberg ran the expanding of the police force.

Praeger arrived with the first load of food, and came storming up to him. "Why didn't you tell me you were a Security Prime! I'm grade three myself."

"And I suppose that would have meant you'd have shipped in all the food we needed free?" Gordon asked.

The other stopped to think it over. Then he laughed roughly. "Nope. You're right. The growers would starve next year if they gave it all away now. Well, we'll get in enough food this way to keep you going for a while-couple of weeks, at least."

It sounded good, and might have worked if there had been the normal food reserve, or if the other three quadrants had been willing to do as much. But while the immediate pressure of starvation was lifted, Gordon's own stomach told him that it wasn't an adequate diet. Signs of scurvy and pellagra were increasing.

Bruce Gordon whipped himself into forgetting some of that. His army was growing. Or rather, his mob. There was no sense in trying to get more than the vaguest organization.

It was the eighth day when he led them out in the early dawn. He had issued extra dope and managed a slight increase in the ration, so they made a brave showing-until they reached the dome.

There were no rifles opposed to him, as he had expected, and the guard at the gate was no heavier. But the warning had somehow been given, and both forces were ready.

Stretching north from the gate were the Municipals with members of some of the gangs; the other gangmen were with the Legals to the south. And they stood within inches of the dome, holding axes and knives.

A big Marspeaker ran out from the gate, and the voice of Gannett came over it. "Go back! If just one of you gets within ten feet of the dome or entrance, we're going to rip the dome! We'll destroy Marsport before we'll give in to a doped-up crowd of riffraff! You've got five minutes to get out of sight, before we come out with rifles and knock you off! Now beat it!"

Gordon got out of the car the Kid was driving and started toward the entrance, just as the moaning wail of the crowd behind him built up.

"You fools!" he yelled. "They're bluffing. They wouldn't dare destroy the dome! Come on!"

But already the men were evaporating. He stared at the rout, and suddenly stopped fighting the hands holding him. Beside him, the Kid was crying, making horrible sounds of it. He turned slowly back to the car, and felt it get under way. His final sight was that of the Legals and Municipals wildly scrambling for cover from each other.

Mother Corey met him, dragging him back to a small room where he dug up an impossibly precious bottle of brandy. "Drink it all, cobber. So one of your Security badges had the wrong man attached to it, and word got back. Couldn't be helped. You just ran into the sacred law of Marsport-the one they teach kids. Be bad, and the dome'll collapse. The dome made Marsport, and it's taboo!"

Gordon nodded. Maybe the old man was right. "If the dome gives them a perfect cover, why let me make a jackass of myself, Mother?" he asked numbly.

Corey shook his head, setting the heavy folds of flesh to bouncing. "Gave them something to live for here, cobber. And when you get over this, you're gonna announce new plans to try again. Yes, you are! But right now, you get yourself drunk!"

He left Gordon and the bottle. After a while, the bottle was gone. He felt number, but no better, by the time Izzy came in.

"Trench is outside in a heavy-armored car, Bruce. Says he wants to see you. Something to discuss—a proposition!"

Gordon stood up, wobbling a little, trying to think. Then he swore, and headed for his room. "Tell him to go to hell!"

He saw Izzy and Sheila leave, wondering vaguely where she had been. Through the opening in the seal, he spotted them moving toward the big car outside. Then he shrugged. He finally made the stairs and reached his bed before he passed out.

Sheila was standing over him when he finally woke. She dumped a headache powder into her palm and held it out, handing him a small glass of water. He swallowed the fast-acting drug, and sat up, trying to remember. Then he wished he couldn't.

"What did Trench want?" he asked thickly.

"He wanted to show you a badge—a Security badge made out for him," she answered. "At least he said he wanted to show you something, and it was about that size. He wouldn't talk with us much. But I remember his name in the book—"

Gordon shook his head and sat up. The book, he thought, trying to focus his thoughts. The book with all the names...

"All right, Cuddles," he said finally. "You got your meal ticket, and you've outgrown it in this mess. Now I want that damned book! I've been operating in the dark. It's time I found out how to get in touch with some of those people. Where is it?"

She shook her head. "It isn't. Bruce—I don't have it. That time I gave you the note, you didn't come when I said, and I thought you wouldn't. Then Jurgens' men broke in, and I thought they'd get it, so-so I burned it. I lied to you about using it to make you keep me."

"You burned it!" He turned it over, staring at her. "Okay, Cuddles, you burned it. You were trying to kill me then, so you burned it to keep Jurgens from getting it and putting the finger on me! Where is it, Sheila? On you?"

She backed away, biting her lips. "No, Bruce. I burned it. I don't know why. I just did! No!"

She turned toward the door as he pushed up from the bed, but his arm caught her wrist, dragging her back. She whimpered once, then shrieked faintly as his hand caught the buttons on the dress, jerking them off. Then suddenly she was a writhing, biting, scratching fury. He tightened his hand and lifted her to the bed, dropping a knee onto her throat and beginning to squeeze, while he jerked the dress and thin slip off.

She sat up as he released his knee, her hoarse voice squeezed from between her writhing lips. "Are you satisfied now, you mechanical beast! Do you still think I have it on me?"

He grinned, twisting the corners of his mouth. "You don't. Don't you know a *wife* shouldn't keep secrets from her *husband*? A warm-blooded, affectionate husband, to boot." He bent down, knocking aside her flailing arms, and pulled her closer to him. "Better tell your husband where the book is, Cuddles!"

She cursed and he drew her closer. He bent down, forcing her head back and setting his lips on hers.

From somewhere, wetness touched his cheek; he lifted his head and looked down. The wetness came from tears that spilled out of her eyes and ran off onto the mattress. She was making no sound, and there was no resistance, but the tears ran out, one drop seeming to trip over another.

"All right, Sheila," he said. His voice was cracked in his ears. "Another week of being a failure on this planet of failures, and I might. Go ahead and tell me I'm the same as your first husband. If I can't even keep my word to you, I can at least get out and stay out." He shook his head, waiting for her denunciation. "For your amusement, I'm going to miss having you around!"

He stood up. Something touched his hand, and he looked down to see her fingers.

"Bruce," she said faintly, "you meant it! You don't hate me any more." She rubbed her wrist across her eyes, and the ghost of a smile touched her lips. "I don't think you're a failure. And maybe-maybe I'm not. Maybe I don't have to be a failure as a woman—a wife, Bruce. I don't want you to go!"

Two worlds. One huddled under its dome, forever afraid of losing that protection and having to face the life the other led; and yet driven to work together or to perish together. The sacred dome!

And suddenly he was shaking her. "The dome! It has to be the answer! Cuddles, you broke the chain enough for me to think again! We've been blind-the whole damned planet has been blind."

She blinked and then frowned. "Bruce —"

"I'm all right! I'm just half sane instead of all insane for a change." He got up, pacing the floor as he talked.

"Look, most of the people here are Martians. They've left Earth behind, and they're meeting this planet on its own terms. And they're adapting. Third-generation children-not all, but a lot of them-are breathing the air we'd die on, and they're doing fine at it. Probably second-generation ones can keep going after we'd pass out. It's just as true out here as it is on the frontier. But Marsport has that sacred dome over it. It's still trying to be Earth. And it can't do it. It's never had a chance to adjust here, and it's afraid to try."

"Maybe," she agreed doubtfully. "But what about this part of Marsport?"

"Obvious. Here, they grow up under the shadow of it. They live in a half-world, and they have to live on the crumbs the dome tosses them. Sheila, if something happened to that dome —"

"We'd be killed," she said. "How do we do it?"

He frowned, and then grinned slowly. "Maybe not!"

They spent the rest of the night discussing it. Sometime during the discussion, she made coffee, and first Randolph, then the Kid came in for briefing. Randolph was a natural addition, and the Kid had been alternately following Gordon and Sheila around since he'd first heard they were fighting against the men who'd robbed him of his right to speak. In the end, as the night spread into day, there were more people than they felt safe with, and less than they needed.

But later, as he stood beside the dome when night had fallen again, Gordon wasn't so sure. It was huge. The fabric of it was thin, and even the webbing straps that gave it added strength were frail things. But it was strong enough to hold up the pressure of over ten pounds per square inch, and the webbing was anchored in a metal sleeve that went too high for cutting. They could rip it, but not ruin it completely; and it had to be done so that no repair could ever be made.

Under it, and anchoring it, was a concrete wall all around the city.

Izzy came back from a careful exploration. "We can work enough powder under those webbing supports, and lay the fuse wire beside the plastic ring that keeps it airtight," he reported. "But God help us, gov'nor, if any gee spots us."

They worked through the night, while Rusty went back to requisition more explosives from the dwindling supply, and while the Kid and Izzy took time off to break into a closed converter plant and find wire enough to connect the charges. But dawn caught them with less done than they had hoped. Gordon went to connect a wire and switch from the battery and coil they had installed, but jerked backwards as he saw a suspicious guard staring at him.

"Let him think we're just scouting," Randolph advised.

There were suspicious looks as the group came back to the Coop, but Mother Corey waddled over to meet them. "Did you find them, cobber?" he asked quickly, and one of his eyelids flickered.

Izzy answered before Gordon could rise to it. "Not yet, Mother. May have to go back tonight."

Gordon left them discussing the mythical search for certain supplies that Mother Corey had apparently used as an alibi for their absence from the building. Sheila started to make coffee, but he shook his head and headed for the bed. She yawned and nodded, fingering the stitches that still ran down the blanket to divide it. Then she grimaced faintly and dropped down beside him on top of the blanket. Her head hit his arm, and she seemed to be asleep almost at once.

He awoke to find Izzy shaking his shoulder. He looked down for Sheila, but she was gone. Izzy followed his eyes, and shook his head.

"The princess took off in a car three hours ago," he said. "She said it was something that had to be done, gov'nor, so I figured you'd know about it."

Gordon shrugged, and let it pass. He found the rest of the group ready, with Mother Corey wishing them better luck tonight. The Mother obviously knew something; but he kept his suspicions to himself, and gave them a cover from the others.

There was no sign of Sheila near the dome. But inside, there were guards pacing along it. Gordon spotted them first, and drew the others back. If they'd found the carefully worked-in powder...

The Kid ducked down and out of the car, worming his way around the building that concealed them. He waited for the guard to vanish, and then went crawling forward. Gordon swore, but there was no sense in two of them risking themselves, only to attract more attention. And at last the Kid came back. He ducked into the truck, nodding.

"Wire and explosive still there?" Gordon asked.

The Kid made the sound he used for assent.

It made no sense; there was no reason for the sudden vigilance inside the dome.

"We might be able to run the wire in," Izzy said doubtfully.

Gordon grunted. "And tip them off to where it is, probably. No, we'll have to do it under some kind of covering, the way I had it planned in the first place, only with one more damned complication. We'll pull another false raid on the dome. As soon as we get chased off, I'll manage to set it off while they're relaxing and laughing at us."

"It smells!" Izzy told him. "Who elected you chief martyr around here? You'll be blown up, gov'nor-and if you ain't, they'll rip you to ribbons for knocking off the dome."

Then he stopped suddenly, staring. Bruce Gordon leaned forward, with Izzy's hands grabbing for him. But he'd seen it, too.

Standing next to the dome was Trench, talking to one of the guards. And beside him stood Sheila, with one hand resting on the man's elbow!

He could feel the thickness of the silence and misery in the truck, but he pushed it away, with all the other things. "Get us back, Izzy," he ordered. "We've got to round up whatever group we can and get them back here on the double. They must be counting on our original time, so they're in no hurry to remove the powder and wiring. But we can't count on any more time."

"You're going through with it?" Randolph asked doubtfully.

"In one hour. And you might pass the word along that we're doing it to save the dome. Tell the men we just found out that Trench is losing and intends to blow it up instead of letting the Legals win."

Rumor would travel fast enough, he hoped. And it should give him a few extra seconds before his forces cracked.

He lifted the switch in his hands and stared at it. It wasn't necessary now. All he had to do was to reach the battery and drop any metal across the two terminals there-if they could get back before Trench-and Sheila-could remove the battery.

It was a period of complete fog to him, but it wasn't until his motley army reached the dome, straggling up in trucks and on foot, that he snapped into focus again. There was no sign of Sheila this time, and he didn't look for her. His whole mind was concentrated down to a single point: Get the dome!

This time, there was no scattering of Municipals and Legals. The Municipal forces were rushing up toward the dome, and surprised Legals were frantically arriving in trucks. There was the beginning of a pitched battle right at the spot where Gordon needed his own cover.

It made no sense to him, and he didn't care. He marched his men up, with the thin wailing of a banshee in his ears.

"Dome warning!" Izzy shouted in his ear. "Hear that siren, gov'nor? Means they're scared we may do it. Give me that damned switch!"

He grabbed for it, but Gordon held firmly to the copper strap. And now the men inside caught sight of the approaching force. For a second, consternation seemed to reign.

Then a huge truck with a speaker on top drove into the struggling group, and the thin whisper of unintelligible words reached Gordon. The whole development made no more sense than any part of it to him, but he saw the Municipals and Legals suddenly begin to turn as a single man to face the outside menace that had crept up on them while they were boiling into a fight.

And suddenly the Marspeaker over the entrance blasted into life. "Get back! The dome is mined! Any man comes near it, it'll blow! Get back! The dome is mined!"

By Gordon's side, a sudden gargling sound came from the Kid. His hand snaked out, caught the strap from Gordon's hand, and jerked it free. Then he was running frantically forward.

Rifles lifted inside, and shots rang out, clipping bullets through the dome. In one place it began to tear, and there was a sudden savage roar from the men around Gordon. He had started forward after the Kid, but Izzy was in front of him, holding him back.

The Kid stumbled and slid across the ground, while blood spurted out from a gash across his head, and the helmet fell into pieces. Then, with a jerk, he was up. His hand reached out, the strap hit the terminals...

And where the dome had been, a clap of thunder seemed to take visible form. The webbing straps broke, and the dome jerked upwards, twisting outwards, and then falling into ribbons. The shock wave hit Gordon, knocking him from his feet into the crowd around him.

He struggled to his feet to see helmeted men pouring out of the houses around, and other men pouring forward from his own group. The few of either police force still standing and helmeted broke into a wild run, but they had no chance! The mob had decided that they had mined and exploded the dome.

He turned back toward the Coop, sick with the death of the Kid and the violence. For once, he'd had more than his fill of it.

Then a small truck drew up, and an arm went out to draw him inside the cab. He stared into the face of Isaiah Trench. And driving the truck was Sheila.

"Your wife took a helluva chance, Gordon," Trench said heavily. "And I took quite a chance, too, to set this up so nobody could ever believe you were behind it. Getting that fight started in time, after you first showed up-oh, sure, we spotted you-was the toughest job I ever did! But I guess Sheila had the roughest end, not even knowing for sure where I stood."

Gordon stared at them slowly, not quite believing it, even though it was no crazier than anything else during the past few hours.

Trench shrugged. "I was railroaded here by Security, told to be good and they'd let me go home. A lot of men got that treatment. So when Wayne was still talking about building a perfect Marsport, I joined up. He treated me right, and I took orders. But a man gets sick of working with punks and cheap hoods; he gets sicker of killing off a planet he's learned to like. I learned to take orders, though-and I took them until Wayne tried to put a bullet through me. That ended that, and I came out to join up with you. You were soused, I hear-but your wife guessed enough to take the chance of coming to me, when she thought you were going to get yourself killed. Well, I guess you get out here."

He indicated the Coop. Gordon got down, followed by Sheila as Trench took the wheel. "What happens to you now?" Gordon asked. "They'll be blaming you for the end of the dome."

"Let them. I planned on that. Too bad Trench got torn to bits by the mob, isn't it? And it's a good thing I've always kept myself a place under a safe incognito out in the sticks. Got a wife and two kids out there that even Wayne didn't know about." He stuck out a hand. "You're like Security, Gordon. You do all the wrong things, but you get the right results. Goodbye!"

Sheila watched him go, shaking her head. "He likes you, Bruce. But he can't say it. Men!"

"Women!" Gordon answered.

Then he stiffened. Coming down through the thin air of Mars was the bright blue exhaust of a rocket. The real Security was arriving!

Chapter XVII
Security Payoff

It was three days before Bruce Gordon made up his mind to hunt up Security; another four days passed after they had sent him back to wait until they received orders from Headquarters for him. There was a man coming from Earth on a second ship who would see him. They gave him a chauffeur back to the Chicken Coop, and politely indicated that it would be better if he stayed within reach.

The dome had been down a full week when he watched the last of Randolph's equipment packed onto a truck and hauled away. The little publisher was back at the *Crusader* again. Rusty was busy opening his bar, and the others were all busy. Only Gordon and Sheila were left.

He heard her coming down the old stairs, and ducked out through the private exit, snapping his helmet in place as he went through the seal. She must have sensed his desire to be left alone, since she made no attempt to follow. She'd asked no questions and hadn't even tried to convince him that he'd be sent back to Earth now.

He muttered to himself as he headed over the rubble toward the previously domed section.

Out at the spaceport, ships were dropping down from Deimos with the supplies that had been held up so long, and a long line of trucks went snaking by. Credit had been established again, and the businesses were open.

For the time being, the hoods and punks were having a tough time of it, with working papers demanded as constant identification. And while it lasted, at least, Marsport was beginning to have its face lifted. Wrecks were being broken up, with salvageable material used for newer homes. Gordon came to a row of temporary bubbles, individual dwellings built like the dome, but opaque for privacy.

As Gordon drew closer to the old foundation of the dome, the feeling around began to clarify into something halfway between what he had seen on the real frontier and what he had known as a kid in Earth's slums.

They had been lucky. The dome had exploded outwards, with only bits of it falling back; and the buildings had come through the outward explosion of the pressure with little damage. Gordon grinned wryly. Schulberg's volunteers were official, now. Izzy was acting as chief of police, Schulberg was head of the reconstruction corps, and Mother Corey was temporary Mayor of all Marsport. The old charter for Marsport from North America was dead, and the whole city was now under Security charter, like the rest of the planet. But the dozen Security men had left most of the control in the Mother's hands, and the old man was up to his fat jowls in business.

Gordon moved automatically toward the Seventh Ward. Fats' Place was still open, though the crooked tables had been removed. Gordon dropped to a stool, slipping off his helmet. He reached automatically for the glass of ether-needled beer. This time, it even tasted good to him.

"On the house, copper," Fats' voice said. The man dropped to another stool, rolling dice casually between his thumbs. "And bring out a steak, there! You look as if you could stand it-and Fats don't forget old friends!"

"Friends and other things," Gordon said, remembering his first visit here. "Maybe you should have got me that night, Fats."

The other shrugged. "That's Mars." He rolled the dice out, then picked them up again. "Guess I'll have to stick to selling meals, mostly-for a while, at least. Somebody told me you'd joined Security and got banged up trying to keep Trench from blowing up the dome. Thought you'd be in the chips!"

"That's Mars," Gordon echoed the other's comment. "Why don't you pull off the planet, Fats? You could go back to Earth, I'd guess."

The other nodded. "Yeah. I went back, about ten years ago. Spent four weeks down there. I dunno. Guess a man gets used to anything ... Hell, maybe I can hire some bums to sit around and whoop it up when the ships come in, and bill this as a real old Martian den of sin! Get a barker out at the port, run special busses, charge the suckers a mint for a cheap thrill."

Gordon grinned wryly; Fats would probably make more than ever.

He finished the meal, accepted a pack of the Earth cigarettes that sold at a luxury price here, and went out into the thin air of Mars. It was almost good to get out into the filth of the slums, and be heading back to the still-standing monument of the old Chicken Coop. He headed for the private entrance out of habit, and then shrugged as he realized it was a needless precaution now. He moved up the front steps and through the battered seal.

Then he stopped. Security had finally gotten around to him, it seemed. Inside the hallway, the Security man who'd first sent him to Mars was waiting.

There was a grin on the other's face. "Hello, Gordon. Finally got our orders for you. It's Mercury!"

Bruce Gordon nodded slowly. "All right. I suppose you know I ruined the dome, was supposed to have killed Murdoch, pretended I was a Security agent..."

"You *were* one," the man said. He grinned again. "We know about Murdoch, and we know where Trench is-but he's a good citizen now, so he can stay there. We're not throwing the book at you, Bruce. Damn it, we sent you here to get results, and you got them. We sent twenty others the same way-and they failed. You were a bit drastic-that I have to admit-but we're one step closer to keeping nationalism off the planets, and that's all we care about."

"I wonder if it's worth it," Gordon said slowly.

The other shook his head. "We can't know in our lifetime. All we can do is to hope. We'll probably get this Mother Corey and Isaacs elected properly; and for a while, things will improve. But there'll be pushers as long as weak men turn to drugs, and graft as long as voters allow the thing to get out of their hands. Let's say you've shifted some of the misery around a bit, and given them a chance to do better. It's up to them to take it or lose it."

"So I get sent to Mercury?"

"You can't stay here. They'll find out too much eventually." He paused, estimating Gordon. "You *can* go back to Earth, Bruce, but you won't like it now. You're a fighter. And there's hell brewing on Mercury-worse than here. We've got permission to send you there, if you'll go. With a yellow ticket, again-but without any razzle-dazzle this time. The only thing you'll get out of it is a chance to fight for a better chance for others some day-and a promise that there'll be more, until you get old enough to sit at a desk on Earth and fight against every bickering nation there to keep the planets clean. There's a rocket waiting to transship you to the Moon on the way to Mercury right now."

Gordon sighed. "All right. But I wish you'd tell my wife sometime that-well, that I didn't just run out on her. She's had bad luck with men."

"She already knows," the Security man said. "I've been waiting for you quite a while, you know. And I've paid her the pay we owe you from the time you began using your badge. She's out shopping!"

The car pulled up to the waiting rocket, and the Security man helped him up the steps with a perfunctory wish for good luck. Then Bruce Gordon stopped as great arms surrounded him.

Mother Corey was immaculate, though not much prettier. But his old eyes were glinting. "Did you think we'd let you go without seeing you off, cobber?" he asked. "And after I took a *bath* to celebrate? I—I—Oh, drat it, I'm getting old. Izzy, you tell him."

He grabbed Gordon's hand and waddled down the landing plank. Izzy shook his head.

"I can't say it, either, gov'nor-but some day, I'm going to have one of those badges myself. Like I always said, honesty sure pays, even if it kills you. Here!"

He followed Mother Corey, leaving behind his favorite knife and a brand-new deck of reader cards, marked exactly as the ones Gordon had first used.

Gordon dropped into his seat, while the sounds outside indicated take-off time. He had less than a hundred credits, a knife, a deck of phony cards, and a yellow ticket. Mars was leaving him what he'd brought....

She dropped into the seat very quietly, but her blouse touched his arm. In her hand was a punched ticket with the orange of Mars on top and the black of Mercury on the bottom.

"Hello, Bruce," Sheila said softly. "I've been shopping and I spent the money the man gave me. This is all I have left. Do you think it's worth it? Or should I take it back?"

He turned it over in his hands slowly, and the smile came back to his face gradually.

"You got a bargain, Cuddles," he said. "A lot better than the meal ticket you bought. Let's keep it."

www.ingramcontent.com/pod-product-compliance
Lightning Source LLC
LaVergne TN
LVHW050636200726
843506LV00010B/1262